THE DEAD WALK!

Weird Tales of Zombies, Revenants, and the Living Dead
Edited by Vince Sneed ۞ Illustrated by Jason Whitley

DIE, MONSTER, DIE BOOKS | BALTIMORE, MARYLAND

Dedicated to **George A. Romero:**
the man who makes the dead walk.

EDITOR & PUBLISHER **VINCE SNEED** COVER ARTIST **ERICA HENDERSON**
ILLUSTRATIONS **JASON WHITLEY** PRODUCTION/DESIGN **DEVILGENGHIS**
ÜBER THANKS TO **JAMES CHAMBERS, C.J. HENDERSON, JASON WHITLEY**

Published by Die Monster Die! Books. 5082 E Federal Street, Baltimore, Maryland 21205. email: devilgenghis@yahoo.com ■ www.diemonsterdie.com

ISBN 0-9759904-0-3 ■ FIRST PRINTING: AUGUST, 2004 ■ PRINTED IN AMERICA

CONTENTS

Introduction:
JUST LIKE IN THE MOVIES
Vincent Sneed

It was an accident, it wasn't supposed to happen this way—but there they were: Susanna Sparrow and her boyfriend Jeff, in the back of Jeff's mom's minivan on the parking lot of Parrishville High School after dark, breathing hard enough to fog the windows. He groped at her with baseball gloves for hands, at the same time whispering something in her ear. It didn't matter *what* he said, just the *way* he said it; low and husky and full of need, just like in the movies.

She didn't put up much of a struggle at first and he kept at it, fumbling in terror but too excited to stop, and then *she* wanted to stop, press PAUSE, *something*, just so she could figure out exactly how far she wanted to go.

And that's exactly the moment her father chose to rap his knuckles against the passenger's side window. Susanna nearly screamed, but started crying instead.

"Susie?" her father said, nothing at all right about the tone of his voice. "Are you in there? Who's that with you?"

"It's, uh, it's me, sir," Jeff said, face draining of color, but unable to *not* answer. He reached across her for the door handle, opened it and crawled out, blinking when Officer Jim Sparrow of the Parrishville Police Department shone a flashlight in his face.

"Nothing happened, sir," Jeff said. "I *swear*."

Sparrow grunted, nodded, but otherwise ignored the boy.

"Susie? C'mon out, sweetheart."

Partially hidden behind Jeff, Susanna spent a moment adjusting her bra, smoothing out her sweater. Then she didn't move, believing for a fleeting moment that if she kept quiet and didn't move that her father might go away.

He didn't, and he repeated his order.

She climbed out of the minivan and stood beside Jeff, head bowed low, not wanting to look her father in the eyes.

What her father said next struck her so deep that Susanna's heart actually skipped a beat:

"Get home, Jeff. Your family needs you."

A moment passed before it sank in; during that moment, Jeff remained still, mouth open, staring dumbly at the policeman.

"Go on, son," Sparrow said. "And keep your car doors locked."

"Yessir!" Jeff stammered. He climbed into the minivan, fired it up and drove off, leaving Susanna alone with her father.

"We'll talk about this later," Sparrow said. "Right now, I want you in the cruiser. We need to find your mother."

With that, Jim Sparrow turned and walked to the police cruiser parked a dozen feet away. He ducked inside, sat waiting for her.

Susanna ran for the cruiser.

"Back seat," her father told her, so she scrambled into the back seat, came face-to-face with her younger brother.

Jim Sparrow Junior grinned. "Gettin' any?" he asked.

"Drop dead, creep."

"Both of you!" Sparrow shouted, banging his hand on the cage separating the front seat from the back. "Susanna: there's a lockbox on the floor." He told her the combination. "Open it up, honey."

Susanna opened the lockbox. Inside was her father's 9mm Sig Sauer, two loaded clips and two empty, and a box of ammunition.

"Load the gun, Susie."

"What's going on, Daddy?"

"Just load the gun, sweetheart, and put the safety on. And don't point it at your brother."

"Yeah," Jim Junior said, patting his own weapon.

She inserted the first clip, slapped it home, flicked the safety on. "Will you *please* tell me what's going on now?" she demanded.

"Dead people," her father said, barely above a whisper, as if he couldn't believe what he was saying. Or didn't want to.

"You'd'a heard it on the radio if you hadn't been in the backseat of Jeff's mom's minivan gettin' all down and dirty," Jim Junior said, suddenly grinning and animated. "It's just like in the movies: dead people getting up out of their graves, walking around and attacking the living! It's so *cool!*"

"No," Susanna said automatically. "That can't happen."

Jim Junior shrugged. "Maybe… But it's happening just the same! Hey! Hope you had fun with Jeff—probably the last chance you'll ever have!"

Susanna resisted the urge to shoot her brother in the face. It was like he'd slipped a different movie into the disk player while she was in the kitchen getting popcorn. And this was exactly the kind of movie he loved, too.

"Where's Mom?" she asked.

"She went to get your grandmother," her father said. "We split up right after we heard the news. We came looking for you while your mother went up to Pine Ridge to get your grandmother. We didn't know things would get so bad so fast."

"How bad is it?" Susanna asked, even though she was sure she really didn't want to know.

"We hit one," Jim Junior said. He pointed to the star-shaped crack in the windshield. There was blood, too, and bits of gray stuff that Susanna at first thought were grasshoppers clinging to the glass. She glanced away.

"The thing hit the bumper, flipped headfirst over the hood and *suh-MASH!* You shoulda seen it!"

"It was Mr. Riley from the grocery store," Sparrow said. "He didn't move to get out of the way, didn't even look like he knew what a car was anymore—just came right at us."

They were on Route 40 now, heading north toward Philadelphia. A familiar sign flashed by on the right indicating that the Pine Ridge Retirement Community was A Wonderful Place To Live! and that it was only a mile further on.

"The front gate better not be locked," Sparrow muttered. To his children he said, "Here's the plan, kids: if your mother and grandmother aren't waiting for us at the Admin Building when we get there, I'll go look for them by myself while you two wait in the car."

"*Daddee—*"

"No arguments, Susie. I'll be all right—I have my shotgun, okay?"

The shotgun didn't make it any better in Susanna's mind but she didn't want to start an argument she knew she wouldn't win. Instead she asked, "And *then* what?"

"We head west. According to the news, the outbreaks are occurring all up and down the East Coast, so we head west. Been a while since we visited your Aunt Sara in Texas, anyhow."

"Sounds like a plan," Jim Junior said.

Sparrow turned the cruiser onto the branch road leading to Pine Ridge. He stopped at the gate. Beyond was the Pine Ridge Retirement Community Administration Building and visitors parking lot. The lights were on but no one and nothing was moving around in there.

"Looks locked, Dad."

"The gatehouse, too." The policeman went silent for a moment, then said, "We'll ram the gate."

"COOL!"

Sparrow backed the cruiser up until he heard a *thump!*, craned his head around to see what he'd hit. Susanna and Jim turned to look, too. The man they'd hit wore the faux-policeman's uniform of the company hired to protect Pine Ridge and its residents. He was also obviously dead; a huge chomping bite was missing from his neck and blood stained the front of his blue shirt dark brown.

The dead security guard shuffled around the car, smacking an open hand on the trunk, the roof, then Susanna's window, searching for a way in, for a way to get to her. Its face had softened in death, the flesh seeming to peel away from the bone as if it were molting, as if it was in the final stages of turning into something *else*.

"Get us outta here, Dad!" Jim Junior shouted.

"I'm working on it!"

It's eyes locked with Susanna's. They were a doll's eyes, hooded by sleepy reptilian lids, staring, staring: at her, the door handle, her again, wanting her in the same painful way Jeff had wanted her.

Susanna screamed.

"Step on it, Dad!" Jim Junior shouted.

"Brace yourselves." Sparrow mashed the gas pedal to the floor.

The police cruiser fishtailed, knocking the dead security guard to the tarmac, surged forward, slamming into the wrought iron gate. The gate hinges shrieked, gave way, and the cruiser hurtled forward into the visitors parking lot.

A solitary figure stalked into a pool of yellow light ahead of the vehicle.

"Mom?" Susanna whispered.

Sparrow yanked the steering wheel hard to one side to avoid running his wife down, struck a light post instead. The post sheared away at the base, swinging the heavy light fixture down across the cruiser's hood, smashing into the windshield.

The cruiser's engine coughed, sputtered, died.

Jim Junior pounded the cage separating him from his father, Sparrow blinked, shook his head, turned to face his children. For a moment Susanna thought that he was dead, that he was one of *them* now, but he smiled at her weakly, a little embarrassed.

"I'm fine, Susie. Missed me by *that* much. You two okay?"

"We're fine, Dad," Jim Junior said, answering for both of them.

"Then let's get your mom and get the hell out of here. Damn! Why isn't your grandmother with her?"

The crumpled door gave with a single kick, then Sparrow was standing, still shaky from the adrenaline rush, clutching the door for support. The dead security guard came from behind him then, wrapping both arms around the policeman in a firm embrace, clamping yellowed teeth to his throat.

Sparrow howled in pain and surprise, thrashing wildly to shake off his attacker. His wife approached from the front, tearing at his shirt collar with one hand, shoving his head back with the other, mouth open wide as a train tunnel. She crunched down on his adam's apple, ripping it away in a bloody chunk. Together with the security guard she dragged him to the ground, his shrieks becoming a watery gurgle.

Susanna wished she was in the backseat of Jeff's mom's minivan, his fumbling teenager's hands pawing at her, their combined breath steaming the windows so they couldn't see what was outside. *That* was the kind of movie she liked best.

"We're getting outta here!" her brother growled, clawing for the door handle that wasn't there.

"We can't," Susanna said, drawing in a ragged breath. She wanted to cry but started giggling instead. "We're in a police cruiser, if you haven't noticed!"

Their mother crept into the front seat of the cruiser, seeing her children through glassy, lifeless eyes, not recognizing them at all. She clawed at the cage, snapped bloodied teeth at them.

"Just like in the movies," Susanna said.

"I'll—I'll shoot out the window," Jim Junior said. "Shoot out the window and we can crawl out. These things are slow; we can outrun 'em easy."

He raised his gun to the window.

And stopped.

"Haven't you seen this movie before? It's your favorite kind!" Susanna was giggling uncontrollably now, making it almost impossible to get the words out right. The look on her brother's face made it worth the effort. "There's always more of them—*see*?"

They came shambling out of the Pine Ridge Admin Building, dozens of them, *hundreds*, drawn by the excitement and screaming, shuffling along on leaden feet, in the blood-stained pajamas and bermuda shorts and t-shirts they'd died in. Some remembered enough from when they were alive to use their walkers and their canes; others dragged themselves along, hand over bloody hand, eager for the feast. With them came nurses and doctors, the fronts of their white lab coats and smocks smeared like butcher's aprons.

They were *everywhere.*

"Just like in the movies," Jim Junior echoed, his eyes glittering, unsure whether to laugh or scream, only that he wouldn't be able to stop once he started.

Susanna clapped a hand on his shoulder. "Enjoy the show, creep!"

THE DEAD BEAR WITNESS

James Chambers

LAST THING WARDEN LANE Grove told me before he slammed shut the cell door was, "You think you're someone special, son? Someone different and unique? You're nobody special. You're just clay like all the rest of us. Sooner you accept that, better off you'll be, because if you think my punishment is harsh, you'll find a rude surprise waiting for you in the next world if you don't change your ways."

This and a month in solitary as punishment for smashing the nose of some Aryan Brotherhood asshole who wanted to "protect" me. Show no weakness to those white supremacist fucks—they will make you their dog or kill you trying.

Warden Grove knew it as well as I did, but I was fresh blood and a media darling, and he wanted to teach me a lesson about getting cocky.

Worst thing about solitary is there's nothing to occupy your mind but thinking about how horribly you screwed up when you were on top of the world. They wouldn't allow me my books or even a Walkman—nothing but the searing brightness of the cell's single bare bulb lit twenty-four, seven. That and all the time I needed to pick over the carcass of my memories, like the last time I saw Evelyn or the look on the bank manager's face when three slugs from my forty-five burned through his gut. Sometimes I got to wondering how it might have gone if I'd been just a few seconds faster.

And that's when I came to understand what Evelyn meant when she used to talk about how the world is a smiling jackal eager for its chance to tear out your throat and lap at your blood. Most people don't see it coming for the clutter in their lives like politics or religion or trying to make a decent living with the deck stacked against you. But Evelyn and I never had much use for all those things telling people the "right" way to live. Better to take what you need and be long gone when the shit hits the fan.

I believe Evelyn held to that right up to the moment I let her and our unborn child die.

THREE WEEKS LATER PAULSON and Gamewood yanked me out of the hole and told me that everywhere in the world the dead had risen to hunt and feed on the living.

Warden Grove's day of reckoning was at hand.

"Bullshit," I said. They dragged me down the hall to the infirmary, while I chased the dime-sized ghost glares burned into my eyes. Wasted from hunger and not having slept more than an hour at a time since they tossed me down there, I wasn't so far gone I didn't notice Paulson's trembling or the glistening film of sweat coating his pale face.

"Whole world...is over...end of...everything," he mumbled.

He wasn't talking to me, really, just muttering to the empty air, and I guessed it was a sick joke, or more of my continuing education according to Lane Grove. Or maybe Paulson liked to get a little high on the job.

Had second thoughts about all that after the horror show at the infirmary.

Couple of hacks brought in Lucio Costas, bleeding like a New York City fire hydrant in summer. His face was ashen and rubbery. Costas was a snub-nosed car-thief on a ten-year chip for his third strike. He was a stupid man with a smart mouth, and it was no surprise someone had decided to slice him open and make good work of it. The guards hefted him onto a gurney for the doctors to work, but a two-foot wide puddle of his blood spilled onto the floor before the sawbones even got his shirt cut open. It didn't take much to see there was no bringing him back.

One of the docs announced the time of death.

Then they ripped him apart like a Christmas turkey.

They set to work like the Devil's pit crew, long, skinny knives and whirring bone saws in hand. Blood spattered and flesh tore. Muscle snapped like strands of stale chewing gum. They peeled back translu-

cent flaps of skin from his bone and sinew. Joints cracked, and foul
patches of gas belched from the recesses of Costas's body. His left arm
came lose and a guard dropped it into a thick vinyl bag, sealed it shut,
and threw it in a laundry cart. Next went his legs, each one amputated below the knee, wrapped in separate containers, then tossed on
the pile.

Every thirty seconds or so, one of the nurses called the time,
counting down the minutes. Sweat dripped from the doctor's faces. It
mixed with Costas's blood and ran in milky rivulets along their silver
tools.

Costas's right arm vanished into a plastic sack. His thighs spread
comically wide as his hips gave way with a loud snap.

"One minute," the nurse said.

They finished with seconds to spare. The doc hunched over
Costas's face wrenched the car thief's head from his neck. Two guards
slipped a body bag over his torso; another held one wide for the head.
And as Lucio's lifeless gray cranium vanished inside, his smartass eyes
flickered open—ivory in the last beam of light that touched them—
and stared right at me, cool as December, like all was right in his
world. Soon as that head crowned the pile of body parts the aluminum
cart started rattling. Slow at first, like when a truck rolls by a house
and shakes the pictures on the walls. But then each of the black bundles began wriggling like a caged rat and the canvas liner bulged as
severed limbs squirmed over each other.

It took the nurse, screaming "Incinerator, now!" to send the disgusted supercops rushing the cart out of the room.

In the infirmary air I smelled the foul odor of raw flesh and the
pungent stink of sleepless terror. The scent of fear is something I am
most familiar with, and but for being so depleted by my hitch in solitary, I would've caught it wafting off my escort like body odor. I
would've gagged on it rising off the medical staff the second I entered
the room. Its choking stink tainted the entire prison. And now that I
had scented it, I couldn't ditch it.

I grabbed the nurse by the arm.

"What in holy hell was that?" I rasped.

"You been living in a cave for the last month?" she spat.

AN HOUR LATER, WITH a clean bill of health—not counting dehydra-
tion, sleep deprivation, malnourishment, and the general stress that
comes with existing in a windowless three-by-five cell for nearly a
month—they sent me back into population.

It was afternoon recreation period, so I went to the television room. That time of day, place should have been full of soap opera fans, but there was nothing but snow on every channel. So, I sat a while, relishing the plush embrace of the couch and resting my eyes in the cool stillness of the room. I thought about Lucio Costas and tried to pinpoint the exact moment when my sanity had deserted me.

An old man hunkered down on an empty chair and gave me the once over.

"Been in solitary, ain't you?" he said. "I can tell. You're out of touch, I suppose. A lot's changed. Why don't you try this?" He handed me an unlabeled videotape. "Television went out almost two weeks back. They stuck a couple of VCRs in here to keep us quiet. Got a couple of old football games on the shelf there, a couple of musicals, one of them Jim Carrey movies. But this the one you'll be interested in. When you're done, stick it in the crack between the wall and the cabinet. I'll fetch it later. Warden don't like this to circulate, y'know?"

The tape contained two hours of news footage someone had recorded while channel surfing. Every broadcast was the same—the corpses of the dead walked the world and preyed on the living with a savageness of insane dimension. It was worst in the cities where mobs of zombies swarmed the streets, but inside of a couple of days it had spread everywhere. The zombies moved with desperate purpose, heedless of their own safety and ignorant of any injury. The unanswerable hunger that illuminated their blank eyes drove them to consume what they had once been. All the reporters asked the same question—"Why?" Sure enough there were theories—radiation, disease, voodoo, parasites, the Apocalypse, cell phones and so on and so on—but no one ever figured it out, as far as I know. Not that it matters. Most people worried about stopping it before it was too late, but as far as I could tell, that point had come and gone and caught everyone with their pants down.

But I watched the whole thing as if it was taking place right then, and I pictured people on the outside, fighting for survival against the legions of the unliving. My imagination ran away a touch, I admit, but I've always been that way. Thing was, what all the other men had experienced over the past weeks—locked up helpless inside while the rest of the world died a slow death—I put myself through in two hours, knowing I had to catch up fast.

The tape rewound automatically at the end. The screen filled with a blank blue field like the empty patch in my memory from my time in the hole.

Damn video did wonders for my doubts about my sanity.

We had been safely locked up, a thing for which not a man among us would have been grateful four weeks ago. And I doubted how many felt differently now. What was there to look forward to when our time was done—families, homes, girlfriends, money?

But then, shit, some of us had lost all of that long before resurrection fever began firing up the brains of the dead.

I went out to the exercise yard to shock my muscles from the atrophy of confinement. Physical exertion clears my head, and I had a hunch I was going to need my strength soon.

Outside was cool and dry, the kind of spring weather that makes you want to drive a hundred miles an hour with the top down. I wondered for half a heartbeat what had really changed—I mean, here was the world, alive and untouched, for all I could see, by nightmares other than ones we bring to life ourselves. But then there was the perpetual odor of rot and the low-toned undercurrent of strange, malformed voices echoing in the yard, coming not from the other prisoners but from outside the walls of the prison. Rifle reports snapped at irregular intervals from the perimeter stations. The gunshots mingled with the crash of hammers. Down at one end of the yard, workers were erecting a scaffold with the lumber meant for the new storage shed. Beside it a hill of old junk and debris was piling up.

I settled onto the bench and began lifting. The heft of the barbell laced strands of pain through my chest, but the grimy iron felt good in my hands as I pumped through my first set. Some con came over to spot me, looking grateful for the break in his boredom. He smoked a cigarette while I went through two more sets. My muscles warmed to the exertion with the last one, so I switched to smaller weights and kept at it, boiling away the cold dread that had been gathering at the base of my spine. I worked my body until the knots in my gut melted to nothing, and then I sat there, panting, while the breeze licked the sweat from back.

That's when Klug approached me, stopping here and there along the way to smoke a butt or gab with other cons or tie his shoe, the whole time keeping his eye on me like a stream of ice water.

Klug was near seven-feet tall and built like a linebacker, as much muscle as he was fat. His clean-shaven head glistened in the sunlight. A bright cobra hood tattoo adorned the back of his neck and skull. Nobody fucked with the King Snake. There was no point. Not a man in the yard could take him one on one, and Klug, for his part, liked his privacy. A genuine live-and-let-live arrangement, and from what I could see, it worked. Klug had been fairly high up on the food chain before they brought him low on some bogus firearms charge, and he went inside with solid connections. Even the guards kissed his ass, and Klug returned the favor by using his influence to help maintain order when it suited him. That kind of shit made for easy time, I suppose, but shots like Klug do you a favor just to obligate you. My first day in I'd elected to do everything possible to stay under his radar.

Guess I screwed the pooch on that one.

"Hear you're a Lohatchie boy," he said. The temperature dropped three degrees in Klug's shadow.

"Yeah?" I asked. "Where did you hear that?"

"Doesn't much matter," he pointed out. "Grew up in Lohatchie. Spent my summers playing around the 'Glades, running airboats in my teens for Gator Joe's. Lived down on Kettrick by the rail yard till I left when I was sixteen. You look about the right age. I imagine we might have passed each other on the street more than once."

"Probably did," I agreed. "Gator Joe's went out of business long time ago, you know."

"Yeah, I heard," he said. "Too bad, too. Joe deserved better than the shit he wound up eating."

A flurry of gunshots snapped on the wind, and Klug craned his neck, intent on the cobalt sky like he was waiting for it to answer some unspoken question. I saw the wheels turning, the machinations of his thoughts gamboling behind his careful, measured expression.

"Waste of good ammo," he commented. "Nothing stops them short of incineration or blowing them into very small bits. Slice them apart and their arms and legs will come after you as best they can. We're just lucky they're slow."

I thought of Lucio in the infirmary, a man cut to pieces but still kicking.

"Old Corntooth told me he gave you the tape, so you know the score," said Klug. "We could be the only ones left, I suppose. Likely there are others out there in situations like ours, but there's no way to know. Warden Grove carried things on like normal for a few days, but when it was clear nothing was going to turn it around, he locked us down drum tight. No one in, no one out, no exceptions. Not even the guards' families. Looked like the screws might mutiny at one point, but Grove kept enough of them loyal to hold the lid on. Pretty soon they all realized whatever family they left behind would probably best be forgotten. They're prisoners, now, just like us."

I said, "I'm tickled by the irony."

Klug cracked what might have been a smile, but I wouldn't swear to it.

"You ever eat down at Mona and Joan's on Banyan?" he asked.

"More than a few times," I answered. "Damn good fries."

"And milkshakes. Nothing beat their chocolate shakes."

"Screw that," I said. "Strawberry-banana. Joan's specialty. The ultimate shake."

Klug smiled for sure this time, cracking his lips and licking his broad white teeth like he could taste the food right then—golden crisp and steeped in oil and salt, sugar sweet and creamy cold.

"Yeah, it's good to be talking to a Lohatchie boy. Man, I bet we're the last two left. Funny us winding up here, now," the King Snake said. "So, I hear you got a place in the wilderness, where if you'd have made it before they caught up with you, they might not have caught you at all."

That took the wind out of me. How the fuck did anyone know about that?

Klug read the expression on my face. "I been in here long enough, I can advise you not to expend a lot of energy keeping secrets. It's not possible, least not from me," he said.

"Well, suppose it's true. So, what? It'd have to be hundreds of miles away, wouldn't it," I said.

"Most fellows haven't caught on, yet, to the warden's grand plan." Klug paused to light a clove cigarette and exhaled a sweetly acrid cloud that dissipated overhead. "Understand this—that man will see to it none of us ever leave this prison alive. We have provisions stockpiled for another week, maybe two if they get stingy, and we got self-contained generators for power but fuel is running low. He can't keep us up here indefinitely without significantly thinning the population or recruiting men to forage for supplies.

"When the dead began to walk, Grove declared the Apocalypse, and curled up squarely in the pages of his Bible to beat back the insanity. We all had to do that one way or another. Ones that didn't aren't around anymore. And for a man with that big a hard-on for God, this has got to seem like some seriously important shit. Protecting us is keeping us from God's righteous judgment. He won't let anyone out to hunt or try to make it to town to find out what's happening. We could be living like princes in here, but he lets the slitbacks collect up around the walls because he believes most of us are meant to die at their hands. It's just a matter of time before he decides to throw open the doors and let it happen."

"Why not do it, already, then?" I asked.

"He wants to prepare us, make sure we repent our sins, and all that happy horseshit," Klug explained. "A few of us have decided to be elsewhere when this happens. The slitbacks go where the food is, meaning where we are. There must be six, seven hundred outside, scattered around the countryside, pressing at the gates, homing in on our scent. Ten, fifteen, twenty more got to be showing up every day. From where I don't know because the nearest town is thirty miles away. They're damn tough to kill, too, and they make more of themselves fast. Couple weeks back a busload of people came banging at the door. Grove ordered the guards to open fire. The ones killed by bullets got up after a few minutes, started eating the live ones."

"So, break out and where do you run? You figure you can get far enough away they won't pick up the scent," I guessed.

"Scent, noise, psychic vibration, whatever the fuck they get off on. Got to be a limit to their range. That's my theory, anyway," he answered. "Better out there testing it than rotting in here waiting to die."

"And if I'm not interested?"

Mild surprise ran through Klug's face. "I haven't considered that. I will if you really need an answer."

I shook my head. "No. Getting of out here sounds just fine. How many?"

"Nine, including you and me."

"Too many. Needs to be less when we get where we're going."

"Well, such things have a way of working themselves out," said Klug. "I know I can trust you to keep this quiet, Lohatchie boy. Tonight, after Grove's dog and pony show, go back to your cell, wait one hour, then meet me in the cafeteria. It's been arranged."

"Okay," I said. "But tell me something—why do you call them slitbacks?"

"You know how they dress bodies in a funeral home? They cut the clothes down the back, wrap them around from the front, tuck it under, and leave it," he explained. "The first ones to come to life were in morgues and funeral homes, all these stiffs standing up and thrashing around while their pants fell down around their ankles and their Sunday best went flopping off. Video made it all over the TV when there still was TV."

Klug blended into the crowd. Faraway gunshots ripped through the afternoon.

I watched the men slaving away at the scaffold, feeling exposed and weak in the harsh sun and afraid I was coming down sick. Fever chills ran through my body, but I think they came when I recognized the structure going up across the yard.

Warden Lane Grove was having a gallows built.

I SAT BY MYSELF at supper that evening.

My first day in, everyone wanted a piece of me. They'd watched me on the news for weeks—"the modern-day John Dillinger," a bank robber folk hero who relied more on his wits than his gun and made monkeys out of the cops.

Yeah, it was a healthy dose of exaggeration, but there was some truth in it, too. I robbed more than a dozen banks over two years and came away clean with more cash than Joe Sixpack could make in a decade worth of overtime. I did it in style, and I did it smart—jumped from state to state, kept a low profile, used a different crew each time, varied my methods, did everything I could to erase my signature. Hit nine banks before they connected the first four. Most of them had been fast, in and out, grabs off the tellers, but you could stretch your time if you knew what you we're doing, maybe take some of the vault, and I did that a few times, too, for the big hauls. It was simple with Evelyn. Girl like her made information easy to come by. We could avoid the places rigged with dye bombs and marked bills, go in on the security guard's coffee break, disable the cameras, little advantages like that.

And no one got hurt—least not until my last job.

Half the public was on my side the day the news broke that the Feds had connected all my robberies thus admitting they'd been out-smarted for a solid eighteen months. I won over the other half by the time they caught me, having accomplished some conspicuous good deeds with portions of the take. Call it buying good P.R., because that's what it was. Mug for the camera, flash a nice smile, let them see you're just an average guy, and it reminds them all how much they'd like to buck the system the same way if they had any balls. That's the beauty of mass communication—blur the lines enough, suddenly real life vanishes, and people think they're watching a movie. Bank rob-ber? No, sir! I was the next great, misunderstood, anti-hero "victim of a heartless society driven to a life of desperate crime." I was goddamn Robin Hood driving a late model Lexus SUV. And I was still reeling from my recent loss. Hell, I got more than a thousand consolation cards while I was on ice waiting for my trial and half a dozen offers to go on talk shows and tell my side of events so "the people could under-stand."

None of that crap interested me. I just missed Evelyn.

I wanted to suffer for letting her down so I plead guilty.

The court handed me a life sentence for killing the bank manag-er and two security guards. My public defender threw his arms up in frustration at me copping to a rap he thought we could beat. Only thing that kept me out of the electric chair was a spark of mercy fanned by the fact that the men I killed had just shot my pregnant wife to death.

But just think—if I'd have walked, I'd probably be dead now.

Tempts me to start believing in fate.

And let me assure you that it's a bad thing to come into stir with a reputation of any kind. Others feel duty-bound to take you down a peg or two, see if you got any juice. But while I was in the hole, word had traveled about what I had done to that skinhead punk, and my first night back no one seemed itchy for a scrap. The whole cafeteria was so damn subdued it made my skin crawl, and I knew it was those wooden beams raised above the prison courtyard dominating the thoughts every of man around me.

We were to gather in the yard for a special service following dinner—Warden Grove's orders. They hadn't strung the ropes before mealtime, but we all knew they'd be hung in time for the night's activities.

Old Corntooth parked himself beside me as I sucked down a forkful of red Jell-O. He smiled wide, showing me how he had earned his name.

"Klug got you, huh? Shots like him usually get what they want," he said.

"Don't know what you're talking about, old timer."

"Uh-huh," he muttered, his smile fading. "I'll tell you the same thing I told Klug. Skip it. It ain't gonna happen. You better off here, cause no matter what they throw at you, you can always find a way to keep your head down and tough it out. You try and force 'em to play by your rules, they jes' going to smash you down. I been in here near thirty years, and I know what I'm talking about."

"You don't even know what time it is. This play is for everything, and keeping a low profile ain't going to save your skinny ass. Maybe an old fellow like you ain't too concerned about that." I dropped my spoon and stood, breaking Old Corntooth's grip where he'd clutched on to my wrist.

He rose and poked me in the chest. "I'm s'posed to be out in six months. You hear me? Then I get my life back, and this shit has to go down, now…" Tears welled in his drooping eyes.

"And you and Klug and them just carrying on like it ain't nothing. It ain't fair," he coughed.

I felt the supercops's eyes on us, so I pushed past the old man as gentle as I could, acting calm and friendly, whispering as I went by, "What's changed, old man? The world is full of empty-headed bodies colliding off each other the way it always was. Gotta find an angle and make it work for you. Give up fighting you're just like them—*dead*. Most of those bastards out there—or, hell, most of them in here— were dead a long time ago."

Corntooth shook his head. "No, no, it ain't like that."

I left him with his shoulders drooping like a week-old balloon.

A crowd was filtering out to the yard, and I'd had my fill of the somber efficiency of the cafeteria. I wanted to raise my eyes and see stars instead of a greasy stone ceiling for the first night in nearly a month. I followed the others into the rose-amber glow of the raging bonfire now consuming the junk pile beside the gallows and stood in the shadow of a watchtower, manned, as they all were, by men with semi-automatic assault rifles. The firelight made the sky hazy, but I picked out enough stars to satisfy. Fifteen, twenty minutes ticked off before everyone was there, grim-faced and determined not to betray the slightest bit of fear. I scanned the crowd for Klug, but caught no sign of him.

Thundering music exploded from the loudspeakers, slow and funereal, some God-awful classical shit that filled us with a sense of powerlessness, meant no doubt to keep us in a docile frame of mind. Warden Grove was something of a showman, having at one time been a revivalist preacher, and he played it well. Ten figures marched onto the platform—three inmates bound in shackles, escorted by two shot-gun-toting hacks apiece. The executioner—a stocky, dark-suited man whose mouth hid behind a blue surgeon's mask—followed. One-by-one the cons took their places below the gallows poles. All three were now outfitted with coarse ropes tied into nooses.

Warden Grove entered like some prince deigning to address his frightened subjects. He telegraphed everything there was I hated about people like him.

"I will waste no time, men," he said into his microphone, "as time is now more truly of the essence than it ever has been. Three sinners stand beside me, gazed upon by a host of sinners. All of you, to the last man, sag beneath the weight of your guilt. I see it, men, hanging upon you, a foul mud weighing down your spirit. The Good Book promises that one day there will be a Reckoning, and on that day the dead shall rise from their graves. That day is at hand! No longer can you afford the luxury of your craven ways. It's time to repent, as these three brave souls behind me have done."

Grove stuck the microphone in the first inmate's face.

"Your name, son?" he asked.

The man had been beaten so bad he could only stand propped up by his escort.

Grove shoved the microphone closer.

"Again, son. Your name?"

"Don... Cooper," he muttered.

"And what path have you chosen, Mr. Cooper?"

"God's path. To repent... my sins," Cooper coughed. "To go...to the Lord...with a clear conscience."

"He has forgiven you, Mr. Cooper, as he is willing to forgive us all. But it is left to you to see that your soul remains in its current state of grace, that you do not again become one of the fallen. Would you do me the humble honor of accepting my assistance in assuring this?"

"Yes...yes, please," said Cooper, struggling to remember his lines.

Grove asked the same questions of the other two men. They gave the same canned answers. None of them looked like they understood what was happening.

"God so loved Mankind, he gave unto us his only Son, and sacrificed him for our sins," Grove roared into the microphone. "And it is our duty to follow his example, by sacrificing ourselves to redeem our tainted spirits."

The executioner draped velvet hoods over the head of each supplicant and fitted nooses around their necks.

"Donny?" one of the men called out. "Donny, I can't see you. What's happening?"

"It's okay, Arthur...I'm still here...and this shit... this shit is almost over. You just...keep your head together," came Cooper's voice, muffled by his hood.

"Men, pray for your fellows, that their souls might find peace," announced Grove.

The executioner sprang the trap doors. The three convicts dropped into empty air. Their necks snapped audibly, and their bodies dangled, kicking awhile then swaying like mute wind chimes. I'd never seen a man hang before, and I'll tell you it's not quick and clean like they show it in the movies. Matter of fact, it's a damn nasty way to die.

Quiet reigned a long time over the crowd. The crackling of the rising fire was the only sound to be heard, unless you listened carefully and caught the moans of the restless dead traveling on the breeze. A number of men looked at their watches, some stared at their shoes. No one stirred, but the corpses, which jerked to life with clumsy, sweeping kicks, and wind-milled their arms like dancing marionettes.

While later a bunch of hacks came out and took position above each hanging body, three or four to a man.

"The unrepentant man is doomed to eternal flesh," cried Warden

Grove. "Such is the fate of the worldly. Only those who choose forgiveness may receive release. Men!"

The screws hauled the flailing bodies up, each grabbing a limb,
while another yanked the noose free.

I was grateful for not having to see the zombies's blank eyes
beneath their hoods, for knowing the dead men could not see the rage
and horror in our faces.

"Free these men of their flesh!" Grove screamed.

The guards heaved the first of the struggling bodies onto the bonfire. It burned slow like green wood and wet leather, kicking and
burrowing into the trash heap. The others followed, all three digging
their way deeper toward the heart of the conflagration like they were
drawn to its center by the heat. Disgusted cries and impotent curses
rose from the crowd.

"These men have been saved, their souls set free," Warden Grove
declared. His chest swelled with pride.

"Who…would like to be *next*?"

I never before heard a silence like the one that answered him.

"Men, I anticipated your reluctance to join the ranks of the saved
tonight. Spiritual matters often require time and deep contemplation
to resolve. I understand. So this will now be part of our daily routine,
until each man among you worthy of saving has been safely sent to his
eternal reward. Remain here for one hour, then you may return to
your cells. Those of you who choose salvation may tell any prison official in order for the appropriate arrangements to be made," Grove
said.

He descended the platform and disappeared inside. He left the rest
of us to perspire for sixty minutes in the warm night and the heat of
the bonfire while the corpses of three men grew thin and black until
not a scrap of flesh remained on their charred bones, and finally they
ceased to move.

LATER I LAY IN my cell, thinking how bright Brockden, my pedophile
cellmate, was to leave me undisturbed. I had promised him on my
third day inside, after catching him using my comb, to make sure he
didn't live to see the end of summer. Can't say I really meant it, as
repulsive as he was, but scaring him served my purposes just as well.

I tried reading, but mostly stared at the ceiling or glanced at my
watch, waiting for the hour to pass. When it was almost time I
dropped to the floor, snaked my hand into the narrow space between
the metal leg of the bunk and the wall, and tapped until the loose
chunk of masonry slipped free. A beat-up paperback waited wedged

inside. Hidden within it where I had hollowed out some pages was the jagged half of a snapped penknife blade, bound with duct tape to a wooden spoon handle. It wasn't much, but it was all I'd had time to acquire before my stint downstairs. I slipped it into the waistband of my shorts.

Sickly-looking Paulson came by on his rounds, pausing at my cell to unlock the door. He tipped me a nod then went on his way. I crept out, ignoring the hatred and envy for the King Snake's new favorite that poured from of the eyes of the insomniac men in the other cells. I passed three guard stations along my way, each one deserted, and I encountered no one in the halls. The Cobra lived up to his reputation.

The scent of Klug's clove cigarette filled the darkened cafeteria.

"That display tonight changes things," he said from the shadows. "We can't wait till next week. We move right away."

He led the way through the kitchen to a corridor that connected with a passageway to the administrative wing. I held back.

"No one will see us," Klug reassured me. "It's taken care of for an hour at least. Now, c'mon."

We crept across the linoleum floor and ducked inside a stairwell that took us up another level. From there we mounted two more flights of steps, finally emerging outdoors atop the wall below one of the guard towers. Two people waited there, one a guard, the other the nurse from the infirmary.

"You're late," the guard snapped.

"No, we're not," replied Klug. "Where are the others?"

The guard indicated the tower and a metal ladder up to the observation deck. We climbed up one-by-one. Inside the glass walls of the watch room waited another guard and two cons hunkered down out of sight on the floor.

"This him?" asked the tower hack.

"That's him, Mason," confirmed Klug.

"I read your file, college boy," Mason said. "That pretty face of yours may play with dumbass TV reporters, but it means nothing in here. I will have no hesitation putting a bullet in your head if you go grandstanding on us."

"Well," I told him, "you can try."

He withdrew a step, a flicker of doubt in his eyes.

"No time for this crap, Mason," intervened Klug. "Cornell's with me. And right now we have things to discuss."

I recognized the two on the floor, Jaime and Scopes, enforcers for Klug. They pulled me down beside them.

"Keep out of sight, asshole," Jaime said.

Klug squatted, too, unfolding a piece of paper from his shirt. He flattened it out on the floor, providing us with a rough map of the prison, and took us step-by-step through the plan. We would go out by the west garage, the loading docks Grove had sealed up when deliveries stopped arriving. The whole area was shut down, lightly guarded at best, and would give us a fair chance of slipping out unnoticed. There were three trucks there. Tomorrow night, Combest, the other guard present, and another one named Georges would sneak in, siphon the gas from two of the trucks, and store it in the third. The next day, Della, the nurse, would pack medical supplies. Combest would meet with Paulson and gather provisions from the kitchen, where Paulson supervised the afternoon work crew. Mason would see to weapons. We would leave between eleven and midnight, with Klug making arrangements for clear passage from our cells to the loading dock. Money was worthless, but there were other forms of bribery and coercion. The last piece fell on Paulson, who sometime in the evening would secure the keys and punch codes for the garage doors and perimeter exits. Then all we had to do was ride, and I got to play navigator.

"We go in two days," concluded Klug. "Before Preacher Grove gets a chance to save our souls."

Mason waved me over to the window. "Come here," he said.

I looked out over the north field. Mason switched on a spotlight. The beam slashed the night, lighting up the aimless slitbacks shuffling along the fence where they circled what must have seemed to them a butcher shop due to open any minute.

"I know you've been in the hole, so I want to make sure you comprehend what we're up against," Mason said.

"Shut that fucking light off," interrupted Klug. "You'll get us noticed."

"Nah, nobody's gonna care. Get bored up here, and it's time for a little target practice. Happens every night. Here, look," Mason said. He handed me a pair of binoculars.

The dead, shambling things looked like mental patients—empty and tuned into some frequency no one else could hear. Mason hefted his rifle and sighted through the scope. The slug caught one of the zombies in the eye and exploded out the back of its head. It fell over and rolled around in the dirt, its stained necktie flapping like a tongue. Mason squeezed off another round, but aimed wide and split the calf of a dead woman passing by, knocking her over. He fired again, taking out necktie's other eye, flattening him to the ground, where he flopped around trying to get up.

"Doesn't stop them," Mason told me. "They smell us just fine, but it evens the odds a bit if they can't see to chase us."

I scanned the herd of slitbacks. The eye sockets of many of them had been blown out by rifle fire.

"And I wanted you to know I'm a good shot," said Mason.

"Yeah? You missed on that second one," I pointed out.

"Think you can do better?"

"Give me the gun," I prodded. "Gonna have to trust me sooner or later."

"Enough," Klug interceded. "We need to go back, now."

What the hell? I'd have my contest with Mason another time.

We clambered down the ladder with Jaime and Scopes, quiet as we could. The administration wing stood empty and still like we had left it. At the cafeteria, the four of us split to return to our cells, Jaime and I moving together toward our cellblock—that's when they jumped us. Two Aryan Brotherhood shitheads, looking for some pay-back, and believe it or not, paid off by my limp-wristed rodent of a cellmate, looking to get me before I got him.

One of them took Jaime off his feet with a pipe to his legs, and the other threw his weight at me, trying to connect with a makeshift sap of rocks stuffed into a rag. He was fat and slow and I dodged every shot, sliding along the floor until his mass shifted enough that I could get my shiv loose. Fat man dripped sweat and squawked about exact-ly what he was going to do me once he made me his punk, how my ass would be his to peddle to all his friends and his first customer would be Brockden. I'd heard more than enough by the time I thrust the broken penknife blade into his neck and forced it until the tip broke out the back, slicing his spinal cord and dropping his dead weight on me like a falling cow. I fought my way loose, figuring fat man's partner would be done with Jaime soon and coming for me. What I found was Jaime propped up against the wall with both knees shattered, but the bloodied pipe gripped tight in his hands. Beside him, laid out with a shattered skull, slumped the second skinhead.

"Shit, bro," I said. "Your legs are all fucked up."

"Get out of here," Jaime wheezed. "The King Snake's gonna need you. You got maybe two minutes before these fucks get up again. I ain't going anywhere after this, so just fucking leave. Now!"

I've never been one to argue with good sense. Jaime was a lost cause as far as escaping went, and that meant he was as good as dead. And it wouldn't do anyone a damn bit of good for me to be found out of my cell after lights out and covered in blood.

I wrenched my shiv free from fat man's throat, threw it to Jaime.

"You may need this," I said.

I jumped shadows back to my cell. When I got there I threw a pillow over Brockden's face without even slowing down and beat him until most of his body turned purple. Only thing that kept me from killing him was knowing the son of a bitch wouldn't stay dead.

THAT NIGHT I DREAMT of Evelyn rising from her grave and pleading with me to find her, but the harder I tried, the more she faded until she vanished altogether.

I wandered through a field of mist. The foggy gray swirls hid something just beyond my range of sight. Giant fleeting shapes moved by me and strange masses loomed high overhead. Voices called out, but none of them knew my name. I walked for what felt like hours until I tripped over something hard.

When I looked up the mists had peeled back and the world was like it always had been, except that everyone had turned into zombies—grinning corpses driving cars, working in stores, running into the post office. A baby rolled by in a stroller with a bottle of blood clutched in his pudgy gray hands. His mother smiled as they turned a corner. Then I realized who they were, but they were gone before I could chase after them. The streets of the city went on forever like a wild maze of concrete and steel growing and changing around me. Alleys became dead ends. Bars appeared in windows. The air grew wet and suffocating.

I snapped awake with Evelyn's laughter echoing in my head.

Figured I was done for the next morning when the screws caught sight of Brockden, but he covered up best he could, said nothing, and hid the limp I'd given him. He'd had one shot in him and it had failed. That sad son of a bitch would've eaten glass if I told him to after that.

Gave me a scare, though, when I was fetched away from breakfast for an audience with Warden Grove.

Two hacks brought me to the administration wing and planted me on a bench outside the warden's office. After awhile another con came out, blubbering like a baby. His eyes were swollen and his face was black and blue. He clutched his left arm to his chest like it was broken.

My turn next.

Standard procedure meant standing stiff-backed and motionless in Grove's office, while the warden reclined in a leather chair, puffing on a cigar. Two guards stood watch.

A window looked out over the south lawn, where the road to town cut a dusty scar through the fields. Slitbacks dotted the grass.

"Good morning, Mr. Cornell," said Grove. "Good of you to take the time to see me."

"Yes, sir," I said.

Grove blew a cloud of smoke toward me. I looked over the room's sparse decoration. It consisted of framed photographs of the warden from his days as a preacher or shaking hands with local bigwigs and state politicians. He had a few diplomas mixed in and here and there were pictures of his family.

"After a good many years preaching, I felt the need for a new challenge," he told me, noticing my interest. "Ten years ago I came here to shine the light of truth on the wicked. It has been most rewarding. Now, you may be wondering why I cut short your stay in solitary. Well, given recent events, it seemed appropriate you should have the same chance for salvation as any other man in my keep."

Grove took a thick file from his drawer and dropped it on his desk blotter. He leafed through a stack of newspaper and magazine clippings covering my story.

"But then I realized that you're a different kind of man than most of those incarcerated here, and so perhaps your road to redemption might not be as simple as theirs. You're an intelligent fellow, Mr. Cornell. But I believe you're crippled by a towering sadness."

He held up a clipping of a photo of Evelyn. "Could I be correct?"

Grove was good, that I'll grant him. He sniffed out your weak spot like a crow digging for grubs.

"Tell me about her," he ordered.

"Nothing to tell, sir," I replied.

"Did you love her? She was with child when she died, wasn't she? Was it *yours*?"

"I don't want to talk about it," I told him.

Grove snapped his fingers.

The hack's club slammed my kidney. Pain buckled me to my knees. I clenched my teeth against a scream.

"I'm a patient and understanding man," said Grove. "Share your pain with me and the Lord. Cleanse yourself."

The guard struck again, glancing his wood off my shoulder blade. Fresh pain blasted through me like slivers of hot glass.

"The way to redemption begins with the admission of sin," Grove continued. "Do you hate yourself for leading the woman to a wretched life that got her killed?"

I laughed despite the burning aches. No one had ever led Evelyn to anything.

"No? The child, then?" Grove probed. "Help me out here, Mr.

Cornell. We both know you don't lose any sleep over the money you stole. Such material transgressions are of little interest to either one of us, I think."

The guard's boot slammed my stomach, lifted me, and left me gasping for air.

"Whether you know it or not, you have arrived at a crossroads. Your body will die and rot, as all men's bodies do. The question is whether your soul will remain trapped within it after your death or be freed to obtain its heavenly reward. I offer you salvation, Mr. Cornell. You suffer no easy pain, but time heals all wounds. I can give you the opportunity to lick yours and knit your soul back together."

A fist crushed the back of my neck, driving me to the floor.

"You are a charming and gifted young man with the ability to secure people's loyalty and capture their imagination. These are skills I would find most useful in my upcoming mission," Grove explained. "My work here will end soon. Last night commenced the final stage. When it's complete, I'll lead a select group of men into the world to free those worthy of redemption and coach any we might find still living toward their everlasting riches. There are many, many good souls out there trapped in foul decaying flesh, and God has charged me with their rescue."

The baton lashed into my thigh. I fell sideways and gasped.

"You have the makings of a leader. Could have been a successful businessman, an entertainer, a politician with your charisma. A man like you could sustain my men's commitment, and help me win the trust of the wanting multitudes, Mr. Cornell. Don't force me to choose a more expedient means to resolve your case."

My thoughts whirled like mud in a rain-swept river. Pain rose like floodwaters. I clung to a desire to lighten the burden I'd borne since the day Evelyn died, and part of me began to buy Grove's insanity. He was right about one thing: I needed to face my guilt for betraying Evelyn. I'd fooled myself long enough about that. But I could never do it in prison, cowering and scraping just to get by when I should be running circles around these madmen and losers. "Play by your own rules," Evelyn had always said, but I'd given up and hobbled myself. Made my debt to her a thousand times worse. Grove's offer could be a way out.

But I already had that, I reminded myself, unless I let get beaten so badly I can't walk, like Jaime. Then that door shuts forever.

"Evelyn," I gasped. "I promised...her...two things. Protect her always...and never...kill a man...in cold blood. Broke both...the day she died."

It was true. Grove would have known if it wasn't. But those few words hurt more than any beating ever could. I had fired on the bank manager in a blistering rage after he shot Evelyn, but those two rent-a-cops had been as shocked as I was when their boss drew his weapon. I didn't need to kill them. I just wanted to because all the light had gone out of my world.

Grove waved off the guard.

"Thank you," the warden said. "Your honesty is appreciated."

He circled his desk, lifted me under the arms, and helped me to a chair. He took a handkerchief from his pocket, wiped the blood from my face, and left the cloth in my hand. He poured a glass of water and held it to my lips.

"Who... decides?" I demanded. Needles of pain flared at the back my eyes. Blood oozed down my throat. "Who says... who's worth saving... and who gets damned?"

"That burden God has appointed to me," Grove replied. "I am here to do His work, and I shall not flinch from my duties."

"And... when you're done?"

"We all go to our reward someday," he said.

Just another way out, I told myself. That's all—a backup plan. Make no more of it. Break out with Klug or throw in with this lunatic, once I'm on the other side of the walls, I can get away clean. Sometimes it's okay to play by the crazy man's rules, long as you don't forget your own.

"You'll begin your mission tonight and assist me at the gallows. The men have heard the Word too often coming from me. A new voice must deliver it—one of their own," ordered Grove.

I hadn't counted on that.

Damn jackal had pounced, and his hot breath was steaming down the back of my neck.

THINGS DIDN'T GO WELL for Jaime.

The guards found him fighting off the resurrected skinheads with my shiv in time to keep him alive, but his blood drove one of the bastards to gnaw clean through his leg above the knee. Damn shame a right guy who could fight like that losing a leg. Least he didn't have to live with it long. That night he came, propped up on crutches, with the first group of convicts the warden paraded onto the scaffold. Jaime played along with Grove's little patch of drama club, and when the executioner fitted his hood, he welcomed it with an oddly gratified expression, like he had finally gotten the answer to some question that had been itching away under his skin for a long, long time. I saw it because I was standing three feet away. Then the traps opened, and Jaime and his two companions dangled into oblivion. Grove let them hang a while, before the hacks threw their quaking bodies on the bonfire.

Better than spending your last days a cripple lying around waiting for the end, I suppose.

Others had the same idea. The man who had passed me outside the warden's office that morning was in the next trio. Some actually bought into Grove's proposition, and the warden couldn't have looked more pleased with the way it was going. But every time he flashed his swinish grin, I thought of Combest and Georges, right at that moment siphoning gas in the loading dock. By the end of the day tomorrow, Warden Grove would be a bad memory.

Midway through the service I took center stage and spouted the words Grove had supplied, mixing them up like he'd asked to make them sound like my own. I know when I have people's attention—you become attuned to the sensation when you rob banks—and I had plenty of it that night in the form of burning hatred from the convicts who thought I'd flipped to save my own skin. Guess they were right, even if I didn't care what the words meant. But why play it their way and wind up dead? What made them different than all the other people wanting to tell me how I ought to live and resenting me for not buying their bullshit code? At that moment I saw no difference between them and the men who had locked us all away, or even the hungry, mindless slitbacks.

Shit, at least the goddamned zombies didn't lie about wanting to eat you.

The three cons who followed my speech were different. They were beaten down, all right, but fresh anger smoldered in their eyes, and the supercops had to drag them out and hold them tight while they roped them up.

"I can only hint at how pleased I am that some of you have chosen to accept my aid," Grove announced. "I have faith that more will make the same decision. But I understand that some among you are incorrigible and incapable of repenting your ways, and I have elected to waste no time with men of such disposition. Men like these sinners behind me. Witness their fate, which is the end of all those who choose the path of sin. May they do some good by their example."

Felt a genuine pang of loss watching those unbroken spirits die. Got a little sick watching them twitch around at the end of their ropes. After a while the screws came and hauled them up. Dragged them, not to the bonfire, but to a pen erected beside the opposite end of the gallows and in they went, tumbling over each other and clambering to their feet. They reached through the bars, straining toward the crowd, their heads tilted at strange angles. No, they couldn't see through their hoods, but there's no doubt they knew we were there.

FOUR GUYS COMMITTED SUICIDE the next day. One managed to do the job right—a wiry kid in for possession who doused his clothes in turpentine from the shop, then set a match to his shirt. The screws displayed uncharacteristic good sense by letting him burn before they hit him with fire extinguishers. Another made a grab for a guard's gun, forcing a shootout. The hacks fought his corpse into submission long enough to set fire to it. Number three swallowed most of a box of rat poison, told no one, and died on his feet washing breakfast dishes in the kitchen. He bit through the throat of the inmate next to him before the other cons cleared out, and two guards returned with scatterguns to rip the dead bastards to pieces. The fourth grabbed a knife during lunch and cut his throat. Panicked inmates stumbled over each other trying to get away, blocking the screws from reaching the dead man before his corpse turned. He killed two more inmates and wounded a guard before they pinned down all four of them.

Made a fine distraction for Paulson and Combest sneaking provisions from the kitchen and Della slipping medical supplies out of the infirmary.

That afternoon I crossed paths with the King Snake in the yard.

"Don't cross me, Cornell," he warned.

"Grove dragged me into his office and gave me an ultimatum. Beat the tar out of me, as you might have noticed," I said. "This shit is just buying time."

"I know all about it. You did what you had to. Okay. Right now I trust you," he said. "So you keep doing what you have to. Stay tight with Grove a few more hours. Just makes it all the sweeter when we pull this off right under his nose. But you try to fuck me, and I will turn your skull into my own personal piss pot."

I started to answer, but Klug was already moving on, not wanting to be seen talking to me too long.

He never mentioned Jaime.

ONE OF THE FIRST supplicants at that night's service was a low-level trafficker I'd encountered many years back and hadn't seen or heard of since. He winked at me and whispered how it was good to go out with a familiar face nearby. He was small and burned fast.

The second wave included Brockden, crossing the platform as

straight and tall as he could, looking like one of the few who hadn't needed the warden's gentle coercion. I suppose I had helped out somewhat in that department. He stared me down the whole time, and when the executioner fitted his hood, he flashed me a final smile that said he'd found a way to cheat me out of killing him.

Guess it meant something to him, then, how he died.

Eighteen more cons took the long dive that night.

One prayed right up until the noose choked his throat closed.

Another pranced around and flipped us the bird while he shouted how he'd see us all in Hell. That one landed in the pen.

Now, there were nine slitbacks crowded in there, bouncing off each other trying to get out, but the cage was too strong. Most of them had worked their hoods loose, and they never took their eyes off the crowd. I knew, then, the real reason for Mason's brand of target practice.

We watched them die. They watched us live.

My first chance to slip away came when the service ended, but one of the guards caught me dead on.

"Warden wants to see you," he said.

Down in Grove's office I found him waiting with half a dozen hacks standing around, and I knew it had all gone to shit when I saw Old Corntooth lurking—bitter and self-satisfied—in the corner.

Grove read my expression in a heartbeat. "Think they're worrying about you, by now?" he asked. "Mr. Klug and the others don't like to be kept waiting, I'd imagine."

"Don't know what you mean," I said.

"Don't lie to me, Mr. Cornell. You can't protect them. Your old acquaintance told us about the breakout, but he doesn't know the specifics. Now, I have seen a side of you others have not, and so I'm willing to give you the benefit of the doubt and believe you were left no choice but to go along with this desperate scheme. Why don't you prove my faith in you, and tell me where to find these would-be escapees?"

Smart thing to do would have been to give them up, work myself even tighter in with Grove, and bide my time till we left on his mission. Not like I owed Klug anything. But it wasn't misguided loyalty that led me the other way. I'd just had my fill of letting other people call the shots, and even if I went down right then, Klug's group would still have a chance to make it out. Mostly I hated to see some tired, broken-down pussy like Old Corntooth get a leg up on the few people I knew who weren't afraid to keep fighting for something other than the shit deal life handed them. And I had a special kind of dislike for the warden.

"Nobody's breaking out," I said. "What's the point? Where would they run?"

"I see we haven't made all the progress I had hoped. Once down this road should've been enough for you." Grove waved on the guards. "But I've never been one to shy away from a difficult case. All dogs can be trained, after all."

I kissed a little farewell off to Evelyn, apologizing for letting it end like this, but I knew she'd understand.

Three hacks slid batons from their belts. One of them tried to draw me out, stupid and clumsy, with a loose snap on his holster, making his exposed gun an invitation to give them a reason.

Or was it?

The hack's badge read Georges, the name of the only guard in on the breakout I hadn't met.

The King Snake's specialty was making things happen, but there was no signal in Georges's steady gray eyes. Of course there wouldn't be. He needed me to make the first move. Wouldn't pay to blow his cover if I wasn't ready to follow his lead.

One way or the other the gun was a way out. I just prayed it was the one I wanted.

When Georges raised his stick, I seized his automatic, rolled across the floor, and fired four shots. Three hit home and three guards went down, and before I had time to finish wondering, Georges clubbed the fourth into unconsciousness. The fifth froze in his tracks, confronted by the barrel of my gun. Georges produced a pistol from his back-up holster and aimed it at the warden. Blood staining Grove's carpet told us at least two of the men on the floor were dead. We all noticed it at the same time and glanced at the clock above the door— wouldn't be long before the dead men developed an appetite.

Grove stood solid and stone-faced behind his desk. "What exactly do you think you're doing, men?"

"Fuck you, old man," Georges said. "Changing of the guard."

"You won't accomplish anything this way—except a lot of bloodshed," said Grove. "Now, I'm not afraid to die. How about you? Or you, Cornell? You going along with this nonsense?"

"Shit! We don't have time for this!" screamed Georges.

He whirled and planted a shot in Old Corntooth's head. The old man hit the wall and slid to the floor, smearing a track of blood behind him.

"Sorry, Fredericks," he said to the last guard then shot him in the chest.

"Hey, man," I told Georges. "We need to go, now!"

But he jumped over Grove's desk and whacked the warden behind the ear with the grip of his pistol. The blow staggered him. Georges grabbed his arm and dragged him out of the office. I followed, slamming the door behind us.

"Leave Grove," I said. "He'll just slow us down."

Georges narrowed his eyes and glared at me. "Who the fuck asked you, pretty boy? You do what I say."

We took the shortest route from Grove's office to outside the administration wing, keeping out of sight along shortcuts and back corridors that Georges knew. Closer we got to the delivery docks the more deserted the place became. The entrance was right where Klug had shown us on his map. Mason and Combest were there, loading packages of food onto the back of the truck.

"What the fuck is this?" Mason demanded when he saw Grove.

"Klug here yet?" said Georges.

"No," Mason answered. "Now, tell me why Grove is."

Georges kicked Grove down the stairs. The one-time preacher tumbled to the concrete floor then lay on his back, groaning.

"Get me some rope, Combest," Georges ordered.

He tied Grove's hands behind his back, knotted his feet together and dumped him in the corner. Mason asked again for an explanation, but Georges shut him down.

"I don't answer to you. Wait for Klug."

He paced the room while the rest of us finished packing supplies. Mason had come through with a stash of rifles, shotguns, and pistols. He handed me an automatic with visible reluctance.

"Like you said, gonna have to trust you sometime," he told me, keeping one eye on Georges.

I checked to make sure the gun was loaded. It was. I tucked it into my waistband.

Scopes and Della arrived next with two satchels of medical supplies she locked in a chest built into the back of the van. That made all of us, except for Klug and Paulson, and so we sat in the dimly lit garage and waited, some of us maybe wondering what kind of world we would find outside these walls. Not me, though. I knew better. The world had been born dead, except for the few shining lights I'd found in it, and I'd allowed the brightest of those to be snuffed out. Didn't expect to find much different out there from when I had first left it. All I wanted was my freedom. I'd come to prison expecting punishment for letting Evelyn down. Instead I got the same bullshit that kept me from living my life in the first place. Debasing my spirit was never going to help me reconcile my broken promises. Evelyn would've wanted me to live the best life I could on my own terms, and that was exactly what I planned to do, what we all planned to do.

Too bad that jackal sniffing his hot nose through my hair didn't give a piss about our plans.

We knew right away what was wrong when Paulson shuffled onto the loading platform stiff-legged and gray.

"Shit," said Mason. He braced his rifle against his shoulder and squinted into the sight. "No one will hear if I fire. No one's even in this end of the building."

Bullets gouged through Paulson's eyes and ripped open most of his skull. He crumpled then rolled over and crawled forward, falling from the loading platform to the floor.

"How do we get out of here? Paulson was supposed to have the keys," said Combest.

"Doesn't matter. Wait for Klug," Georges said.

"Maybe Paulson got the stuff," Mason suggested. "Son of a bitch looks like he died on his feet. Must have been sick."

"Yeah, he was," I said, recalling how he had been sweating and trembling the past two days.

Mason got a shotgun from the truck and edged toward Paulson. He pressed the barrel against the dead man's hip and fired, nearly severing the leg. The shot knocked Paulson flat, and Mason shifted the gun over a shoulder and took off an arm. He reloaded and blasted the other, then sighted over his neck, and ripped the corpse's head most of the way loose. It didn't stop Paulson but he couldn't move very well, and Mason found little trouble beating off the advances of the dead man's limbs while he searched his uniform.

"Got it," he said, holding up an overloaded key ring and a small notebook. He wiped the blood off it onto his pants. The punch codes were written inside.

"We got everything we need," urged Della. "Let's go."

"No!" screamed Georges. "We do nothing without Klug!"

"Klug could be dead or worse," Della argued. "The longer we wait—"

Georges slapped her. The wet smack resounded through the garage, and Della stumbled.

Mason and I moved at the same time, but I was closer and that's why Georges wound up on the floor with my foot on his throat rather than with a bullet in his head. Someone needed to take control of this show before things got out of hand.

"Mason," I said, "point your gun somewhere else, give Combest the keys then get the truck ready."

He didn't want to do it, but he did. Combest took five tries to find the right key and open the lock. The electric doors crawled upward. Night poured in. The narrow driveway stretched into it, turning into darkness toward the prison gate. I expected that fresh air to smell like freedom, but instead I choked on its stench. We couldn't see the slit-backs right away, but we could smell them.

"What the hell?" said Scopes.

Three figures drifted toward the open doors. Four more followed. Scopes grabbed a flashlight and caught one full on in the beam—the fat Aryan punk whose neck I'd gutted. His partner trailed behind him.

"Slitbacks," he said.

More figures staggered into the faint light, among them were the victims of some of the cons who had committed suicide, inmates who had died less publicly than Grove's showcase sacrifices, guards who had maybe refused to go along with the warden's plan. Guess he had dumped them all here for cheap security in case anyone tried to do exactly what we had in mind. About fifty of them blocked our path. He must have started stockpiling them early on.

"What do we do now?" whined Combest.

"Close that goddamn door, first of all," Klug's voice boomed down from the loading platform. "And Cornell, get your foot off of Georges."

The King Snake came towards us like his namesake, sly, easy, and lethal.

He crouched over Warden Grove, lifting his face from the ground and holding it close to his own. "Gotcha, motherfucker, I win," he said then punched Grove in the nose and bounced his head off the floor.

"Son of a bitch, it worked, Klug," sputtered Georges.

"Damn right," the King Snake said. "Now get those guns off the truck and get ready. No one's going anywhere."

"What the fuck are you talking about?" bellowed Mason.

"We have Grove. That means this whole fucking pit is ours. We put him out for show on his own gallows, hang his ass out where anyone who wants to can beat it with a stick for a few days, and we'll have this whole place in our pocket. I have men waiting for my signal. Now I have guns to give them. We're going to turn this place into a fortress," said Klug.

"What about escaping?" asked Della.

"To some cabin in the woods? When we can stay here, forage in town, and build an empire? I never meant to leave, sweetheart. Just wanted Grove looking the other way until we got close to him. Knew he was interested in Cornell so I played that card for what it was worth and it paid off better than I ever expected. Escaping was a last ditch backup plan at best." Klug winked at me. "Sorry I couldn't let you in on it, brother, but I needed you believing we were leaving for real when Grove moved on you. Now, you all can do what I say and come along for the ride or you can die right here."

"Bullshit," said Mason.

"You think so?" asked Klug. He took Georges's gun and fired before anyone could stop him. Combest screamed once then fell. Klug moved across the room, kicked Combest's body outside then hit the door switch. The panels crawled downward. Combest was still alive, moaning and too shocked to move.

"I told him to shut the fucking door," said Klug. He removed the keys from the control box and put them in his pocket. "And I fucking meant it."

It wouldn't have hurt the King Snake to let us go, but he wasn't one to give something away for free. Maybe if he'd known that Mason's family had been among those on the bus turned out by Grove at the prison gates, he'd have tapped someone else to secure his arsenal. Maybe he would've understood Mason felt the same way I did—that he just wanted his freedom and didn't care what anyone else thought he ought to be doing. Damn hard to bully someone who has nothing to lose. Man in that position tends to hit back where it hurts most.

"Well, then, fuck you, too!" Mason yelled. He raised his rifle and blew away most of Lane Grove's face in spray of hot, red gore that painted the concrete.

Klug gaped. Not even the King Snake could think of everything.

"Motherfucker!" he screamed.

Scopes charged toward the stash of weapons on the truck, but Mason blasted his legs, crippling him.

Georges pulled a snub-nose from his ankle and fired wild, shattering one of the truck windshields. Shots ricocheted off the masonry and everyone ducked. I grabbed Della's hand and pulled her around the far side of the truck we had loaded. Mason vanished behind one of the other vehicles and squeezed off rounds in rapid succession, forcing Klug and Georges behind a stack of crates in the opposite corner. They left Scopes writhing in pain on the floor.

When the gunfire ceased echoing I heard two things—the first lazy thumps of slitbacks beating on the garage door and the voices of live men barking in the inside corridor.

Up to then that jackal breathing down my neck had only been playing with his food. But his hunger had finally outweighed his boredom and it was time to sink his fangs in deep.

The inside doors of the loading area exploded with a crashing whoosh and half a dozen guards burst through in a cloud of smoke. Klug and Georges opened fire before the hacks got their bearings, forcing them back. Two of them dropped on the platform. Georges spread some cover fire while Klug wriggled out and grabbed a rifle off one of them. Then the King Snake unleashed his fury and the guards returned in kind. Bullets whined through the air. Sparks flew as lead pocked the metal doorframe. Bits of masonry spun loose from the walls. Klug's mouth hung wide in a silent scream, and he paid no attention to the shot that grazed his shoulder and left a trail of blood soaked into his singed shirtsleeve.

Through it all Paulson's head wobbled below the crossfire like a bird's egg. His eyes strained for sight of food. His limbs squirmed around him like worms.

Klug and Georges would run out of ammo soon at the rate they were firing, and when their guns died, the guards would advance again. Seemed wasteful until I understood they were watching the clock, holding off the hacks till the dead men on the platform got up and started running interference. I might have done the same, and that got me moving, because I knew the next step would be to get to the weapons. And unless Klug's disposition had a gotten a whole lot cheerier as a result of being shot at that meant going through us.

Mason and I made eye contact, drawing the same conclusion—only way out was the yard. We had the truck. Klug had the key to the door.

I shoved my gun into Della's hands and told her to cover me.

"No problem," she said. She handled the gun with confidence, getting a shot off every few seconds to keep Georges from turning his attention our way. I slipped into the exposed opening at the back of the truck and found the three spare fuel cans that had been prepared. I lined them up within reach of the door, grabbed one and dropped to the floor, ducking and crabwalking toward the yard exit. The pungent fumes burned my nose when I opened the cap, and I tried not to splash fuel on myself as I emptied the can to make a puddle halfway along the length of the door. The slitbacks were standing just inches away on the far side of a thin sheet of aluminum. The metal rumbled under their fists, and their sorrowful moaning drifted through.

Running back to Della, I saw Warden Grove pick himself up. The remains of his head poked upward like a broken flowerpot, and he shuffled his way toward the nearest food source—Scopes. Grove pounced on the wounded man like a rodent, ripping his flesh with the splinters of his teeth. Scopes only stopped screaming when Grove chewed open his throat.

The gunshots were dying down. Georges had emptied his snub-nose and produced yet another weapon, and I wondered where the hell he hid them all. A truck engine rumbled to life. I had time to wave once for luck to Mason before he revved the motor, popped the clutch, and blasted in reverse across the loading area. The truck body smashed through the crates that had shielded Klug and Georges. Chunks of wood twirled in every direction. Klug twisted around, face contorted. The back bumper caught him below the waist, lifted him and pinned him to the cinder-block wall. His rifle sailed loose and disappeared below the wheels. I thought the impact might cut Klug in half, but then the truck came to an abrupt halt.

The crash had knocked Georges sideways into a mess of broken crates. He tried to aim his gun when Mason climbed out of the cab, but it dangled from his broken wrist like a useless toy. Mason shot him, anyway, hitting him in the neck.

I grabbed a shotgun from the stash and trailed Della to the corner.

We got there in time to watch the King Snake realize that he was trapped unarmed with a corpse that would soon be hungry for his flesh and that we were leaving without him.

He didn't like either circumstance.

Mason shoved his hand into Klug's sweat-dampened shirt pocket, fishing for the keys and took them straight to the control box when he found them. Soon it would dawn on the supercops that they weren't being shot at anymore.

"You can't leave me here, Cornell," pleaded Klug. "I know this shit wasn't supposed to go down this way, but we've got to put that behind us. C'mon, man! Ain't no part of Lohatchie left but you and me, now. We got to stick together."

Felt like I should have something smart to say, then, but I stayed silent and stared at him like he was a bug pinned to piece of cork-board. He screwed his face into a twisted wreck of anger, and then all at once let it go as he started laughing. Only took me a moment to catch onto the joke.

I ducked sideways with maybe a second's breathing room, just in time to avoid the gore-drenched hug of Warden Grove approaching me from behind. Klug stopped laughing when Grove's momentum carried him into the wreckage. The preacher zombie tripped and started crawling his way toward the King Snake. After all, what's the difference between Klug and me to a slitback? Fresh meat is fresh meat.

With the corner of my eye I spotted the two dead hacks dragging their pale bodies upright. Scopes would be next, I remembered. Time to move.

Della sent a couple of potshots at the guards to keep them hiding then ran to the truck. Mason was ready at the control box.

My first two matches extinguished in the gas puddle, but the third ignited a low wall of blinding hot flame that licked at the door. Mason hit the switch and we hauled back to the truck as the door inched up. The fire spread down a ten-foot length between us and the yard, and as the opening widened, the first slitbacks pushed inside. They burned like sinister jack o' lanterns. The aroma of cooking flesh polluted the air, and others fell into the conflagration where they drove the flames higher. The smart ones trailed around to the clear end. Soon all the zombies shambled to one side, and the yard emptied out in front of us.

The first slitback to reach the truck knocked on the passenger side window and Mason gave him the finger. Della hunkered down behind the seat and I sat behind the wheel with the engine running. Only three slitbacks stood in our way when I gunned the motor. Heat rippled through the truck as we breached waist high fire. Zombies crunched under the tires, bouncing us like speed bumps.

And then Mason was pulling my arm and screaming, tugging on the wheel so we swerved right and more slitbacks smacked off our fenders.

Combest's torso appeared in the glow of the headlights.

The punch codes.

I slammed the brakes hard, and brought the passenger side as close to Combest as I could. Mason popped the door and dropped to the ground. He fired on the closest zombies, launching chunks of flesh into the darkness, then rifled Combest's shirt. The notebook was gone. He heaved the body over and patted the dark grass, feeling for the paper and cardboard. The slitbacks closed in, and I slid into the passenger seat and blasted them with the scattergun. Blood gushed from their wounds, but they kept coming.

"Forget it," I screamed. In moments they would overrun us. "We'll crash the gate."

"No!" Mason yelled. "Got it!"

Then he was back in the cab, shoving me toward the driver's seat and tugging the door closed behind him. I punched the gas and we rocketed into the yard, plowing through slitbacks. The truck jounced and skidded. Twice bodies caught up in the wheel well almost took away control, but after that the ride went smooth as we raced down the hard pavement of the driveway. The first fence loomed ahead, a darkened guard post beyond it, and I skidded us to a halt two inches from the heavy chain link.

Mason leapt out, clutching the wet notebook and punched in the codes.

The slitbacks came faster than I thought they could. A dozen wobbled toward us.

"Shit, there are more of them?" asked Della.

Mason sidestepped the trundling gate to enter the pen, and I rolled the truck in after him. Moments later the fence slid closed, and we were sandwiched between the yard and the outside world.

But there, beyond the outer gate fifty, sixty, a hundred slitbacks glommed against the fence like they had expected us.

Mason roared and fired bullet after bullet into them until he emptied his clip. I thought he might reload and keep firing, but instead he slung the rifle over his shoulder and rubbed his head.

"How the hell do we get past them?" he asked.

Della climbed out of the cab. "What do we do now... ," she said.

"Now," I answered. "We blow up the truck."

It was the first thing I thought of and it struck me as the kind of rare inspiration that should be trusted even if you can't quite figure how it's all going to work out. I didn't know what chance we would have on foot outside the prison walls, but I heard Evelyn's voice telling me not to give up, happy again because I had stopped lying down to take what came my way.

Or as Lane Grove might have put, the Lord helps those who help themselves.

"That's the best you can come up with?" Della challenged.

"Well, yeah," I replied. "Go back, we die. Stay here, we die. Only choice we've got is keep going forward."

"Fuck," she said. "Then let's make it work."

"We take what we can carry," I said. "Then light the gas tank, open the gate, and hide in the station booth. Let in as many slitbacks as will fit and wait for the fuel to blow them to cinders. Then we run out through the visitor's door."

The guard station included a small airlock type of arrangement that protruded beyond the gate. It was used to admit people on foot without passing them through the pen. It wouldn't protect us for long, but I hoped it wouldn't have to.

The chain link buckled under the weight of the zombies that had chased us across the yard. There were Scopes and Grove, and I saw Klug in the distance limping along with half his torso shorn open.

"Town's thirty miles north of here," Mason told me. "Gonna be a hard run with the countryside crawling with slitbacks. My house is less than half that distance east. We make it there, I think we can get a car."

"All right, then," I said. "We're staying at your place. Let's start packing."

We took guns and extra ammo. Della insisted on bringing the medical supplies over my objections, but I figured any wound you couldn't walk off was as good as being dead. We stowed enough food to hold us two days then prepared the truck. Fetid hands clawed to break through the chain link on both sides of us. The groans and half-formed yelps of the dead filled the air. Mason and Della put our gear in the guardhouse while I tied strips of padding from the truck together and soaked them in gas to make a fuse. I threaded it into the truck's gas nozzle and shoved it down as deep as I could with my rifle barrel. Della took the third can of gas, jumped up on the hood of the truck, and splashed fuel over the mob of slitbacks. Mason entered the code for the gate and punched the button. It creaked sideways, squealing under the weight of the zombies. I lit the fuse, and we ran into the booth.

The slitbacks stumbled in, tripping over one another in the confined space. The gates spread and more followed, clotting against the front of the truck and blotting out the headlights. The pen became a writhing tangle of shadows moving toward the guard booth, where we crouched below window level. With luck the wire-reinforced glass would hold up to the explosion.

Damn good thing it at least proved bullet resistant. Three shots must have struck it before we realized we were under fire.

The spotlight in the nearby guard tower flickered to life and we saw the hacks up there pointing down at us. They must have hoped to cut us off.

The light drew the attention of the slitbacks away from the booth, but there were so many of them, there was no way to return fire without exposing ourselves.

We were stuck waiting. And it was taking a hell of lot longer than I had expected for the gas tank to blow. We heard the zombies right on top of us, lowing like sick cows and batting weak fists against the windows. They knew we were there. Every few seconds another shot from the guard tower ripped through one of them and sprayed blood onto the window glass, turning the spotlight ruby in the dark space we occupied. The gunshots came more rapidly, and I knew the windows couldn't hold much longer. We grabbed our weapons and prepared to fight.

Night erupted into blinding day.

A wall of heat cascaded over us.

The weakened glass shattered, and heavy, webbed chunks rained down. Burning metal and flesh flew into the room and crashed against the far wall.

The explosion had been less powerful than I anticipated. The truck went up like a charcoal barbecue doused with too much lighter fluid rather than a bomb, but the desired affect was achieved. All the slitbacks in the pen were alight from head to toe and they were packed so close together the flames danced among them, reaching out to those still beyond the gate, turning the mass of them into horrible scarecrow torches. The confines of the pen had driven much of the explosive force upward where it hit the guard tower. The spotlight had fizzled when a piece of debris shattered it. Patches of flame burned in the darkness above us.

We ran.

There were four slitbacks outside the visitor's door. We knocked them over and pushed past them. Other slitbacks came toward us, but we batted them away, or shot their legs out from under them. The farther we moved from the prison, the fewer there were. Most were moving toward the gate, walking in two lines around the prison walls, drawn by the light and noise or beckoned by those who had been there first. We took a path through the woods, one Mason knew well enough to navigate by night, and came out on the road about two miles away from the prison. It was deserted. At a steady pace, we would reach Mason's house by morning and there make plans to go back into the world. One thing Klug got right was my hideaway deep in the Everglades north of Lohatchie, and if all the world proved a cesspool of decaying flesh and cannibal zombies, then we could head there, leave it all behind us, and make a new life.

Walking along in the moonlit stillness, I tasted air free of rot or fear for the first time in days, and I knew again how it felt to be a man. Somewhere that smiling jackal was laughing over the good scare he gave me, knowing all along it was only a matter of time before he decided to deliver what he had promised. But for now it was enough that I could no longer hear Evelyn's voice in the back of my mind because the only time she kept quiet was when she was satisfied.

ZOMBIE BEACH PARTY
Neal Patterson

Pale blue skies. Wheat tan shore. And in between, roiling foam atop the fiercest waves on the west coast. It was summer, and the old gang was back. The tinny sounds of jangling guitars emanated from transistor radios as bikini-clad beauties jiggled their toned fannies to the latest boss tunes. Volleyballs were spiked with abandon, and young men tested their mettle on the curling waves that charged endlessly toward shore. Some were good, but Freddie was *damn* good. With an uncanny sixth sense of each wave's capricious whim, Freddie finessed his board against the turbulent wall of water, caressing its ever changing form like the curves of an undulating belly dancer. Senses heightened, acutely aware of the slightest alteration, Freddie always commanded his board to shore.

After taking the best of a dozen waves, Freddie triumphantly charged up the beach to his girlfriend, Gigi, who had been watching him intently from her beach towel.

"What do you think of your daring boyfriend *now*?" Freddie queried, driving his board into the sand dramatically. "I haven't wiped out so far this summer."

"It's amazing, Freddie!" Gigi beamed, but her smile quickly faded.

Freddie dropped to his knees beside her, "What's the matter, puddin' pop? How can you be down on a gorgeous day like today?"

"It is gorgeous, Freddie. It's the most gorgeous day of the most gorgeous summer of my life. But everything comes to an end sooner or later. And when we head back home, what do we do then? High school's over, and you haven't even thought about college! What about our future?"

Freddie smirked, "C'mon, Gigi. Why do you want to bring everything down with talk like that? We have plenty of time for that stuff later. We've gotta swing while we can."

A volleyball bounced across Gigi's legs, followed quickly by a lanky Texan in a fishing hat and tight swim trunks.

"*Lunkhead!*"

"Sorry guys," Lunkhead apologized, sheepishly. "Lost control of my ball. I couldn't help but overhear, though. You know, Freddie has a point. With our government's insatiable desire to feed the military-industrial complex, we've set ourselves on a course of nuclear proliferation that may well result in the destruction of the entire planet. Therefore, an attitude of living for today and damn tomorrow is not at all unrealistic."

Gigi rolled her eyes. "Oh, Lunkhead! You say the craziest things!"

"Speaking of crazy," Freddie said, pointing down the beach. "Look what's coming this way."

It was a man in a gray suit walking up the beach. As he grew closer, his graying temples and salt-and-pepper van dyke betrayed his advancing years. He strode with great dignity despite the sand moving underneath his wingtips. Everyone stopped what they were doing and approached the man as if he were a gorilla escaped from the zoo.

Brad, the most serious of the group, was the first to speak up. "I think you may have lost your way, friend."

"Oh, on the contrary," the man replied with a slight lisp. "I've traveled many miles to reach this exact spot. You see, my name is Professor Price. I teach Ancient Cultures back East. I've come to settle the estate of my late aunt who owned the house down by the cove."

Professor Price pointed to a weathered, cedar shingled house in the distance.

"Funny, I never noticed that house before," Freddie muttered.

Torchy, the buxom red-head of every teenage boy's dreams, wiggled up to the elderly man. "Say, why don't you shake off those banker duds and join us for a game of volleyball?"

"I'd love to, my dear, but I'm afraid I have a previous engagement." Price moved closer to Gigi and gently kissed her knuckles. "Perhaps this lovely young lady can direct me to the Way Out A-Go-Go?"

"The Way Out A-Go-Go?!" Lunkhead squealed. "That place closed last summer!"

"Head over that hill to the main road," Gigi explained, a bit breathless. "Follow it down to Seagull Lane. Make a right and it's about four blocks down."

"Thank you, young lady," Professor Price replied. "And a good day to you all."

As Professor Price disappeared over the hill, Freddie scratched his head. "There's something odd about that cat."

"I think he's kind of charming and gallant," Gigi mused.

"I'm warning you, Gigi, you stay away from him!" Freddie fumed. "This doesn't add up. And where did that house come from?"

"You don't notice anything that you can't hang-ten on!" Brad cried.

Freddie sniffed, "Maybe if you paid more attention to the waves and less to your hair, you might be able to make it to shore once in a while."

"Say, this beach is getting kinda crowded," Lunkhead said, gesturing to the other side of the beach.

Strolling along in a clumsy gait came a short, squat, balding man wearing a sandwich board. The writing became more clear as he neared the group:

IMPRESS YOUR FRIENDS—BECOME A REAL LIVE SUPER-SLEUTH!

The man bowed his head, sporting a grin like a '55 Buick. "Hi gang, Big Dick here!"

"You're telling me," Freddie whispered to Gigi.

"What's with the walking advert?" Lunkhead asked.

"Oh, this is my new business venture," Big Dick announced. "Impress your friends! Become a real super-sleuth!" He turned around and pointed to the back of his sign:

ENROLL IN THE BIG DICK DETECTIVE SCHOOL TODAY!

"Detective school?" Brad cried. "What good would that do?"

"Some businesses come and go, my friend," Big Dick swung into his pitch. "but there's always chiselers, deadbeats, and philanderers who need to be tracked down by a good gumshoe. I can turn anyone into a first-class Sam Spade for just twenty-nine ninety-five."

Freddie's gears quickly meshed. This could be the career opportunity that I need to impress Gigi, he thought. If I could become a successful private eye, Gigi would be crazy *not* to marry me!

"All right. You're on, Mr. Dick!" Freddie declared.

"Please, I'm just plain Big."

"Oh, right."

"Say, I won't be outdone by this Neanderthal!" Brad interjected. "Sign me up too!"

Lunkhead then stepped forward. "I suppose man's never ending suspicion of his fellow man could provide ample opportunity for a life long means of financial reward."

"Stop talking like a goof, Lunkhead," Freddie scolded.

"What I mean to say is, I'm in."

———

"Now, the key to any good private investigator is the ability to study your surroundings," Big Dick expostulated from a rickety lectern at the front of his makeshift detective school. "Not to just *see* the world around you, but really *observe* the world around you."

Freddie, Brad, and Lunkhead dutifully took notes from their public school surplus chairs. When the three future detectives showed up for their first class at the address Big Dick had provided, it turned out to be the dilapidated Way Out A-Go-Go.

"Anything could be potentially important," Big Dick continued. "A man sitting in a car for a long period of time. A woman running down the street. A knocked over trash can. All these things could be perfectly innocent occurrences. On the other hand, they could be vital clues. Therefore, you must never take anything... for granted... nor should you..."

The lecture was drowned out by the growing roar of motorcycle engines from outside. The din became too great to bear as the cycles pulled up in formation outside the building. The four men approached the large picture window at the front of the room. A group of cyclists in leather jackets were dismounting their bikes. As they turned their backs to the men inside, Freddie, Brad, Lunkhead, and Big Dick shared a sense of queasiness. On the jackets, emblazoned in garish chartreuse, was the name The Subversives. The gang of three men and two women lined up as if at attention on the sidewalk. With some commotion, a compact bulldog of a man pushed his way through the group and quickly scrambled to regain his composure.

"Oh no!" Big Dick groaned at the sight of the man. "It's The Subversives, and their leader, Commie Qazi!"

With the snap of his fingers, Commie Qazi lead his minions into the newly-christened detective school. As they entered, Big Dick rushed toward them, oozing charm from every pore.

"Why look gang, it's The Subversives!" Big Dick gushed. "And to what do we owe this honor?"

"Enough with your pladitudations, Dick," Commie Qazi said flatly. "We only recently discovered that you have illegally and unethical-like purchased this establishment. We are here to reclaim this property as our rightful hangout."

"Now wait a minute, Qazi," Big Dick sputtered. "I purchased this building fair and square from the previous owner. He was more than willing to sell it to me for a song."

"I think I know why," Brad murmured to Freddie.

"I do not want to hear your technicalitudes, Dick," Qazi continued. "The Subversives have claimed this site as their honorarious place of hanging, and we will not be moved!"

"Yeah!" the phone booth of a man beside Qazi stated.

"It's all right, Pinko," Qazi consoled the man. "I can speak for myself."

Big Dick stiffened. "Look, Qazi, I don't want no trouble. But I have a deed, signed and legal, that says this is my property. So unless you want to enroll in my detective school, I'm going to have to ask you to leave."

Qazi's face invented a new shade of red. He began to hyperventilate with a wheezing sound only known to certain species of pig. Nervously, he proceeded to hitch up his black jeans. "Do you hear how this man chooses to speak to me?!"

"Calm down, Boss," Pinko said. "You know what happened the last time."

The red got redder and the pants rose higher. "No one, but no one, talks to Commie Qazi in that tone!" Hitch 'em up, hitch 'em up! "You are sealing your own fate, my friend! You are leaving me no alternative but—"

When the pants reached his nipples, Commie Qazi abruptly froze. Pinko rolled his eyes.

"Oh no!"

One of the girls exclaimed, "He gave himself *The Melvin!*"

As if it was rehearsed, the group of bikers picked up their leader by his arms and legs and carried him, statue-like, out the door.

"You ain't heard the last of us!" Pinko threatened as they disappeared out the door.

"Does anyone know what just happened here?" Freddie asked, as the four men gaped at each other in bewilderment.

———

Since the Way Out A-Go-Go had closed, the teenagers had moved to the Purple Frog as their new night-time haunt. It was a more up-scale club than the Way Out, attempting to cater to both the surfers and the older resort patrons. To that end, one side of the building was devoted to a restaurant of fine continental cuisine, and the other side had a bar and dance floor. Freddie and Gigi were on the dance floor, shaking and gyrating to the tunes of *Dennis O'Dell and the Surf Mops*. Although Gigi's perfectly lacquered hair would not move, she was beginning to perspire, so the two retreated to their usual corner table.

"You're the swingingest, Gigi," Freddie panted.

"And you're the most wonderful man in the world!"

Freddie was taken aback. "Go on."

"Well, I never thought you took anything I said seriously. But now that you've started in detective school, you've proven to me that you really do want to settle down and start a career. I'm so proud of you."

For once, Freddie looked serious. "Gigi, I know sometimes it seems like all I care about is waxing my board and chasing the best wave, but I care about you more than anything else in the world. In fact, when this summer's over, I was thinking—"

"Why, there you are, my dear!"

Professor Price was all at once present in front of their table. Once again, he gently kissed Gigi's hand. "I'm so happy to see you. This is the first time I've gathered the courage to venture out in this town. It's so nice to see a familiar face."

"Yeah, nice seein' ya', Doc," Freddie barked, trying his best bum's rush.

Gigi scolded Freddie with her eyes, then quickly recovered. "Would you like to join us, Professor?"

"Well, actually, I have a table waiting in the restaurant. I was wondering if you cared to join me… oh, your gentleman friend is welcome to join us, too."

"Sorry Doc," Freddie jumped in. "But Gigi and her 'gentleman friend' would prefer that you go scout out someone more geriatric for your dinner mate."

"Freddie!" Gigi glared. "You have to excuse his rudeness, Professor. He was raised by wolves!"

"There's only one wolf at this table, and it ain't me!"

Gigi ignored Freddie. "As a matter of fact, I think I would like very much to join you for dinner, Professor."

It took a second before Freddie could retrieve his jaw from the floor.

"Splendid!" Price exclaimed. He offered his bent arm to Gigi. "Come along my dear. Will you be joining us as well, Mr.—?"

"Just Freddie," he replied through gritted teeth. "And no, I suddenly have other plans."

A combination of anger and hurt flashed across Gigi's face. Freddie struggled to maintain a poker face. Before anymore could be said, Professor Price whisked Gigi from the table and into the restaurant.

It didn't take long for Brad and Lunkhead to circle the table.

"Gigi volunteering at the nursing home?" Brad asked.

"Can it, Brad," Freddie grumbled.

"It's not surprising," Lunkhead mused. "Since women tend to mature sooner emotionally than men, while also reaching their sexual peak at a later age than men, women of late adolescent age are often more attracted to older men who are mentally and emotionally mature while also less sexually driven than men of their own age."

"You are such a *lunkhead*, Lunkhead," Freddie jeered. "Everybody knows that young women want a guy with rock hard abs and a super-charged, chopped deuce coupe... *and* who can surf."

"Oh yeah," Lunkhead replied, smacking his forehead.

"I think one thing we can all agree on," Brad stated. "That Professor Price is really *creepy*."

"Yeah," Freddie cradled his chin in his hand. "He talks about an old aunt living on the beach, but I swear that house was not there until yesterday morning."

Brad nodded. "Come to think of it, I never noticed it before, either. And how could he have had an appointment at the Way Out A-Go-Go when Big Dick had turned the place into a detective school?"

Hearing his name, Big Dick turned around from the neighboring table. "Hey guys, taking my name in vain?"

"Hi Dick," Freddie muttered. "We're just trying to figure out what the story is with that Professor Price guy. He never came to your detective school, did he?"

"Price? Never heard of him. But hey, I've got a great idea for your final project. You can investigate this Professor Price. If you turn up anything juicy, it could be an A-plus for all of you!"

The three boys brightened. *The Mystery of the Peculiar Professor* was afoot.

———

Big Dick rolled his 3' x 4' mobile cork board to the front of his classroom and proceeded to tack up the photos and index cards that the boys had compiled over the last few days.

"I got some great shots in front of the house," Lunkhead said, perched awkwardly on the edge of one of the desks. "There are several of packages being delivered. Pretty large and heavy from the looks of them. The door is always answered by some butler-looking guy."

"About that house," Brad interrupted. "I checked the public records. There's no documentation to show that a house was ever built on that site."

"Great stuff!" Big Dick ejaculated. "What've you got, Freddie?"

"He's certainly been seeing a lot of Gigi lately," Freddie reported glumly, handing over photos of the two at the Purple Frog. "It looks like it's getting pretty serious. What could she see in him?"

"I hope she doesn't get too serious," Brad said. "This guy is plain no good. I noticed him on several occasions buddying up with our pals The Subversives at various discrete locations. I even saw money changing hands."

"Remuneration for unlawful acts of physical force?" Lunkhead offered.

"That's doesn't make sense," Freddie cried. "It more likely he's using The Subversives as hired muscle. And he's getting my Gigi involved!"

"All right, calm down boys," Big Dick said. "We've got a bunch of suspicious looking things, but nothing connects the dots. It could mean something; it could mean nothing. What we need is to dig deeper."

"Like how?" Brad asked.

"Like get inside that mystery house and prowl around."

"Don't you need a search warrant for that?" Lunkhead asked.

"Dummy, that's only for the police. We're *private* investigators!"

Lunkhead smacked his forehead.

"I know," Freddie exclaimed. "I'll pose as one of those delivery guys. Then I'll make up some excuse to get inside, like the package can't be signed for by anyone but Professor Price. That should get me past the butler."

Big Dick was bouncing with excitement. "Great! Let's move!"

———

Freddie scrounged through the Army-Navy Surplus store for anything that would pass for a special delivery man's uniform. A khaki shirt and pants, patent leather shoes, some pins and badges, and a cap. Then he dug through the dumpster behind the store to find a cardboard box that he could fashion into a package. By the time he had wrapped up his box with tape and labels, it was dusk. He threw on his makeshift delivery man's costume and headed for the mystery house, hoping his evening delivery would not appear suspicious.

"Can I help you?" the balding manservant greeted him with a voice that reminded Freddie of molasses rolling off a tin roof.

"Yes sir," Freddie replied, a crack in his voice. "I have a package."

"I'll sign for it," the butler stated.

Freddie spoke fast. "Uh, no sir, this package has, uh, super premium insurance. It can only be signed by the addressee, who in this case is..." Freddie made a show of reading the name on the label. "...a Professor... Prince?"

"*Price*," the butler corrected.

"Oh yeah," Freddie glanced at the label again.

The butler smirked in a bemused fashion. "Very well, will you please wait in the library while I fetch Professor Price?"

Freddie nodded and cautiously stepped inside.

Big Dick watched the proceedings pensively through binoculars from his Buick Skylark across the street. Brad was sitting in the passenger seat, craning his neck to glimpse what he could.

"Can you see anything through the windows?" Brad asked.

"Nope," Big Dick sighed, "he's got dark curtains. Stay cool, Freddie."

The inside of the house was pretty much like any other summer home in the resort, except for the heavy baroque furniture cluttering the relatively small rooms. The butler ushered Freddie into the library and promptly disappeared. Freddie marveled at the tremendous volumes lining the floor-to-ceiling bookshelves on all four walls. There were even books neatly stacked in piles on the floor. Most were ancient, dusty tomes with leather bindings and gold lettering.

Seconds passed like hours as Freddie slowly paced the room. Anxiety gripped his chest. Must stay calm, he thought. During his fifth stroll around the room, he stopped at a pedestal cradling an especially large and dusty book. The dry, amber pages crinkled in Freddie's hands as he turned the pages.

Some of the passages were written in English; others written in a language Freddie could not recognize. He needn't know the writing, for the illustrations said it all. Horrific etchings of torture, dismemberment, and violent, sadistic death. Corpses rising from their graves and attacking women and children. Villages ablaze while the walking dead wrenched limbs from agonized villagers.

Freddie slammed the book shut. This was more than he had bargained for. He dashed from the library and weaved through the maze of furniture toward the front door. He was fixated on the door when a robed figure blocked his way. Looking up, he recognized Professor Price.

"Don't you want my autograph?" Price grinned.

Freddie struggled to speak. "I don't care what you're up to! I just want out!"

"Too late, my boy," Price chuckled. "You're already very much *in*. But you could be of some use to me, after all."

A steel rod poked in Freddie's back. With a slight glance back, he spied the butler holding a revolver. Instinctively, Freddie's arms went up.

"We're having quite the party this evening," Price continued, strolling into the parlor. "A real *shindig*, as you young people might say. And I have the perfect date."

Professor Price emerged from the parlor clutching a young woman by the elbow. She wore a flowing, green evening gown and, despite the pale white powder on her face and the heavy mascara, Freddie would recognize Gigi anywhere. As Freddie fixed on her eyes, he saw panic, but also an unspoken pleading.

"You've gone too far, Price" Freddie cried. "Let her go! Why don't we have this out like men... or maybe you don't consider yourself a man!"

Price chuckled. "Spare me the melodrama, son. This isn't one of your drive-in movies. You have no idea with whom you are dealing." With a grand flourish of his left hand, the walls around them faded away. In a shimmering instant, the house was gone and the four were standing on Main Street. Only the books remained in orderly piles.

"Ah, my books—shipped in from around the world. I suppose they have served their purpose." With another swipe, the books erupted in flames, then rapidly were ashes.

Before Freddie could comprehend what he had just seen, the ferocious rumble of motorcycles introduced the arrival of The Subversives. Commie Qazi gave a wave from his chopper, apparently pleased with his recovery. Freddie also noticed Pinko sitting in the back seat of Big Dick's Buick, holding a gun on his two captives.

"Freddie, be a good boy and climb on the back of Mr. Qazi's bike," Price breezily ordered. "My manservant will drive Miss Gigi and I in the brougham."

With his friends held at gunpoint, Freddie had little choice but to snuggle up behind Commie Qazi on his shuttering motorcycle. Price, Gigi, and the butler climbed into an antique Packard. With the growl of engines, the unlikely caravan headed down main street. It was only minutes before the vehicles turned onto Seagull Lane and stopped in front of the Way Out A-Go-Go.

"Mr. Dick," Price ordered as he climbed out of his car. "please unlock the door of your establishment."

With Pinko's gun in his ribs, Big Dick unlocked the front door and they filed inside. Immediately, Price ordered The Subversives to move all the chairs, desks, and other furniture to the walls, clearing the floor. Then, he told everyone to form a circle in the center of the floor.

"Now, I'm sure some of you are wondering what all this is about," Price began. "I am a connoisseur of the occult. Until recently, it was little more than a hobby. That is, until I discovered a little-known legend regarding a pirate ship that once pillaged around the South China Seas. It seems the captain of the ship found amongst his booty an ancient book of sorcery. In it, he found incantations that would raise the dead. One such incantation could create zombies that would do his every bidding. Not long after, his entire crew was felled by a severe virus while they were out in the middle of the ocean. The captain decided to use the incantation to bring back his crew so that they could sail the ship to a safe harbor.

"Sadly, the captain did not use quite the right incantation, and he turned the crew into a violent, bloodthirsty zombie mob, fighting and feeding on itself. The captain was even attacked, losing his left arm. Hiding from the zombies in a tiny storage space, the captain studied his book while the ship sailed aimlessly for months. Finally, riddled with infection, he found an incantation in the book that would put the zombie crew to rest. With his dying breath, he uttered the incantation. The captain and his zombie crew were unaware when the ship crashed on the California coast.

"I intensely researched this story until I discovered the exact spot where the ship crashed. And that spot is... *right beneath our feet!*"

"Gee, Professor," Qazi groaned. "That's some campfire story, but I thought this was about getting our hangout back from this Dick here."

"Silence," Price bellowed. "now secure my fair Gigi to the post over there."

With a shrug, Qazi gestured to Pinko who obediently tied Gigi to a support post.

"Freddie, save me!" Gigi squealed, but Freddie was held fast by one of The Subversive goons.

Price flipped through his book and smiled when he reached the appropriate page. "Fortunately for me, unlike our pirate captain of yore, I have the benefit of careful, academic research. I can now confidently recite the correct incantation that will revive the zombie pirates and put them under my control."

Closing his eyes, he uttered words in an ancient tongue. As he spoke, the floor took on a slightly orange glow. Freddie thought it was moonlight filtering through the window, but it soon deepened in intensity. He also sensed heat through his shoes.

Professor Price's voice rose as he forced out the final words of the incantation. Shooting his fist into the air, the room shuddered with a stomach wrenching rumble. The solid orange circle on the floor became a fiery ring surrounding a pit about ten feet deep. With fire licking their toes, the group looked down into the pit before them.

There was motion in the darkness. Bodies in tattered, soiled rags twitched and shuttered. They began to rise and shuffle about. The pirate zombies were moving without purpose within the pit. Some limped pathetically on legs with shattered bones. Others swung lifeless, scarred arms about like sausages. All were caked in mud and congealed blood. The room was silent save for the low, agonized groans of the walking dead.

Qazi sniffed and attempted his bravest stance. "Congrats Professor. You woke up a bunch of stiffs. Now what does this have to do with us getting our hangout back?"

"You fool! Don't you grasp the gravity of this moment? The moment when I have again raised the pirate crew—when I alone will command an army of pirate zombies that will be the terror of the world! And you... *you* can be a part of my triumph!"

A slight smile played on Qazi's face. "Yeah, we could be feared and worshiped by everyone. What do we do now, boss?"

Price grinned without humor. "First, we need more zombies. Throw our friends here into the pit."

With a tremendous effort, Freddie, Brad, Lunkhead, and Big Dick fought to free themselves from the clutches of the gang members, but it was no use. The beefy motorcycle fiends tossed them to the waiting zombies. The undead roared as their first meal in several centuries landed before them. The once-promising detectives fought vainly against the onslaught of the pirates.

Qazi cackled as he stood on the edge of the pit watching the melee. "I warned youse guys! Commie Qazi always gets his revenge!"

"I've had about enough of you," Brad shouted to Qazi, kicking away a peckish zombie. With his strongest effort, he leaped and grabbed hold of the rocky pit wall. Using muscles toned by months on the waves, he struggled hand-over-hand up the side.

"C'mon, surf boy," Qazi taunted. "I'm waiting!"

Professor Price was already pondering the next phase of his plan. He approached Gigi and touched her perfectly coiffed hair. "We will be leaving soon, my dear. Then you and I will be the King and Queen of all we survey."

"You—you're *mad!*" she breathed, recoiling as Price moved in for a kiss.

The front door shattered, interrupting their moment of intimacy. It was the gang from the beach, and they were not happy.

"Hold it right there!" one of the boys cried. "You've got our friends, and we want them back! Let's get 'em!"

The rallying cry released an explosion of flying fists and feet. Qazi turned to join in the fracas, but he was held fast. Brad had made it up the wall and grabbed hold of Qazi's ankle. There was a struggle, but Brad's coiled arm-muscles performed a bone-breaking yank. He and Qazi both tumbled back into the pit.

Bodies crashed over Big Dick's surplus furniture. Miraculously, Professor Price dodged any attack, carefully weaving behind Subversives. He found a ladder in the back room of the former night-club and hauled it over to the pit. With great effort, he heaved it into the dark hole.

"Arise, my zombie soldiers!" Price shouted. "It is time for us to conquer the world!"

A horrid, acrid smell rose to Price's nostrils as the dank, ragged pirates climbed up to the surface. He was not fully prepared for the sight of their rotting, discolored flesh and milky eyes. He steeled himself, knowing that he had come too far to weaken.

"Attack these meddling kids!" he screamed.

One by one, they shuffled up the ladder and fell into the tumult. Spurts of blood soon decorated the walls and ceiling as the zombies tore into the flesh of the teenagers. Even The Subversives were not immune to their hunger. Only Professor Price, speaker of the incantation, was left alone. He began to enjoy the sense of power from the terror that he could unleash.

Gigi, helplessly tethered to the support post, was an unwilling witness to the carnage. She felt as if she would pass out when a sight before her suddenly shocked her upright. Commie Qazi, now a newly-created zombie—thanks to some nibbling on his leg—was shuffling toward her.

"She's a pretty one," he whispered, dragging his lame leg behind him.

Gigi struggled, her flesh burning under the taut ropes. Qazi's acrid breath touched her nose. She looked up and saw his bugging eyes glaring at her. His mouth salivating as it moved toward her jugular. Millimeters from her neck, he bolted upright in shock. He was frozen in his place. Gigi was stunned, but relieved to see Freddie step around from behind Qazi.

He pointed to Qazi's bunched up pants. "I gave him *The Melvin*."

"Oh, thank God," Gigi forced out, breathlessly.

Freddie immediately moved behind her and undid her bonds. Rubbing her burned and bleeding arms, Gigi kissed her hero... only, his cheek was oddly cold. Gigi had little time to contemplate the moment as Freddie was already chewing on her bloody arm flesh.

———————

Hallowood-by-the-Ocean was no longer a resort. Soon after the zombies spread from the Way Out A-Go-Go across the town, tourists and residents fled for their lives. The National Guard was mobilized and the town was sealed off. The Governor nervously waited for the moment when he would have to order his troops into battle against the zombie hordes that would inevitably seek further sustenance beyond the town limits.

Thankfully, a savior came in the form of a chubby, balding man possessing a tattered, old book. Calling himself Big Dead, he said that he had the power to contain the zombies within the town limits, but for a price.

Speaking of Price: he was nowhere to be found. It seems that Big Dick was not deemed palatable by the pirate zombies and made it out of the pit unscathed. By the time he'd escaped, Professor Price was teetering woozily from the vile stench of the zombie pirates. Seeing an opportunity, he wrestled Price's sacred book from his hands and knocked him unconscious with it. Perusing the book, Big Dick found an incantation that would put the zombies under his control. He then ordered them to toss the good Professor into the pit, after which Big Dick sealed the pit forever. Thus began his new business venture.

The zombies were happy to remain on the beach, passing the days with surfing and volleyball games. The only thing the Governor had to do was provide freshly dead bodies to be airlifted to the beach. Each night, the traditional clambakes had been replaced with armbakes or legbakes or whatever was provided. And the tinny sounds of jangling guitars emanated from transistor radios as gray-skinned beauties in threadbare bikinis jiggled their decaying fannies to the latest boss tunes.

Zombie summer would never end.

THE LAST BEST FRIEND

C.J. Henderson

THE SMALL BUT ENTHUSIASTIC throng of men packed themselves in around the oblong box in the center of the room like refugees crowding an over-laden dinner table. Their eyes shone from a fairly standard variety of emotions. Some reflected disbelief shaded with greed, others' flashed a more refined image of desperate hope mingled with avarice. Fear and dread were present as always, along with the ever-turning crank of desire, the true motivator of the type of men now jammed body-on-body around the intricately locked mahogany box.

"Gentlemen, your most energetic enthusiasm warms my heart to its happiest depths."

The speaker was a tall, compactly built black man wearing an outlandish top hat and feathered vest, standing far to one side of the knotted crowd. He was younger than some present, older than most. As the majority of the assembled turned at his smooth, velvet-like voice, his handsome, moustached face smiled widely, allowing his inner self the satisfaction of a hidden moment of amusement at the crowd's expense. He had earned it, he felt. He deserved it. True, the joke might all be of his making, but it pleased him, so he continued to grin.

"You are eager, which is delightful to me, but, why not? Truth to tell, you all certainly deserve such emotion this night—yes? After all, you have waited now a very long time, eh?"

"Too long, Lowe," snapped one of the crowd. "We were promised a return on our investment six months ago. So far we haven't seen crap. That better end tonight."

"Oh, I promise you, good Mr. Conti, sir, all 'crap' comes to an end this evening. You have not been admirably patient, it is true. But, you have been patient enough to allow for the promised work to be completed."

"Well," asked another in the bunch, his fingers bridging, then intertwining, his anxiety easy to read and amusing to the grinning man known to those assembled as Baron Lowe, "what are we waiting for then?"

Yes, thought the smiling man; what, indeed?

With a clap of his hands, the group's host summoned two servitors. Both a shining, deep ebony black, they moved through the tight-packed crowd, letting it be seen that if they were not allowed to approach the oblong box with their sets of keys that its contents would never be revealed. The mostly white crowd allowed them passage, parting the way a line of sports cars will for a tanker rig on a crowded highway—with no generosity in their gesture, merely self-interest.

"'And I saw the dead, small and great, stand before God;'" quoted Lowe mostly to himself as the various locks were opened, "'and the books were opened and another book was opened, which was the book of life.'"

The two retainers inserted their keys with a rhythmic unison, unlocking the box's restraints smoothly as if the action were a thing learned through much practice. All around them, the throng began to press forward again, their fanatical anticipation shining in their eyes.

"'And the dead were judged out of those things which were written in the books,'" continued the evening's colorful host quietly, "'according to their works.'"

At that point the last of the varied locks was finally defeated. Without a word, the servitors lifted the heavy wooden lid from the oblong box, then moved it toward the back of the room, away from the greatest body of those gathering, back toward the man called Baron Lowe. The group took no heed of their actions. Having served their purpose, the pair had disappeared from the crowd's radar. With the lid removed, the throng's patience evaporated as they rushed the box, all competing for the first glimpse of its contents.

"'And the sea gave up the dead which were in it...'"

What the assembled saw was the well-dressed body of a man, tall, thin and emaciated. His eyes were closed, and his skin discolored, but he was readily recognized by those around him.

"'And,'" the evening's grinning host whispered as he signaled for his retainers to take their positions at the secured doors, a raised finger cautioning them to wait for just the right moment, "'death and hell delivered up the dead which were in them...'"

The man within the oblong box was so quickly identifiable because most of those assembled had been present three days earlier when he had been murdered right before their eyes, hung by their host with a thick length of hemp which broke his neck, emptied his bowels and stopped his heart. They had all seen it; had examined the remains for themselves—knew in no uncertain terms that the man had been absolutely dead at that time.

"'And they were judged every man according to their works.'"

As the assembly stared, their host took a backward step toward the door through which he had entered. He did not move with guile; there was no need. The throng's eyes were all fastened intently on the dead man's body—on the dead man's moving, shifting body.

"He's done it! He's alive!"

"This is it, all we were promised."

The dead man's head, striped with distorted purple welts, lurched to the left, and then, its eyes opened—wide and unblinking. The assembled screamed with delight, their mouths all grunting different sounds signifying relief and joy. At the same time, the assembly's host signaled his men to open the pair of assembly doors where they had stationed themselves.

The throng went wild as the corpse grabbed at the sides of the box, pulling itself erect.

"Life!" screamed one of the crowd, "it's goddamned life everlasting!"

As the throng cheered, the reanimated corpse reached out for one of the waving hands flapping near its head. Catching hold of it, it's bloated face smiled as it drew the hand to its mouth and snapped off two of its fingers. At the same time, the two retainers stepped aside as the cleverly-fashioned secure doors opened. The design of their posts allowed the pair to easily side-step the parades of animated dead shambling into the arena. The corpses moved slowly, many with an awkward gait, but the room was not large, and in moments they had it filled.

Men screamed and dodged, many stumbling directly into the grasping arms of the oncoming horrors. Some struggled, but it did not matter. Their necks were ripped asunder, eyes gouged, chests and spines and skulls torn open before they could think. Blood splashed across the floor in torrents and slavering, rotting tongues lapped it up eagerly.

"'And death and hell,'" said the grinning man in the flamboyant hat as he disappeared through the room's back door, locking it as he did so, "'were cast into the lake of fire.'"

And with those words, the old man laughed—a deep and cleansing sound that echoed across the courtyard before him—the pitch of his noise responding to the wild screams piercing the night behind him.

"You wanted immortality, gentlemen," he announced as he walked away. "Well, now, those of you who survive…enjoy!"

Outside the obscured building, the man called Baron Lowe and his men walked off into the pelting rain, the terrible cries bleeding out into the night from the solidly locked complex of no consequence to them whatsoever.

1.

AS HIS CAB PULLED away, the nervous young man in the ill-fitting suit picked up his bag. Never having left his home village before that morning, now he stood in New York City, his mind snapping over the million differences between his homeland and this strange new place which he had seen just on the trip from the airport to the Manhattan corner on which he stood.

No time to waste—

The thought flustered the young man. Quickly he turned around to face the yellow-and-black-painted-brick building behind him. Walking up to the front door, he knocked, then waited. When no one responded he knocked again, then suddenly cursed himself for his failed memory.

"Oh, misery," he spoke the words quietly.

If I can't even get this much of it right…

Worry permeated the young man's mind. He had a message to deliver to a man he was told he would find within the bowels of the building before him. He had been given a ritual to perform, and already he had bungled an important step. Now, if people were to be believed, his life was in danger.

"This is not a cigar shop I'm sending you to," his uncle had warned him with an almost frightening gravity. "The people within are truly dangerous. There are those who have tried to gain entrance there without performing the ritual and they have never been seen again."

Grasping the doorknob before him the young man found that it turned readily, as he had been assured it would. Entering the foyer within, he closed the door behind himself, then paused before the interior door. As he waited, he spoke nervously to the far-too-close walls around him.

"I am most sorry for the knocking," he said to the air. "I knew not to do it, but I forgot myself. Please do not turn your back on me because of this mistake—I, I beg of you, do not ignore me, for my message is most insistent."

The young man pulled at his collar, his mind flashing with a rush of thoughts he could not contain.

"Do it right or dey will not respond." He remembered his uncle's words, heard them in his ear once more. "Not respond at best, that is. I trust you to do dis thing, but I warn you that you must be serious, and treat your mission seriously, and treat dey people you will find in dis place most seriously, or you may never be returned."

He had not thought much of what his uncle had told him then. Indeed, he remembered his sneering answer, "you are saying they would harm a simple messenger?" When his uncle's mood did not change as he had imagined it would, he had barked, "and these are the people you expect to help us?"

The young man shuddered, remembering also the stinging slap he had received. He had felt ashamed then. His uncle was a well-respected and venerable man, but one too elderly and frail to make the journey to New York. That he had chosen his nephew over other candidates showed great faith. Ashamed for a moment, still the youth had been proud of that fact.

Now, he was merely worried—worried and a bit frightened. As he continued to stand quietly in the foyer, looking over the various apartment names on the building's tenant roster, he did not push any of the buzzers. Nor did he knock again. He had been taught the routine. He remembered it. Now he would simply stand and wait until the old woman came.

Eventually, because he had done as he had, the locked inner door clicked internally and then opened cleanly, propelled by the stick-thin forearm of an elderly black woman.

"What bring you here?" she asked.

The woman's appearance upset the youth even more than the waiting had. Although in his mid-twenties, the firsts he was encountering that day were beginning to pile up faster than he could handle them. After all, he had never been further than twenty miles from home before. Never been on an airplane. Never worn a suit and tie. Never before been told that if he said one word out of place he would be killed without a second thought. And, until he looked into the old woman's eyes, he had not believed such a thing could be.

"What brings me wh-where, grandmother?" he answered the old woman, palms sweating, tongue drying.

"To dis place?"

"What—" the youth hesitated, a centuries long split-second passing before he started again, "w-what place be that?"

"You choke to name dis place?" asked the woman harshly, her eyes drilling under the young man's flesh. "You run from de thought to name dis place?"

"This place has no name, grandmother," calm, calm, he screamed within his mind. Say the words, "One can not name what is not there."

A pause with the weight of mountains settled on the young man's back, and then suddenly, the old woman smiled, saying;

"Den enter what is not..."

"And be where there is nothing."

The ritual completed, the youth found himself shaking. Tears formed in both his eyes. With control he would pride himself over later, he allowed neither of the droplets to roll down his cheeks, but kept then in place through force of will. Unconcerned, unimpressed, the woman asked;

"Why be ye here?"

"I ha-have a message."

"For me?" snapped the old woman. "For Boney Pete, for Santa Claus, for St. Michael? Can you speak?"

The last word ended with a tiny but moist mote flying from the woman's lips to splatter against the young man's face. His lips stiffening, shoulders straightening, he threw his words forward like a weapon.

"For Pa'sha Lowe," he practically screamed. Without reaction, the woman merely turned on her heel.

"My son is this way."

As he watched, the old woman walked down the unadorned hall behind her. The young man continued to stare for a long moment, then, making the sign of the cross, he forced his legs to move one after another and followed her down the dark hallway. As he moved along, the youth ignored the doors to either side, not knowing what lay behind them, suddenly keenly aware they were none of his concern. Reaching the end of the hall, he followed as the woman turned to the left and headed down a moldering well of stairs marked: Danger...Stay Off...Danger

He ran his hand along the railless wall as they descended. The stairs seemed sturdy enough, as if the sign were a distraction of some sort, but he continued to steady himself anyway. Finally, after several more twists and turns, he was lead into a darkened chamber.

"Pa'sha, baby," called out the old woman. "There is a... someone to see you."

At the far end of the room, an enormous black man turned from a worktable covered with half-built handguns and other, more formidable weapons, a large smile filling his round face. He stood with an abrupt motion, revealing a six-and-a-half-foot height hung with three-hundred-and-thirtysome pounds of solid meat. His quiet voice seemed out of place coming from his massive frame.

"And who are you, little brother?"

"My name is Christophe Boyer. My uncle is François Boyer. He sent me here."

Pa'sha stared at the younger man, his brow creasing. His mother made to speak, but the weaponeer casually silenced her with a wave of his hand.

"Tell me, Christophe, what race are you?"

The younger man pulled at his tie, his nerves tightening as he answered matter-of-factly, "I am mulatto. What is it to you?"

"Just gathering information." When Christophe's face remained unchanged, Pa'sha told him, "That you were Haitian was announced as soon as you opened your mouth. Your accent is as clean and clear as the streams that feed the Trois Rivières. Now that you have told me you come from money—"

"What?"

"Oh please, little brother, our island has an old saying, 'the rich black is a mulatto; the poor mulatto is a black.' Whether your people are still prosperous is not important. Knowing what you think of your background gives me advantage, yes? Has François taught you nothing of the world?"

Pa'sha made a dismissing gesture, moving his head from side to side while waving his hand slightly. His mother smiled, turning to withdraw. A look in her son's eyes, however, caused her to stay.

"Now," the weaponeer continued, concentrating on his guest, "while I hold all the cards, and you have yet to draw from the deck, tell me why it is you are here."

"My uncle sent me to tell you that there is a great need for you in your old home."

"This tells me why you made a trip, but it tells me little else. Might there be some specifics to your tale, or did old François forget to give you any?"

Christophe bristled at what his young ears heard as ridicule. His thin fingers curling unconsciously into fists, his voice lowered as he said, "No one may speak of François Boyer in such a manner."

Pa'sha was amused at the younger man's naivete, but he managed to hold back his laughter. He could not mask his smile, however, as he answered, "Calm yourself, boy. I would no more insult my sweet god-father than I would cook and eat a ribboned rooster. Now, stop wasting time and tell me why you be here."

"It is your father," answered Christophe, his tone humble, eyes lowered, fingers once more hanging loosely at his sides.

"My Pa'pe?" said Pa'sha, eyes unblinking, brow creased. "What trouble could he bring to our island?"

"There is rumor thick as delta silt. The old seals have been broken, the old religion filled with flame." The younger man's voice began to grow louder, his words running faster. "Many have flocked to him for the secrets of life, only to disappear. Important men, rich men, white men... but, you know, you don't be making the rich, important white men vanish, even on Haiti, and not turn to find trouble sitting your doorstep next morning. De Baron Lowe be bringing plenty trouble down on everyone."

Pa'sha turned toward Mama Joan, staring into her eyes. His moth-er returned his gaze, defying God, Jesus and the Holy Spirit as well to dislodge any of the tears she had ever refused to shed over the hus-band she had not seen in so long. After an eternal second, Pa'sha turned back toward Christophe.

"I don't think it be mine Pa'pe that is causing trouble for anyone."

"I have no reason to anger you, and," the younger man's eyes bounced from the weapons piled on Pa'sha's table, to the size of his corded arms, then back to his eyes, "it would be a most damned fool's errand to do so, but I must tell you again, as my uncle has told me to, it is de Baron that has done these things. It is he who must be stopped."

"My father," answered Pa'sha, chips of anger flinting his voice, "can not be your problem. My father is dead!"

"No, sir," answered Christophe quietly. "Not anymore."

2.

"SO, MY GODPA'PE," SAID Pa'sha, speaking to a compactly built, older black man in a cleric's collar, "what for you need to bring me home with such a tale, eh?"

Across the gloomy, overly warm barroom, the priest sat back in his wheelchair and smiled weakly, his arms raising, outstretched. Pa'sha crossed through the place's few patrons to face François Boyer, bending as he did so, encircling the old man with his huge arms. The two hugged each other quietly, refusing words, each holding back wells of emotion. Two fans, one rusting, one new, fought the stifling heat within the room as best they could.

"I be sore pleased," whispered Boyer, his voice wavering. "To have you home again. Here again."

The men broke, Pa'sha pulling a close-by chair to himself. As he pushed his massive frame in between the arms of the old wooden piece, he held his breath as his weight settled against its squeaking joints.

"I don't ask why for you no return before dis," Boyer added. "Past is past, and time spent crying on be just more dead minutes. I be old enough, and too glad to see you now to worry on when I couldn't."

"And why be you so glad?"

Pa'sha stared at his godfather with a dreading curiosity. The weaponeer knew something terrible was happening. Christophe's agitated mood both in New York and throughout the trip back to Haiti had given him that much.

Besides, thought the big man, no one would call me back to this place without a damn fine reason.

"Because there be a long darkness coming, snorted from de nostrils of a raging quartet of horses, terrible beasts that no man can ride, that no woman wants to see, that no child should ever know."

"That be one powerful reference you make," said Pa'sha. "I'm sure you know that."

"I've spoke de mass near fifty year, I know which book I'm quoting. I do so 'cause it's powerful frightened that I be. Dis place be conquered now, at least by night. De first horse, de white horse, it dances in de square every night, its rider swinging his bow, ruler of all he surveys. And de red horse be right behind him, his horrible voice braying for all to hear."

Pa'sha simply stared, understanding his godfather's metaphor all too well. Raising his hand, he signaled the bartender that he could use a cold beer. The scarecrow of a man brought a large mug to the table filled with a golden brew so rusty in color the weaponeer could tell he would need more than one of the lime slices in the bowl in the table's center. Fighting back the heat with a deep swallow, Pa'sha pointed to Boyer's drink, asking if he needed another. As the old man shook his head while taking a polite swallow, Pa'sha, pointing at the spent 40mm shell casing in Boyer's hand, said;

"Perhaps for the best. It must be a powerful drink to be served in so potent a glass."

"Just a left-over from when your president, de one your country said was unfit to rule, but who ruled on and on anyway, sent his army to us to teach us how best we should rule ourselves." Boyer brushed an amber droplet from his moustache, continuing, "It was quite an experience. Out of nowhere, suddenly a shadow passing across de land, and all Haiti wondered if dis time around America would burn us all to death, the way it does its own people when dey resist its will."

"And, was anyone burned to death?"

"Not nearly enough."

Pa'sha eyed his godfather for a moment, then laughed aloud when the old man smiled, no longer able to hold back his own amusement. Taking up the brass cylinder before him, Boyer lifted the gunmetal cup to his godson, banging it harshly against Pa'sha's beer mug.

"To life, Pa'sha," he said, "to just de one, and no more."

"One is all I need."

Both men tilted their arms and worked at draining their drinks as Christophe entered the bar. The younger man joined them at their table, signaling the bartender to bring him a beer as well. Pa'sha doubled the order.

"I will never understand why you like this place, uncle."

"I like de name," replied Boyer, amusement still twinkling in his voice.

"That Dark Inn," Christophe responded, his eyes darting from one shadowy corner to another. "Well, it certainly be a dark enough place."

"Is that all de name means to you?" When the young man answered in the positive, Boyer snorted, waving his nephew off with friendly disgust. As Christophe turned to Pa'sha, the weaponeer told him;

"The name, I would guess, it be a salute from the poem by Walter Scott, 'To that dark inn, the grave!'"

"What does Haiti need a white man for to name its taverns?"

Pa'sha sighed. He thought of answering Christophe for a moment, then sighed again and let it pass. Boyer chuckled.

"Wisdom has entered your life, I see."

"It usually comes to those of us who live long enough." The large man took a long pull from his newly arrived mug. With a pause, he smacked his lips, then finished the last of his second beer, biting the two pieces of lime that slid down to the rim. The weaponeer sucked their juice, pulling at the citrus fibers as they mingled with the last golden red drops. Settling the mug on the table, he asked;

"So, now tell me, why am I to believe that my dear Pa'pe has not only left his own dark inn, the one I helped lower him into, but that he is now the magnet drawing us all over the edge toward the inferno?"

François Boyer raised his weary head, staring unblinking at his godson. His eyes looked tired, tired from age, tired from staring out over a world gone just a bit madder with each passing day, tired of having to drink in more pain than the soul to which they were the mirror could bear.

"Because, my poor boy," he said, looking on, feeling older, hating the world more with each word, "dere be zombies walking de land."

"Zombies," Pa'sha spat the word like a curse, signalling for yet another beer. "Please, there be no connection between such dazed fools and my Pa'pe. Drugging the living is one thing... no one makes the dead to walk again."

"Someone does," answered Boyer with a shudder. As Pa'sha started his third beer, the old man whispered, "this be not dey same tribal nonsense we lived with when you left us. Dis be somethin' new. Somethin' evil."

"Uncle's words be most true," added Christophe. "I have seen dese things. The dead walk."

"Do not play with me, boy."

"He be not playin' you, Pa'sha. Some new and horrible darkness has come to play with us all. Christophe has seen with his eyes young, and I've seen it, too. And more. When de stories came in, of de dead walking once more, of blood spilled, of sacrifices made, of men disappearing, and all of it being laid at de feet of a whisperman named Baron Lowe, I made de journey to de poor patch where we laid your father down."

Pa'sha sat still, his head bent, one eye struggling to face the words spilling toward him.

"He was not dere. Only de piece of limestone we set to mark his place, and a deep hole, already flooding with weeds, that was all that waited for me."

"And you have seen him," snapped Pa'sha, his blood suddenly hot, muscles knotting. "You have watched him staggering on moulder legs, pointed to his peeling skin, dangling entrails? Were his eyes still in his head? Teeth in his mouth?"

"There are those who have seen..."

A large fist slammed against the table. Heads turned at the explosion, but only slightly. The day was hot, and those few patrons inside were accustomed to pain dancing cheek to cheek with belligerence.

"Take me too them. Find me these witnesses."

"People speak only in de third person about dese things. You know that, boy," snapped Boyer, his strength rushing from his body. "Who will swear to seeing de dead climbing from their graves? Who will attest to witnessing de march of the zombies? Voodoo? Here on Haiti?

Don't you know dat be all the old past ways, long forgotten? We be so much more civilized now."

"And so civilized you are, you cower from threats you say do not exist." Pa'sha signaled the bartender, calling for a round of the 40mm rum drinks. "Well, I agree. I scoff right with you. My Pa'pe is not crawling across the land, dead eyes staring to nowhere, dead hands clutching at air…"

"Pa'sha, please—"

"No!" The weaponeer slammed his fist again, grabbing the first of the drinks being placed on the table by the barman. Tossing it off quickly, he reached for another of them. "If I am to do something—anything—then I must believe. And I do not."

The large man tossed back the second rum, barely feeling the burn as its blurring fingers wrapped themselves about his reason. His massive fist encircling the last drink, he growled; "You know the words… 'Except I shall see in his hands the prints of the nails, and put my finger into the print of the nails, and thrust my hand into his side, I will not believe!'"

As Pa'sha tossed back the third drink as well, he rose from the table. The quick ascent staggered the weaponeer for a moment, but he caught himself on the edge of the table, then turned and headed for the door. Boyer called after him.

"Where are you going, boy?"

"To the cemetery," he snapped. "To take a head count."

3.

PA'SHA STUMBLED OVER A mossy rock in the darkness. His hand grabbed automatically for the wooden gate to the abandoned church cemetery, ripping the rusting screws of the upper hinge from the grey wood. As the fungused boards splintered under his weight, the weaponeer was thrown off balance, plummeting unceremoniously to his knees on the overgrown gravel path. His fall was broken by the dense foliage that covered the long forgotten patch. Indeed, so long had the place gone untended, choking vegetation hid most of the grave markers still standing.

"Oh, Pa'pe," he sighed, "My fault this is. A true thing I say now—yes?"

Staggering to his feet, Pa'sha moved on through the darkness which hid most of the graveyard's features. Although the moon was shining brightly, it hung at little less than a quarter in the sky, illuminating just enough to mark the weaponeer's way if he concentrated on what he was doing. His brain was somewhat freed from the effects of the trio of drinks he had downed so rapidly on top of his beers, but still the big man had trouble in pulling all the pieces he had together within his mind.

Too many things made no sense to him. That zombies roamed the Haitian night was nothing new. But in his time he had lived on the island long enough to know the truth about such matters. He knew, for instance, that voodoo was based on a belief in a Christian God mixed with lesser Haitian and African deities—the loa. He knew that the native religion was concerned with possession of the living, and that the houngans and mambos, the priests and priestesses of the faith, did not concern themselves with the Hollywood nonsense of the walking dead. Pretending to powers on that level was something left to the sorcerers—the bocor—and even most of them made no pretense about being able to actually raise the deceased from their final slumber.

"But someone," the large man muttered, "someone wants people to believe that my poor Pa'pe—twelve years rotting in the heavy dark—that he now be bocor himself, and powerful enough to rise up flesh without blemish or maggot, terrible enough to take the place of Jesus in the pulling of men from their charitable sleep, setting them to the pain of living once more."

"You make that sound like a bad thing."

Pa'sha froze. The thin voice, one almost recognizable to the big man, had come from somewhere in the darkness, somewhere too close to be considered comfortable.

"It is more than a bad thing," replied the weaponeer, wary, suddenly immensely focused on the fact modern travel restrictions had left him virtually unarmed. "It is a horrible thing. A screaming blasphemy."

"It is a truth," the voice whispered.

"Then it is a damned truth," answered Pa'sha, his eyes straining to spot anything loose and sturdy which he might pull to himself, "and you are a damned thing for spreading it across the land."

"You have come a long way to walk in dey darkness this night," the voice spoke again. Listening to the words carefully, Pa'sha heard a cruel slyness in their tone, a smug self-assurance which warned him to immediate caution. No longer looking for the speaker, the weaponeer busied himself with his search for any kind of defense. Spotting what appeared to be a recently erected cross, he did not bother to question who might have been buried in such a forgotten spot, but instantly grabbed at the affair, wrenching it from the ground. Little more than two sections of painted two-by-four, Pa'sha pulled the boards apart, holding one to the ready in each hand.

"We all walk in darkness, my friend," answered the weaponeer, continuing on to the far corner of the long abandoned cemetery, the place where last he had seen his father. "It is realizing that this never changes that makes all the difference."

Only some thirty yards from his father's resting place, Pa'sha picked up his pace, threading his way carefully between the mostly crude and crumbling monuments scattered haphazardly about the overgrown necropolis. Although he did not allow it to show, the weaponeer was beginning to experience a slight sense of dread. Many of the mounds he passed had been torn open, dug away, defiled by someone or something. It was a sight that would not have left him comfortable, even in daylight.

"You know what you will find at dey end of your quest, don't you, Pa'sha Lowe?"

"No man knows his destiny," responded Pa'sha with authority. If they did, what would be the reason in continuing on?"

"Like yourself," answered the still-hidden voice, chuckling at something private and faraway, "they simply must see things for themselves."

And then, as Pa'sha neared his father's plot, he stopped at its edge, his conscious mind finally accepting what he had been told—what his instincts and emotions had accepted long before. Seeing the gaping wound in the ground where his mother and he had so long ago planted various flowers and then watered them with tears, he shouted;

"End this game! Show yourself, and tell me why for you needed to drag my poor Pa'pe from the cool bosom of that sweet dark rest the Lord saw fit to give him?"

"Nobody dragged him nowhere, my poor, sad foolish one," the chuckling voice answered. "The trumpet call came, and didn't he do his duty and answer it. And I was sore pleased to see dey glee with which he took to doin' my holy work."

Off to one side, a figure moved from the shadows, approaching Pa'sha with a steady gait. "You say all men walk in darkness," it called to the weaponeer. "Well den, maybe I be no mere man."

With a clap of his hands, the dark form somehow encased himself in a sudden light, the fingers of which splashed across the cemetery. As Pa'sha stared, he saw a man dressed in splendid silks and feathers. The brilliance surrounding him made his features and many other details a mystery for the weaponeer, but still much was left which could be made out. One thing Pa'sha noted immediately was that around the glowing man's feet walked an odd assortment of chickens, some all black, some whose feathers were streaked with white and even yellow. On each of his shoulders sat a long-tailed bird, both with fierce claws and large beaks, both with crested heads and staring eyes. Various lizards and a number of large spiders peeked out of the man's many pockets while a vast cloud of insects spun madly above his head.

"Where is my father?" asked Pa'sha.

"So impertinent," laughed the glowing man. "But, since squeaky wheels are supposed to get dey grease, perhaps I should send some good and trusted guides to take you to him."

The glowing man made no gesture, spoke no words. The light shining from him changed in no way Pa'sha could discern. And yet, from all around the graveyard the rustling of grass was heard as two score pairs of feet began shuffling forward.

"This foolish lump who now offers us his face after showin' only his backside for so long thinks he has power here. Instruct him, my children."

Eighty legs moved forward, tightening a crude circle around the weaponeer. Hefting the longer of his two boards, Pa'sha immediately scanned the cemetery, looking for the quickest way back to the front gate. As the first of the surrounding forces approached him, the large man matter-of-factly swung one of his the two-by-fours with a surprising speed, shattering the head of the closest figure, spraying himself with its blackened blood and shattered teeth.

Zombies, thought Pa'sha, his own blood freezing, mind numbing. These thing really be zombies!

The first assailant slumped to the ground, its hands still clawing at the air even as its body crumpled against the soil, fingers still trying to drag it forward. At the same time two more of the stumbling figures reached for Pa'sha, but he stepped back from them, again swinging his larger board with violent accuracy, caving in first one's head, then the other's, both with the same blow.

The bodies folded in on themselves like the first, but there were still many more coming, and not all of them appeared as fragile as those first he had dispatched.

I've got to get out of here.

"And how will you do that, mere flesh, with so many of your brothers lookin' to keep you here where you belong?"

Pa'sha froze. The glowing man-thing had read his thoughts. Shuffling, rotting bodies continued to push through the wild grass and weeds, crushing their way toward him, but still, he could not move, could not think fast enough.

"What are you?" cried the weaponeer, his eyes riveted to the glowing man. The approaching zombies forgotten, he screamed at the figure;

"What are you?"

"I am dey truth and dey light, and dey revelation's herald. I am your destiny, dear Pa'sha, your ancestor. I am dey hand on dey future's door, and I'm turnin' dey knob right now, boy, and I'll be draggin' your damned soul down to the pit where it belongs—right next to your damned Pa'pe!"

"No!"

Pa'sha screamed the word as suddenly both his hands swung out in a blind fury. The shorter of his boards caved in the chest of one of his attackers, knocking the rotting thing backwards into a few more of those shuffling forward behind it. The longer board crushed its way through one head on Pa'sha's other side, and then another still, but it jammed there, the nails of it caught in the shattered skull and brain of the dead man grabbing for the weaponeer's throat. The now blind thing twisted violently as it remembered pain, the sudden turn wrenching Pa'sha's weapon free from his hand as the zombie stumbled off into its fellows.

"Kill him, my children," mouthed the glowing form, the words broadcast for Pa'sha's benefit, "Tomorrow night, at the devil's stroke, when we march from King Henri's Citadelle, he must be at our side. So, drag him to us, make him understand dey glory of dey judgment to come!"

"Yes," growled Pa'sha, slamming his remaining two-by-four against his palm, "come on to me, you stinking remains, you come and try to teach me something."

With a roar Pa'sha leaped forward into a mass of the approaching zombies, slamming away with his board, tearing skin, breaking bones, scattering those coming at him with the unexpected savagery of his attack. Blood splattered from his arms as broken nails raked along their lengths. Hair was torn from the big man's head, his left ear and cheek laid bare, his back cut open by grasping hands and snapping teeth.

The zombies fell one after another, however, their ribs shattered, legs broken, skulls ripped free. Pa'sha ignored how their headless bodies would thrash about, how arms shorn from torsos would continue to drag themselves along the ground — spidered fingers crawling blindly —searching for him, feeling, clutching. He ignored the sprays of fluid that would splatter against his chest and face as he smashed away at his enemies. And, he ignored the questions in his mind, the reasoned voices nearly paralyzed by those things they were witnessing which they could neither explain nor accept.

"I will not think on these things," he growled, more at the glowing man than to himself. Panting, he dug his feet in as he added, "I will not think on anything, do you hear me, except your destruction."

Pa'sha gasped down a great breath of air. The weaponeer was running out of strength, his endurance sorely taxed. Still, he noted, he had severely routed the glowing thing's forces. And then, as Pa'sha sucked several more deep breathes into his burning lungs, the ground began to shake as a hundred hands, some still wrapped in skin, some nothing more than bones and gristle, began clawing their way to the surface of the cemetery.

"I cannot be destroyed, boy," answered the grinning figure. "Can dey wind be destroyed? Dey mountains?"

"For the wind," gasped Pa'sha, "one builds a wall. And for the mountains …"

Pulling his pocket watch free, keeping his mind clear, the weaponeer turned its stem counter-clockwise, then jerked it loose altogether. Tossing it into the mass of human light before him, he shouted as he leaped away;

"For the mountains there are other means!"

4.

"AND THEN WHAT HAPPENED?"

"The watch did as she has waited to do, she exploded most nicely, sending force and flame in many directions, and chasing away whatever the thing be that came to me at my Pa'pe's grave."

"But what happened?" asked Christophe. The young man was bent over Pa'sha's back, cleaning the wounds the large man had taken. As he pulled bits of twig and leaves and broken fingernails from his skin before cleaning and bandaging the various cuts and scrapes and bitemarks the weaponeer carried, he said, "To the thing, the zombies, to you?"

"Nothing much more to tell, I'm not so saddened to say. Gladly would I tell of triumph and battle, but for me to use my sweet Vivian, this means I had nothing left to give. She has always been my hole card, as it were. Like many women, to turn her loose is to bring down upon the world much noise and great confusion. Vivian traveled with me so that if all were lost, I still might have an option for which my enemies might not be prepared."

Pa'sha jumped involuntarily as the ointment Christophe was applying burned him unexpectedly. Apologizing for his lack of control, he finished his story.

"Also like the best women, my Vivian had a fiery core that made her most special. In her case that core was phosphorous. It set a great many fires which resulted in a most beautiful bounty of smoke. All of it helped cover my escape from the cemetery most nicely. I started running before she exploded, and kept running afterward. When I stopped at the graveyard gate to see what all had transpired, I found the glowing bastard thing had disappeared in the explosion."

"You destroyed him, yes?"

"I sorely wish so, Christophe, lad, but I do not know. I could not chance to look. There were still zombies everywhere, of course, many on fire. Quite a few seemed lost, but many still were putting forth the effort to continue their affair with me. I was tired, wounded and very confused. And frightened as well. It was time to withdraw."

Pa'sha closed his eyes against another burning stab of cleansing pain. As Christophe pronounced his ministrations finally at an end, the weaponeer thanked him for his help, adding an apology.

"I must ask forgiveness of both you and uncle François. I was rude and stupid earlier, and neither passion nor disbelief are adequate defense for such ignorance."

"It was... I mean..." embarrassed, the younger man struggled for words. "It was understandable, anyone..."

"Thank you, Christophe," answered Pa'sha. "You are kinder than I deserve. Now, tell me, have the zombies ever yet come so far into the city as here?"

"No, sir. Not really... once some were... no, not that anyone knows of for certain."

"Good, let us trust things remain of that fashion." Rolling over onto his side, Pa'sha told the younger man, "My first day home has been not so much a success, eh?"

"You are still alive," offered Christophe. Pa'sha roared with laughter.

"Finally, our island has a philosopher equal to walk with the Greeks. Ah, boy, you lighten my soul more than it deserves. Can I ask of you two boons?" When the younger man agreed he could, Pa'sha said, "Safe we should be 'til morning, I think. But still, I would wish for you to keep vigil until the sun cleans away evening's shadow. Uncle François and I will have much to do come the morning, and we need what rest the world will allow us."

"You said two boons?"

"Yes," answered Pa'sha, his eyes heavy with the need for sleep, "Some packages will arrive tomorrow for me. If you will sign for them and wake me when they come, I will see what I can do about ending all this misery before it crawls much further."

"Packages?" asked Christophe. "What are they? I mean, what is coming; what is in them?"

"Boom boom," answered the weaponeer.

"Boom boom?" repeated the younger man.

"Yes," replied Pa'sha in a dreamy voice. "The most beautiful boom boom."

And then, Pa'sha drifted off, and Christophe's remaining questions were answered with snores.

————

THE SEVEN LARGE FEDERAL Express boxes waited for Pa'sha in François Boyer's dining room, entirely blotting from sight his grand oaken dining table.

"Ah, the most dependable men of Fed Ex," said the weaponeer with satisfaction, rubbing his hands one against the other, "when it simply has to be there the next day."

"What is here, my godson?" asked Boyer. "And who sent it? And how did they know you were here?"

"I sent them, godfather," answered Pa'sha as he tore open one of the over-sized, oblong boxes.

"But what is it you sent?"

"When the 10th Mountain Division came to Haiti as part of Operation Uphold Democracy, ah, what a delicious name—how I miss the delicate irony of the Clinton administration. But, pardon, I was speaking of the 10th Mountain, and how they came armed with a most effective rifle, the M16A2, a most wonderfully designed piece of equipment. Even when fully loaded, it weighs under twelve pounds, and yet maintains a maximum effective range of 400 meters, in the right hands, of course."

Pa'sha pulled one of the four M16s from the first box. Handing it over to his godfather for examination, he then started in on another of the boxes.

"But here is what makes it a true wonder." Pulling forth another handful of deadly metal, he held it out for inspection as well, announcing, "the M203 40mm Grenade Launcher. For only the addition of another three pounds, one can most effectively increase the destructive capabilities of the modern warrior."

"And why would you send such a thing here to yourself?" asked Boyer, turning the weapon in his hand over and over. "I thought you did not believe in zombies."

"Before I arrived, I truly did not," answered Pa'sha. "But I have always believed in you, and if the word from your house was that zombies were dancing in the street, well, who am I to not bring along a few musical instruments to help make the party more lively?"

"And what do you believe now?"

"I believe things have changed greatly here in our island paradise since I attended seminary…"

"You?" Christophe's surprise poured out of him, a noise so amazed it bordered on the insulting.

Pa'sha smiled.

"Yes," he answered quietly, his strong voice fading. "My Pa'pe, he was a wonderful man—the sun would not set until he was safe home. He was an usher for the church and a right hand to the priests, like your uncle François here, for all my years. I knew from when my eyes came only to his knees that I would be a priest one day. All for him." The large weaponeer looked toward a blank spot on the wall, seeing something else for a long, still moment. Finally, however, he began to unpack his boxes once more as his voice returned.

"But, then he was murdered. There was much of it to do with politics and the government. Port-au-Prince has always been the devil's pit it is today. I called on the authorities to avenge me, and they laughed. I called for the people to rise up, and they divided their response — some laughed, most slunk away, and at least one called the authorities so they could come and beat upon my poor coconut head until it sensibly stopped talking." Pa'sha continued to pile weapons on the table, throwing boxes to the floor, attaching the launchers to the rifles as he finished his story.

"At that point I prayed for justice, but none came. Since the authorities and the people would not help me, I left Haiti. Since God would not help me, I left the church."

"And now that you have returned to your home," asked Boyer.

"One thing at a time, Godpa'pe." Turning to Christophe, the weaponeer handed him a great wad of cash and ordered, "I need you to go to That Dark Inn and gather all of their brass serving cups. Do not spend every dollar doing so if it is not necessary."

When the younger man hesitated, Pa'sha explained.

"It is a reasonable price that is charged to send weapons through the mail. Ammunition, however, incurs a most magnificent charge. I was hoping to pick some things up locally since the M16 was used here by the Americans, and then by the UN peacekeepers afterwards. But, having seen our enemies last night, I am thinking perhaps a special touch shall be needed. See what you can do, eh?"

Christophe ran for the door. Stopping in the doorjamb, he turned, looking at Pa'sha. He held his pose for a moment, then suddenly broke into a large smile and continued on his way. After a few seconds, Pa'sha said;

"I think perhaps the boy is getting the idea."

Boyer smiled in response, then laughed. After a moment, Pa'sha laughed, too, then went back to work.

———

PA'SHA, BOYER AND CHRISTOPHE worked throughout the remainder of the morning and all the afternoon, preparing the special shells the weaponeer had decided to cobble together. As he explained it to his godfather, "These zombie creatures, they are a new thing to Haiti as you said. They are truly the dead raised from the grave. I do not know how, nor do I care. My only idea right now is to put them back where they belong. And with the beautiful children I have in mind to create, that should be a thing most easy."

The first thing Pa'sha set Christophe to work at was cleaning the 40mm brass shell casings gathered from the tavern. They needed new primer, which the weaponeer replaced with fulminate of mercury he simply took from bullets friends of his godfather had on hand. When still others Boyer trusted arrived, they were put to work packing the shells with gunpowder which would become their propellant. After that, the projectiles were filled with various loads.

Some were stuffed with white phosphorus, some with magnesium —both very flammable. Another set were filled with bundles of nails wrapped in paper tape. Still more were filled with dime-sized slugs. While the others worked on packing these, Pa'sha labored with a small welding set, piecing together sets of ball bearings by joining them with a coil of thin steel cable some three feet in length when stretched out. These he would load into one of the 40mm shells, chuckling as he did so. When questioned, he explained;

"I can not guarantee that these children of mine will perform as I envision. Offspring so rarely live up to their parents' dreams, but the idea is that when fired, the ball bearings will spread out, joined by the cable, which will hopefully cause some wonderful mayhem."

All gathered grinned, or at least nodded with satisfaction. As the afternoon wore on, all of the special rounds were sealed with wax and labeled as to what type of shell they were. Finally, as the small band who Boyer had gathered to face what was coming finished their preparations, Pa'sha held up one of the 40mm packages they had created.

"Now," he told them, "since these sweet rounds were made for a weapon that was never designed to fire them, we may find that some of them could be, oh, shall we say, problematic."

"He means difficult, troublesome," one man told a friend.

"Are these things children or wives?" asked a balding fellow good-naturedly. As all the men chuckled, Pa'sha continued.

"My friends, just remember that these are low-velocity shells; they do not have the penetrating power of a common pistol round. But, the size and weight of the loads will make up for that."

"And let me add something," said Boyer. As all heads turned, the old man said, "I can not go with you to Henri's castle tonight. Wheelchairs, they be not meant for climbin'. But I will be with you in spirit, and I will be prayin' for you, beggin' Jesus to stand your sides and help you in dis righteous act. God's gentle mercy be with all you, and all you... you watch you selves, and end dis thing tonight.

"Tonight."

The men nodded, some clapped their hands. Everyone thought the idea of a last drink was a good one, and two bottles were passed until they were drained. Then finally, when not a single drop further could be brought forth, the seven gathered in the hot room who could stand did so and made for the door with their weapons on their shoulders, ammunition on their belts, and prayers on their lips.

5.

HIGH ABOVE THE ISLAND'S once-fertile northern plains stood the Citadelle, built by King Henri Christophe at the beginning of the 19th century to defend against invaders who never came. It was the largest fortress in the Western Hemisphere, Haiti's most revered national symbol, a brilliantly constructed monument to cruelty that had cost some 20,000 conscripts their lives and which now stood in ruins, mostly unvisited, practically forgotten.

"I was named for the king, you know," panted Christophe as the seven worked their way up the 3,000 foot mountain, Bonnet-a-l'Eveque, upon which the Citadelle sat like a crown.

"I was named for my grandfather," responded one of the older men in the crowd. As the slow procession continued, one of his friends said, "But your grandfather's name was Umbura."

"My mother's father."

"Oh, that is different," responded the man. After a second, though, he added, "But his name was Michael, and your name is Louie."

"This is true," admitted the first speaker. "But he had always wanted to be called Louie."

The small troupe laughed, even Christophe, who knew their nonsense was aimed at him.

"Too bad the cannon are still not above, eh?"

"It depends," answered Pa'sha. "If the zombies are waiting there for us, perhaps giving them cannons would not be a good idea."

"Waiting for us there, cannons or not," added another man, "is still a good idea. For them, that is."

The others had to agree. The Citadelle was an impressive fortress, stretched across a mountain peak with sheer cliffs on three sides, its only point of access easily defended by any within.

"She had over 350 cannons at one time," Christophe said. "They say it took three months for each of them to be moved from the island floor to the mountain's top. Some of them are still up there, but they are worthless now."

"We will be worthless if we do not reach the top before darkness descends," snapped Pa'sha. The others, sensing his mood, fell silent, understanding the wisdom in his words.

They seven still had at least a half hour's climb ahead of them. Making merry had its merits, but they were drawing too close to the Citadelle to fall off their guard. On top of all that, Pa'sha was trying to pull together all the facts he had into some kind of scenario which made sense.

Trying to make sense of the walking dead, a voice within his mind asked him. And have you explained this thing yet?

The weaponeer scowled at the question. Indeed, all the facts he had left him confused. His father, a most religious man, rises from the dead and promises rich men everlasting life in exchange for great sums of cash.

But why would a dead man need cash, he wondered. Things keep pointing toward the coming of the Apocalypse. But again, if one is bringing about the final judgment, what need is there for cash? To buy a new suit in which to meet Jesus?

And again, how could it be his father? Yes, the weaponeer did believe the dead could walk. Although he had never seen the bocor who could manage the feat when first he lived in Haiti, he had seen enough the night before to convince him that some powerful new evil had visited his home with abilities far beyond those of the local sorcerers.

But, the reports of this murderous Baron Lowe talked of a man. A normal, human man. Not a zombie—not a rotting corpse. The man he had been told of during the day was an articulate figure, clever and theatrical. The zombies he had seen the night before had been growling, numb things. Animated beasts, puppets, not planners and thieves.

There was much more that puzzled the big man. Why was the glowing man bringing forth the zombies? Why were they marching from the Citadelle? Why at midnight? The end of the world was the end of the world—when it finally happened it was to happen everywhere at once, across the face of the entire world—and it was to be directed by powers somewhat far beyond the glowing man and his flock of chickens.

There is something here I can not see, thought Pa'sha. But, if I keep moving things, sooner or later that which is hidden shall be moved into the light, and I will see it then.

Hefting his weapon, checking the breech, he thought to himself with finality, And then this will all be dealt with, one way or the other.

After some twenty more minutes, the seven were finally within the walls of the Citadelle. They had beaten the falling sun by a margin great enough to allow them to set a number of powerful lights in place. After that, Pa'sha placed a man at each of the lights, both to act as sentry against the zombies and guard for their illumination. He then went over the use of the flares each man had, reviewed how and when to use their various types of ammunition, and then just sat back to wait.

They did not need to wait long.

It was Louie who first heard the distinct chatter of barnyard fowl. Cocking his weapon, he turned his head this way and that, calling to the others, asking in a loud whisper if they heard what he could hear. All could hear the clucking and pecking sounds, though none could tell from which direction they came. Nerves began to wear; trigger fingers began to sweat. And then, an orange shimmer began to grow within the walls of the Citadelle.

As the men watched, a seed kernel of light burst free from the ground, vines of illumination growing quickly upwards, wrapping around each other in the form of a man until finally the glowing figure Pa'sha had met the night before stood in the center of the Citadelle's vast and overgrown courtyard.

"Ah, Pa'sha," it called, its voice mocking, "such a good boy. Always so dutiful."

No one spoke. The weaponeer held back on giving the signal to fire. After all, he thought, he had dropped a powerful bomb in the very center of the creature before him only twenty-four hours earlier, and the act had obviously had no lasting effect. Before he tried something so futile again, he wanted to know as much as he could about his foe.

"You talk most familiar for a thing I don't know but as a graveyard thief," the weaponeer called out. "What for you bothering people with all this nonsense, eh?"

"You call dey end of humanity nonsense, boy?"

"The end of the world don't need no financing," answered Pa'sha. "Plenty people pouring enough money into that I'm thinking Heaven don't got need to spend no cash. You ain't no angel, thing. God's right hand won't be where you sit."

"I sit where I choose, and my legions will cover the Earth while

I recline in admiration. You what I came for, boy. You ready for to get in line?"

"You saying you want mix it up, we be most excellently ready for that, zombie-man."

"You too clever by far, Pa'sha Lowe. Like your daddy-man. Two big pains in dey ass." The glowing man threw its arms out to its sides, fingers pointed toward the fortress's floor. The seven defenders shuddered as the ground responded instantly, trembling and cracking.

"But dat pain goin' ease itself, dis day. And I be the laughin' one." All about the Citadelle, torn and ragged hands began to push their way up out of the soil.

"Tonight the big night of sacrifice," shouted the glowing figure. "I went to some fine big trouble to ensure all the most tasty meat be here for the last offering. When you all be dead, I be a god, and my revenge be finally complete."

Everywhere around the seven, zombies began to rise from the ground. Struggling to understand what the glowing thing had just said, Pa'sha threw its words to the back of his mind as he shouted to his fellows.

"No more waiting, good brothers. Fire as you will."

The Citadelle erupted as seven rifles blazed as one. Wasting no time, the defenders blasted at the zombies as they dug their way up out of the ground, taking off their heads, shattering their chests, before they could even gain their feet. Limbs were torn apart and sent flying, spines were disintegrated, skulls shattered.

Working his way down to the Citadelle courtyard, Pa'sha used his ammunition carefully, lining his shots to take out two or more of the zombies at a time, firing his rifle rounds in bursts of three only, doing his best to explode the heads of the rotting monsters so as to rob them of both their eyes and teeth.

"You are formidable, true," called out the glowing figure, "but you have bullets and bombs in numbers finite only, and the dead of Haiti number far beyond such as you can count in lead or explosives."

"Then I will break all their necks for them once more, and then yours, monster."

"You can not stop me, Pa'sha boy," answered the floating form over the violent noise ringing from every corner of the mountain-top castle. "So far, you have done everything I need for you to do. Think you can stop now?"

"I have done nothing for you."

"Please, you have made everything possible."

"How?!" The weaponeer screamed the word, even as he fired

another of his specially cast shells. Released, its ball bearings tore across the courtyard, the steel cord holding them together slicing near a half dozen zombies into sections before it shattered, one of the balls flying off and burying itself in a wall, the other dragging the cord with it, plowing through the body of one last zombie, its tail wrapping around the thing's head, whipping its decayed face.

"You have been most helpful to me," answered the glowing thing gleefully, "I need sacrifices, you brought them here to me. I needed you back in Haiti, you came with speed most enviable."

Pa'sha slid a purely explosive round into his launcher and fired. It struck the ground directly beneath the glowing figure, sending a cascade of shrapnel and fire upward, all of it passing through the floating form with no discernable effect.

All around the weaponeer, the others battled with the ever-approaching zombies. No matter how many they slaughtered, blew apart, decapitated or otherwise maimed, however, a dozen more crawled upward out of the ground or staggered in from the surrounding hills. One by one the men ran out of bullets. One by one they ran out of the special rounds they had helped make hours earlier.

"This is why I told you I would be here," laughed the glowing figure. "Only so much could you carry to dis height. Far from dey graveyard, you thought, forgetting dey thousands who died to build dis place. Now, you have no where to go; my poor dogs are all about, and you are quite finished."

And, at that moment, one of the seven screamed. Out of ammunition, he had taken to beating back the zombies clawing toward him with his M16. Eventually, though, no matter how many he piled at his feet, their animated limbs twitching beyond reason, the grasping hands caught hold of him.

The others ignored his screams as his chest was torn open, his organs pulled out of his body, eyes plucked, blood slurped, fingers munched upon—not because they had no compassion for him, but because they were all but minutes from the same fate.

"You wondered at dey need for money," the thing laughed again. "All magic takes offerings. Money is magic, boy, didn't you know that? It's not real. It don't exist except in men's minds. The things I pray to, dey give me power, but only enough to get for dem what dey wanted."

"And what do these things want?" Pa'sha bellowed the question, still firing, still directing his remaining forces.

"I'll tell you, boy."

As the glowing figure spoke, the zombies stopped their forward march. All about the remaining six defenders, the walking dead froze where they stood, heads rigid, hands unmoving, feet solidly in place. Their eyes staring, mouths half open, flies buzzing about them, worms slithering out of their flesh, dropping to the ground, the zombies waited at their master's command as the glowing thing revealed his final jest.

"What else, Pa'sha...they want *you*."

The weaponeer made to speak, then fell silent for lack of anything to say. Some of the still remaining others called to him, but he gave them all the signal to hold their fire. A scant ten yards across the courtyard from him, the thing continued on, explaining itself.

"Foolish boy, I gave to you few helpers so you would be easily scooped up. Enough to make you feel you commanded a force, not enough to stop my beasts."

You gave to me?

"Twelve years ago, your daddy-man was tricked into supporting my bid for de immortal. All along, he think he be helpin' one in need. Too late he figure dey truth. No escape for de old Lowe. But, his soul too pure. With him knowin' de truth, no deal for me, no power. God things take his soul and laugh at me, let me know mine is next, unless I can give them you."

No, thought Pa'sha, *not this, Jesus. Let this be anything but, but... this.*

"I make you think de government kill you daddy. You forget de church, turn your back on de only thing what can save you. I wait, wait for the stars to become right again..."

Not you...

"Wait for dey right time, de appointed moment, gather money to buy de proper offerings, rare gems, sacred things used since de beginning of time..."

Not you...

"Now, my altar is built, and de things dat want you soul so bad, holy boy," the glowing figure moved toward a large mound of rock centered along the back of the courtyard. At it, the two human servitors who had aided him all along, decorated a large flat section of stone, placing upon it several wooden chests. "Righteous boy, stinkin' little saint, consecrated fuckin' bastard...now," the thing paused to laugh one moment longer, then threw open the two chests, "dey wait no more."

Sickening black lights oozed forth from the twin boxes. Within, two sections of the same crystal, separated for tens of thousands of years called to each other, pulsating from the sudden nearness of each other, yearning.

"Thirty some years, I work for dis moment."

Two of the defenders aimed their weapons at the glowing figure and released their remaining bullets in continual streams. The lead passed through the form, tearing up the ground, shattering another zombie, killing one of the illuminated thing's servitors. The floating figure was not harmed in any way. Almost without thought, the thing sent its zombies forth to devour those who had fired. The others watched, helpless, faces twisted with grief. The glowing man laughed at their pain.

"De gods, dey mark your daddy-man, I give him to dem. Dey mark your soul, I help smother it. Turn you from the church, break your shield... you could have denied me, so true—if you had but hung on to de faith, all done for me. But no, too weak you were, blame God. After that, all is mine, just need bring you back at de right time..."

The black lights began to entwine, dazzling bits of brilliance trapped in the ebony tentacles of merging power. At the same time, the zombies began to move once more, all of them heading for Pa'sha.

"Now, it all be finished, godson, all but the throwin' of you to dose what you been promised to, and de collectin' of de power I done waited so long for to be mine!"

"NO!"

The sudden scream coming from deep within Christophe's throat, the young man threw himself from an upper wall, a lit flare in each hand. His aim all too true, he landed atop the altar, his body shattering as he hit the solid slab. Ignoring the pain of his newly broken bones, he stabbed with his flares, driving one into each of the gem boxes.

"Christophe, don't—"

Boyer's plea came too late. The chests rocked violently at the touch of the burning chemicals, exploding outward with a force which made all within the Citadelle turn away. The young man was incinerated instantly. At the same moment, the protective glow that had surrounded the floating man vanished, dropping him to the ground. Above Bonnet-a-l'Eveque, the sky darkened over, the stars fading behind a rushing billow of gray, ichorous clouds.

Boyer lay on the ground where he had fallen, crippled once more. He gibbered in a tongue none of the others in the Citadelle understood. It did him no good.

"Run, my brothers."

The remaining pair of defenders joined Pa'sha in making their way toward the gaping front doorway of the dying structure. Behind them Boyer shouted pleas, begging for their mercy.

"Pa'sha," he screamed, "Help me!"

A thick revulsion building in his throat, the weaponeer turned to view the scene in the courtyard behind him. From all corners of the

Citadelle, zombies staggered forward, marching toward Boyer. In their center, the man who had pretended to be his own best friend, who had played the role of loving uncle and concerned godfather, screamed until his throat ripped, tasting his own blood as rotting teeth dug into his flesh at a thousand points at once.

"I'm so sorry, godpa'pe," Pa'sha spat the title in disgust, "but as you said, I be too weak to do much for you now."

The large man turned his back once more, heading for the exit. He could not fathom how such magics worked—how two simple stones could hold such power, and still be so easily negated. Neither could he understand the greed and hatred which had driven his father's best friend to betray him, to condemn him to torments Pa'sha could not imagine, to sacrifice his own nephew, and to hate the weaponeer to where he would do those things he had done.

Behind the retreating men, the screams grew to a mad shrill tenor the trio could not bear. In the sky above, massive thunder peals exploded, heralding scores of devastating lightning strikes, but still none of it could drown out the terrible cries which followed the men all the way to the bottom of the mountain.

The three staggered in the lashing rain, desperate to keep each other from falling over the trail's edge. As a score of lightning strikes came down at once, all pummelling the castle ruins, Louie said;

"You know, they say ol' Henri, his ghost still walk de Citadelle. Maybe now, maybe he gonna have some company, you think?"

"Yeah, maybe," his companion answered. "Dey can be best friends in Hell."

Pa'sha stared up through the driving rain for a long moment. He thought on what he would tell his poor mother, twelve years a widow, all for nothing. He thought for a moment on Christophe's sadly wasted life, as well. He remembered his years in the seminary, equally wasted, like his years since. All his life flashed through his mind in a split second, ending on the words spoken by his fellow survivors a moment before. With a sigh, he quoted a line he suddenly remembered from the distant past:

"My name is death;" the poet had written, "the last best friend am I."

And then, he continued onward through the mud, ignoring the thunder, turning his back on the lightning, desiring only the cleansing feeling of the driving rain, praying for the sacred blessing of forgetfulness.

THE RIGHTEOUS RISE

Robert M. Price

I have the privilege of membership as a Fellow of the Jesus Seminar, the most publicly notorious arm of the scholarly think-tank called The Westar Institute. Our research, shared in popular editions for over a decade with a hungry public, has brought us grateful praise from an audience of seekers dissatisfied with traditional church pabulum, and equal or greater indignation from the wider church public, including, one must admit, erstwhile colleagues who hastened to distance them-selves from us once we began to expose for public scrutiny the long hushed-up conclusions of critical scholarship. Even within this schol-arly fellowship, my own theories have tended to be so marginalized, influenced by the Dutch Radical School of the nineteenth century, that I have learned there is only so much I may share even with these beloved colleagues and fellow explorers into the shadowed past. This, probably destined to be nothing more than a superfluous note to myself, prefaces my translation of an astonishing document discovered a number of years ago by unknown persons, from whom it eventually passed into the hands of John M. Allegro, one of the first delvers into the Dead Sea Scrolls, and the only one not a devout Roman Catholic. Though my own academic career did not overlap with Dr. Allegro's, as a young man I came to admire his work, in some ways more radical than my own is now, and I was thrilled to shake his hand at a confer-ence in Ann Arbor, Michigan, shortly before his death. His early books on the scrolls, some occasionally reprinted even now, are not controversial. His mature work was far more polarizing, even shocking: *The Sacred Mushroom and the Cross, The Dead Sea Scrolls and the Christian Myth*, etc. Having come into possession of the document that follows here, he had first thought to prepare a critical edition and make it known to the public, but failing health as well as discouragement over the universal repudiation of his work among the lock-step phalanx of conventional scholars led him to put aside these plans until it was too late. As practically the only admirer, I am sorry to say, of Allegro's work, I easily persuaded his heirs to hand the project over to me. Once I saw what it was he had uncovered, I began to rethink my resolve. I now see that Allegro must have realized it would have been an utter waste of time to publish the manuscript, for the sheer impossibility that anyone would deem it more than a fiction and a hoax. Nor am I seeking publication now as I write. I suppose this brief preface is just to satisfy the curiosity of any of my own heirs who may in future days chance to pick up these sheets. Indeed, such a reader will most likely think the whole thing my own invention. Well, by the time you read this, I shall in any case be quite beyond caring.

––––––––

These are the sworn last words of Joseph of Arimathea, member of the Sanhedrin of the Fifty, on whose account the Almighty Power does ever suspend righteous judgment from a sinful world. In the recounting I am about to write, I shall seek to leave out nothing of any weight from such recollections of my brethren as may be required unto the sense of the narrative. You will forgive an old man's inability to recover precise words, though many of them I could not forget if so I wished.

It was the day the death of Jesus the Nazorean was being accomplished, and I lay tossing on my cot. My wife and sons had hidden me in the inner court of the dwelling in case Pilate's men should seek me out during the tumult that shook the city, for not only mortal men but nature itself rocked and swayed with indignation. Yet of these things I lay oblivious as visions, fueled by the fever, rushed upon me like the nightmares of the wicked. Truly, it was not fever heat I felt but the very flames of Gehenna. I danced upon a merciless griddle, and my flesh seemed about to drop away from blackened bone, yet relief did not come to me. I felt as if I were one with that sow that Antiochus, may he be cursed, had caused to be sacrificed upon the altar of defilement. I shrieked, but there was no sound. It was all I could muster to remember my own name. But it was not my own name. In the grip of fantastic mania I believed myself to be Menandros the Essene. This was not a name unknown to me, but rather of a lamented friend, in his day a member of the Sanhedrin of the Fifty Righteous like myself. Here was a mystery: that one of the Righteous on whose account the world still stands—committed to the hell of fire! And yet I knew too well the reason for his, for my, presence there.

But suddenly, as my fever broke, and my forehead bathed itself in a crown of welcome sweat, the pangs of Tophet loosened themselves. And through the eyes of old Menandros I glimpsed, not the inside of my own house, but the dank and foul-smelling interior of a rock-cut tomb. The fit of the stone door was imperfect, and sunset rays gave some light to the scene within. My immobile form lay idle on a stone bench cut from the hill wall. My hands began to move first, and it was an easy matter to shrug away the rotting linen bands that had embraced me. I feared to extend arms and legs lest I look upon limbs ravaged by mold and maggot. But they were clear, bearing naught but the familiar wrinkles and spots I had grown accustomed to in life. A life to which I, or rather Menandros, had now returned. And then I awoke.

Beholding my fevered seizures on the cot, my family kept vigil around me for what remained of that dreadful day, now and again one of them creeping toward a window to receive a whisper of the latest tidings. So strange and distressing were these that I knew not what to credit. Had tale-bearers already been at work embellishing them? One said that mild quakings shook the earth, the which I, too, had felt, though at the time I did imagine these tremors to be part of my dreams. Pilate's men might still be observed roaming the narrow, cobbled streets, but they seemed now more intent on keeping general order than in rounding up those who had confessed faith in Jesus as King of the Jews. Of these I was commonly believed to be one, as so I was, save that I knew there was rather more to the Nazorean than most thought.

My fever returned about the third hour. I dreamed again, and once more I was not myself but took the name of another of my old fellows of the Fifty, another man whose loss I had mourned these last years, Abramelin of Socho. I felt no heat this time but instead a great parching of the throat, like a man wandering long in the wilderness. But wandering was denied me, for I was bound, my feet tied to some boulder or weight below me—in a depth of water stopping just above my wetted beard. The water around me was clear, clearer than the Lake of Genessaret, so that passing fishes were easily to be seen. Some paid me a moment's curious regard as they swam past my ungainly twistings and turnings, all in the effort to lower my chin and lap up some of the delicious water. But naught availed. Just above my head, like refreshing drops of rain, suspended by some magic, hung ripe and luscious fruits. I craned my neck till it pained me greatly, and still I found no means of satisfying thirst and hunger. And throughout all was the rueful memory that it might always have been so, and the leaden certainty that it should always be so, and the self-reproach for what I had done to place myself, or rather Abramelin, thinking with his thoughts, in such a place.

But at once there was a change, and I felt a welcome sense of free movement. I heard at some distance the common sound as of a clay pot shattering upon impact, as if thrown from a window, and then I felt no wetness and no binding of my limbs. Still I thirsted, but it was no more such agony. I sat up from the dusty ground, clearing away sharp shards of clay which pricked my back. And I saw through the gloom a line of irregular glazed jars, all about the same size, with names and holy symbols emblazoned thereon. They were ossuaries, containing the bones of the dead. I whispered thanks to the angels and got up, testing the strength of my spindly legs. The door was not hard to open, and I (which is to say, Abramelin) slipped into the night, heading instinctively for the Holy City as if in answer to some call.

My niece Tabitha caught me walking in my sleep and woke me from this dream. She was not much distressed, having learned over many years to expect the strange from her old uncle Joseph. The rest of my relations were just returning from outside, where the darkness had emboldened them to venture. And yet it was not night-time. From nowhere, it seemed, an eclipse had eaten the sun. Unwelcome in the season of Passover, when the full moon ought to be visible, the prodigy augured divine displeasure, but beyond this, whispered opinions divided: was the Most High showing his displeasure against the blasphemer Jesus or against those who had persecuted this prophet of God? That each man must decide for himself, or so Jesus would have said.

Helping me back to a bed whose clammy touch I would as well escape, my sister and her daughter charged me to lie there and regain my strength. How could I, I tried to reason with them, when my friend must soon breathe his last atop the lonely gallows hill of Gol-Gotha, so named for the circle of standing stones amid which the latter-day Romans had taken to crucifying their Jewish subjects. Nonetheless I drifted again into fitful sleep. As I did so, I thought I heard the fearful whispers of those about me that new and more terrifying reports had filtered in from passersby. For in the unnatural darkness that banished the day, the priests and Levites had in alarm sought the counsel of the Most High in the Temple Sanctuary, offering sacrifice and chanting psalms. And after they had so performed for an hour or so, as if in answer to their displays the great veil of purple, blue, and scarlet, whose topmost section was woven with gold in the form of laden grapevines, began to split open, without visible cause, from top to bottom, revealing the forbidden Inner Sanctum. Here none but the High Priest dares enter, and even then but once a year to offer the blood of atonement. The priests on duty, it was said, stopped in their tracks. They caught a glimpse of what lay within and fled in terror, precipitating a stampede of the gathered crowd, which not even the Temple police were able to stop.

More Roman troops were called forth from the adjacent Antonia Fortress to make sure the fleeing crowd did not ignite into riot. But they found themselves less than eager to intervene when reports began to reach them from still other panicked Jerusalemites that certain familiar faces of the sainted dead were being recognized here and there throughout the city. I knew as I heard these bedside mutterings that they must be the product of my fever-madness. And yet as I plunged deeper into sleep's enfolding layers, I felt that I understood even the strangest of what was happening on this fateful day.

Now I saw before me, sitting by her fire, the wizened, toothless face of a woman who was no relation of mine. No relation to Joseph, that is. But she was known to me at that moment, for she was the old mother of Nectebanus the sage, dead these last three years, and I was Nectebanus. Her distress showed widely across her face, and she asked me, asking Nectebanus, why the sun should be dark at such a time of day, and why her son should be alive again. I know not what he may have told her as I took my leave of their company at this juncture. But I was beginning to think I knew the answer to her questions.

Three tau-marks stood etched crudely against the sky, darker blurs against the gray void, drained of the sun at the very height of mid-day. Two silent forms gathered their strength to hold onto another useless hour of life. The man between them mumbled something, perhaps words of scripture to comfort himself on this, the crumbling ledge of eternity. The three of them were all but naked, mere strips half-protecting their forgotten modesty. Each alike was tied with abrasive rope to the crossbeam. What visibly distinguished the others from the man in the middle was the laurel wreath of nail-length thorns twisted gingerly into this peculiar shape and perched atop his pockmarked scalp. Mingled blood and sweat flowed down to irritate the wretch, so that he now and again shook his head feebly from side to side to shake off the stinging, salty fluid.

Watchful Roman eyes were fixed upon this man from below, where a centurion, despising his task, waited for these scarecrows to die. He had derived some small amusement a couple of hours before when the two men on the ends traded insults to one another, chiefly crude remarks about each other's genital endowments. Their bravado had ceased when the sunlight was eclipsed in some unnatural fashion. Now he listened carefully to the middle figure, who had begun to speak only once the light was gone. The Roman held his hastily lit lantern aloft and focused on the bruised lips of the torture victim, seeking to read the stammered Aramaic that fell from them now and then. He idly wondered if one so close to the lip of the next world might see something and try to forewarn the living. He could make out little. But he did notice, of a sudden, that with one of the man's periodic attempts to shake away the sweat in his eyes, his mock crown had almost been dislodged. For some reason the centurion felt this must not be allowed to happen, and he set down the lantern, tried to make sure of his mark, and hoisted his lance up to push the crown back into a more secure position with the sharp tip of the spear. What he could not see for the deep shadows was that his spearpoint had raked the forehead of the crucified man. Something else he could not see was a short line of what would have appeared to be healed scars, just at his hairline, forming the Hebrew word emet, "truth" or "faithfulness." Little did the Roman know his lancehead had nicked the flesh to the right of this scar, omitting the tiny rightmost letter. In an instant, the man slumped dead, no more fighting half-heartedly for breath. The centurion thought it odd and hoped Pilate would not think he had somehow killed the man before his sentence of suffering was complete. And then he noticed it was growing lighter.

Some measure of composure returned to my family once the light of the sun was restored about the ninth hour. The quaking of the earth had subsided as well, and word reached us that Jesus the Nazorean was dead, mercifully dead given the design of crucifixion to kill its victims from exposure over several days' time. Things seemed to be returning to normal—save for one lingering shadow of nightmare. Rumors persisted that many of the righteous of past days had been seen alive again in or nearby the places they had once dwelt, received alternatively with terror or delight, as at the return of one long prodigal. And every name was known to me. They were my brethren of the Sanhedrin of the Fifty Righteous on whose behalf the world continued, ever since the Holy One of Israel did swear unto our father Abraham that he should not destroy the Cities of the Plain if fifty righteous should be found within. The Angel of Death had thinned our ranks in recent years till I was the last left alive.

I rose from my sickbed, now in truth feeling much invigorated, perhaps from determination, and I brooked none of the attempts of my loved ones to hinder me. It was not the first such occasion. Now, as before, I wended my way as rapidly as my old limbs would take me through winding alleys in the oldest portion of the city, that in which the unclean ruins of the shrines of ancient Jebusite gods used to stand, and where rock-strewn passages yet opened upon nether secrets, provided one knew where to look for them. And I did. All the Fifty had known. And as I carefully sought each precarious step, I recalled the equally dangerous steps that had led to my previous course of action and its present aftermath.

Some three years before, when the Fifty Righteous were convened in prayer and advisement, I did mourn greatly, and another inquired of me, "O Joseph, praytell, wherefore is thy countenance fallen?" In truth I had grown thus sombre following the reporting of several of our number who, as was their wont, spent the year traveling to and fro through the earth. Our own lot was to act as salt savoring the world with a view toward making the same pleasing to God. If not, the world should still go on despite the magnitude of its sins, but our role would be little more than that of hostages, for whose sake, because of his ancient promise, the Almighty must needs spare mankind. And I for one was greatly crestfallen at the state of things, at the plague of evil and oppression that stretched like the empire of the Evil One across the boundaries of Rome, Parthia, Hind, Cathay, and whatever other lands might exist in God's wide knowledge.

I voiced among my brethren the hitherto unspoken fear that such a world might one day be found not to yield so scant a harvest as fifty righteous in a single generation. Our ranks were old and gray-bearded, with few on the horizon to replenish us. We must, I urged, undertake bold measures to purify the world in the sight of God, lest worse come to worst and all be lost. If God had ordained us as captains of a ship now tossing amid a great storm, surely our task was to find a means to see the ship safe into port, not to witness its final disappearance beneath the churning waves. All were weary, as I was, and though weariness often brings with it a paralyzing complacency, these were the Fifty Righteous, and they did not ignore my pleas. The question was what, precisely, we might do.

If my diagnosis was not controversial, the same cannot be said for my prescription. I had devoted much study to the scriptures until I concluded that much power might lie idle and dormant until some mighty man of valor should step forth to don the mantel of history, even as Saul, and Jephthah, and Gideon before us. They, too, lived in trying times, times when their people, though full of vigor, yet languished for the lack of any firebrand to ignite it. We the Fifty ought, I judged, to anoint such a champion, who might draw upon the forces with which God had endowed us, and to act mightily and heroically in ways closed to a group of aging and secret adepts. In recent years, many had instinctively looked to men of the stature of Athronges the Shepherd King and of John the Baptist to fill such a role, but these were struck down too easily by the mighty fist of Rome. Nay, the times required one with visible powers that should give a clear sign of the presence of God among men. And thus I proposed that we create us a champion such as we sought. There was a way, as all knew.

I had come to the meeting prepared, and now I brought forth the hoary scroll of Yetsirah, a collection of secrets surviving from before the flood, formulae bequeathed to the Nephilim by their fathers, the fallen Sons of Elyon. There were others like it housed in the repository where we met: the venerable Book of Raziel which Noah received from the archangel Raphael, containing cures for every illness; the terrifying Stelae of Seth of which none ever speaketh; the dreaded Key of Shalmanu, which Solomon stole away to summon the demons to build him a temple against the will of God. But I knew the Sepher Yetsirah held the secrets used by the Almighty Creator himself to make mankind, and which might with trepidation be employed likewise to repeat that endeavor.

And so I proposed to the assembly. Much debate followed. Several of the brethren begged time to familiarize themselves with the contents of the writing, which they had hitherto shunned, considering it blasphemy. It was a matter of months before we met again to reach a consensus, and yet more months before we had prepared the needful ingredients and arrangements, which I may not set down here. But at length, there beneath the streets of ancient Salem, even Jebusite Jerusalem, which once did echo the sandaled feet of Melchizedek, there lay before us the roughly molded clay homunculus, a puppetlike suggestion of the form of man. It reclined in a shallow tub of water enriched with divers substances. Chalk symbols ringed the basin, while corpse-fat candlesticks ringed these at a further distance. The head was propped so that the face from the cheekbones to the scalp-line was exposed. I had stooped down to engrave in the firm clay four letters, e-m-e-t, truth. This word of power should impart life and power to the Golem we had formed, and whom no man might stop save by effacing again the first of the letters, reducing the word to met, death. On this one we would set our hope. Into this one we had contrived to transfer our powers and vitalities, that he might succeed in saving a world which we had grown too old and tired to save.

I rose to my feet, and my friend Hibil-Ziwa handed me the text of Yetsirah, from which I read slowly. "And the mighty angels each did take of his own virtues and combined them into the form of a man which they had made from the clay of the bed of the River of Life. And they breathed life into what they had made, saying, 'He shall be called Enosh, for he is the first of men.' And a Voice did sound from the Four-Faced One seated on the sapphire throne, saying, 'Let all God's angels worship him!'" Whereupon I did make the final needful gesture, and all of us did kneel, our old bones creaking, to the rough chamber floor. And as we knelt, the figure within the circle did slowly rise, his eyes glowing with wisdom and power. And I feared much to speak now, but I must, saying, "You are like the man, though you are made by man, hence you shall be called bar-enosh, the Son of Man!" He turned to look at me with magnanimity.

Tripping only once or twice, distracted by memories, I succeeded in descending unto the adytum I sought, and once there, recollection melded seamlessly with reality, for here, as accustomed, were the restored circle of the Fifty Righteous, and I was unsure for the moment whether perhaps again I dreamed upon my sickbed. But no, the forms were real, their welcoming hands and words all too convincing. None knew precisely what had transpired in the world above, though many had some surmise to offer. We gathered in council as we had of old, the thoughtful gazes and wise words of Menandros, Hibil-Ziwa, Abramelin, Nectebanus, and all the rest a welcome delight in these most straitened of times.

I jested, apologizing for being the last of us left alive. But Eliadnor of Tyre corrected me, a gleam in his eye once he had brushed a clinging cobweb from it, "Nay, brother, you are no straying sheep, but you have returned to the flock."

"Rather, I should say that the rest of the flock has returned to me!" said I, still jovial. But this is not what my friend intended. Abramelin spoke next. "Perhaps, old friend, you knew not how very ill you were in these last days! How do you suppose you were able to visit with several of us in spirit and to witness the moment of our returning?"

Quoth Menandros the Essene, "Forsooth, you, too, became like us! You died, and your soul hastened to join us in the Pit of Tophet. But then somewhat intervened, restoring both you and us. Mayhap it was the clemency of the Lord, which causeth the prisoner to pine but which cometh at last." Here the man closed his eyes and lowered his head, meseems, in prayer. But I could no more hold my tongue.

"Nay, it was not as you suppose! But it was mine own will and working that regathered us here, though I am no less surprised than you at the result!" Here I explained to my brethren, all more astonished than hitherto, if that were possible, how we had come to this pass.

The appearance of the Son of Man amid the multitudes of Galilee and Peroea was marked with great acclaim. At once he was a sensation, healing both the bodies and the souls of those who sought his ministrations. And as he sought to rid the world of its affliction with evil, he scrupled not to beard the beast of sin in its lair.

And it happened one day that Jesus entered a village called Magadan. And on the street he chanced to recognize some who were highly praised for their righteousness in the synagogues of Bethany, of Caphar-Nahum, of Nazareth, and of Chorazin. And he asked what business brought them here. Now the chief occupation of the men of Magadan was that of fishing, but none of these men had any employment in that trade. Now one man, dismayed to see Jesus, answered him some false excuse, and so did the next. And Jesus waited and saw where they went in. And he inquired of one of the men of Magadan, of what business might be transacted in that dwelling, and he was told, "Yonder is the house of Mary Magdalene, she who is known as the Great Harlot who hath grown wealthy on the trade of the nations, for all do come to see her ply her trade." Jesus gazed in the direction of her house, which was large and fronted with Greek pillars, and he said, "She seemeth to be the veriest embodiment of Lilith, who causeth God's servants to go astray." And withal, Jesus, too, went to her door and entered. And he began to overturn the tables of those who took payment and the couches of the harlots. Beaded curtains he seized and wielded as whiplashes to turn the flutegirls and the sinners out half-dressed into the streets, where they were much discomfited. At the ruckus, the Magdalene herself emerged from the inner chambers like Goliath alerted to the arrival of his mortal foe. "What have you to do with us, Jesus the Nazorean? I know who you are, O son of dust!" And Jesus replied, "And likewise do I know thee all too well, Magdalene, for that thou art not the harlot in the brothel, but rather even that very brothel in which seven wicked spirits cavort despite thee!" And he said some words invoking the Prophet Elijah, whereupon the Magdalene pitched over in convulsions as seven dybbuks fled from her supine form. And as they fled, one knocked over a pair of hanging lamps and set the place ablaze. As Jesus took Mary Magdalene to safety, now in her right mind and free of the band of devils, he uttered these words:

"So shall the fire of untoward lust at length consume itself! He who has ears, let him hear!"

Not long afterward, these tidings reached my ears, and soon I heard also of the sad passing of my colleague Abramelin. I thought not to connect the two events at the time, but upon reflection, I was able to determine that the death followed hard upon the heels of the deliverance of the harlot, even in the selfsame hour, though many miles removed.

And Jesus came with his growing circle of disciples to the house of Simon in Caphar-Nahum, where Simon's daughter had long consumed the resources of the family with lingering illness, for she was sorely crippled since birth. And Simon had told him about her, hoping he might see fit to heal her. But as they entered the house, Simon's mother-in-law told him, "Trouble not the teacher the more, for the child is dead." And she wept much, but Simon only looked at Jesus. And Jesus said, "Where is the child?" And they showed him to the inner room, and he took with him Simon and Andrew and Jacob, and he bent over the girl's twisted form and said to her, "I tell you, daughter of Simon, get up!" And the girl arose and made to embrace her father. And all rejoiced, save Simon himself, so that Jesus asked him, "What troubleth thee, Simon?" And Simon replied, averting his gaze, "Forsooth, master, I hoped you might heal her of her affliction as well, yet she is no better, albeit she lives again." And Jesus said to him, "Do you think the Son of Man came to make men's lives easier? Nay, rather, harder, for only so may they learn endurance and compassion."

This I heard from Simon himself soon afterward, who had in the interval come to accept the wisdom of his lord. On the same occasion it was Simon who reported to me the death of Hezekiah ben-Imlah, another of the Fifty. He saw no connection.

One day Jesus entered a village of Judea, where a beggar approached him from a narrow alley, saying, "Jesus the Nazorean! Have mercy and heal me! Surely such is the will of God, is it not?" Jesus stopped in his way and looked at the man, answering him, "It may be. Let us see." And he touched the withered leg of the man, who said, "I injured it while I slept, I know not how." In a moment, his leg was sound like the other, and he went on his way rejoicing, leaping with the very leg that had hobbled him. Now Jesus lingered in that village, teaching. And it was not long before men told him of a rash of thefts and burglaries. And Jesus said, "Be vigilant, for if the master of the house had known in what hour the thief would come, he would not have suffered him to carry away his goods." And so Jesus himself kept watch that night and, sure enough, he caught a man looking though his things. No longer feigning sleep, he said to the robber, "What seek you? Have I not already given you such as I possess?" For in truth it was the lame man he had healed a few days earlier. And at once the man's leg withered up again. "If it is the will of God, it is better to beg from others than to steal from them."

I smiled when they repeated the episode to me, but at once my spirit was quenched by the news of another old friend's death, this time Hibil-Ziwa of the Rechabites. I began to fear.

When next I met with my brethren of the Fifty, there was great rejoicing at the seeming success of our endeavor, for they had all heard similar stories, and yet there were fewer gathered than in former days. And as the weeks and months went on, and the fame of Jesus the Nazorean grew, our numbers declined proportionately. If any besides me understood the linkage, they remained as silent as I did, reckoning that the price we were paying was a small one in view of the good we beheld accomplished on all sides. I gladly acquiesced in what seemed to be happening to us, since it was plain that the saving role of the Fifty had been transferred to more capable shoulders. The world might go on quite well without a crowd of old men huddling in secret. Our Golem would succeed, was succeeding where we had done nothing save to delay the inevitable slide into the Abyss. So Jesus increased from strength unto strength, while our number dwindled.

Oh, I knew well enough that when all of us whose powers energized him were exhausted and dead, Jesus' own powerful deeds must cease. All things must come to an end. Our wager was that, when that time came, Jesus should have effected so much good in the world as to have fended off the advances of darkness and of the Evil One. One is so often blinded by the glow of optimism, alas. Little did any of us foresee that, as Jesus weakened, leaving miracles behind and devoting more time to teaching his disciples, the crowds would begin to grow cooler to him, missing the bread and circuses he had first provided them, as they must have regarded them. At length, they should play into the hands of our enemies, Rome and the Powers behind their masks, and our defenses spent, the Darkness should rally for one last assault.

All this came home to me with resistless clarity once all the Fifty but myself had passed away and, as I subsequently learned, entered the torment which our blasphemous usurpation of the divine prerogatives had earned us. Once the word arrived that Jesus had been arrested at the Olive Press of Gethsemane, I knew I must act quickly if there was to be any chance at all of undoing the damage my brethren and I had done. In the silence of the tomblike cavity beneath Old Jerusalem, I stood without witnesses and chanted softly from the Sefer Yetsirah, seeking to unleash and direct a bolt of the primeval life-force like unto that we had at the first released to make the Golem stand up. I hoped to revivify the Nazorean at the moment of his death, or as near to it as I might venture. I finished as much of the ritual as I could, without anyone to take the antiphonal part. My spirits still low, I crept back up the way I had come and retired to my cot, suddenly enervated. And so my fever dreams began.

As I now told my old friends and fellow-workers, my spell had gone astray. I had unleashed the Power of Creation, for which no doubt I should be doubly damned, but I had been a modicum too early, and the effect was unanticipated. Instead, it was the disintegrating forms of the buried Fifty which returned to life, creating havoc in the city as they ventured a hesitant return to their accustomed domiciles, then sought refuge in the last place it remained to them, even here. Our Jesus was dead, but we lived, for how long none might say. And no longer could we claim the distinction of the Sanhedrin of the Righteous, since we above all other men had transgressed the laws of God, relying upon our own rashness, mistaking it for wisdom. Surely our mere presence in the world could no longer serve to stave off its doom. If anything, we appeared to have hastened it.

But then, as the tattered form of Dositheus the Samaritan now observed, Jesus himself had done nothing but good. He could not have attracted to himself the damnation of a righteous God. And where I alone had failed, and died, might the restored college of Fifty succeed? Might we not again pool our life-forces, our knowledge of the arcane elements, to bring back the Nazorean from the dead? Miracles would likely remain beyond his grasp, but it was evident now that such had never been the strength of his ministry to the heart and the soul in any event. If we could but secure him a few added years in which to complete his teaching! Who knew? Perhaps he might succeed in building a new Sanhedrin of Fifty Righteous. And if he did not, if the world no longer possessed a guarantee of salvation despite its depravity, perhaps that was just as well. Perhaps the children of men would finally understand the gravity of their need. Perhaps the long stalemate of good versus evil, which the cumulative weight of the Fifty had only served to maintain in balance, would issue in a final struggle, for better or for worse. That might even prove to be the real will of God.

With no alternative available, the risen sages agreed to pursue my course, and we made as many of the ritual preparations as we could. The thing took some hours, but at length we were done. At once I left for Gol-Gotha, hoping that I might prevail upon the hegemon Pilate, a man not unknown to me from better times, to let me take charge of the corpse of Jesus, lest it be cast, as seemed likely, into a common lime pit. As I returned to the surface, I mused that I should never more see the Fifty, that already they must be collapsing again, this time in an unknown tomb that should hide their mysteriously missing corpses forever from the sight of men.

Despite the day's tumult, or rather perhaps because of it, the usual official barriers were easier to make one's way round, and finally I gained audience with Pilate. He was thoroughly exhausted with the strange business of the day. He had heard the superstitious rumors and sought to calm the fears of those who spread them, applying force as needed, and he was most heartily sick of it. With my request scarcely out of my mouth, he waved his permission and dismissed me with a paper hastily inscribed by one of his attendant scribes. I needed but give it to the centurion on duty, and he would assign a soldier to carry the body to my own nearby tomb.

Once the body of Jesus lay prone on the stone shelf of the tomb, I gave it a cursory examination, then noticed the torn flesh on the forehead. At first mistaking it for another wound of the thorny crown, I soon recognized the incidental effacement of the crucial letter, without which the mark of divine truth had changed to the mute seal of death. I was no surgeon, nor had I any tools to repair the wound, but I felt that the flesh of the Golem had begun to return, almost imperceptibly, to its original clay, something I had not anticipated. So it was a simple matter merely to smooth the flesh and reinscribe the torn letter. And at once the skin was warm again beneath my fingertips. His eyes opened. His mouth said one word. "Joseph." Then his glowing eyes blinked, and he spoke again. "I am he that liveth and was dead."

I put my finger against his lips and whispered, "No, master. Not now. I have but little time. You may not have much more. And we have much to accomplish. Let us go forth."

Where, you may wonder, did they go? Allegro said he had bought the manuscript from a trader (many of the Dead Sea Scrolls came into scholarly hands that way), not from an Arab smuggler, but from an antiquities dealer who swore the thing came from Nepal. Make of it what you will.

HUNTING SEASON

Brian Keene

Pop and I were up hours before the sun. I'd gone to bed early the night before, but was too excited to sleep. I'd tossed in anticipation, and it seemed that when I finally did fall asleep, he was there shaking me lightly.

"Jason, wake up son. It's time."

I opened my bleary eyes. Pop stood beside me, shadowed in the light of the full moon shining through my window. Yawning, I got out of bed, shivering as my bare feet hit the cold wooden floor. I heard Mom bustling about in the kitchen, and my stomach rumbled as the smell of eggs and bacon drifted into my room. It had been a year since we'd had real bacon! She must have been saving it all this time.

I stood looking out my window at the pre-dawn world inside the containment fence. A thin layer of snow covered the yard and the tree-tops in the forest beyond the compound. The harsh February wind whistled sharply, blowing tufts of snow around in the darkness.

I dressed quickly, glancing around my room as I did. The candle's flame made funny shadows across the walls. My boyhood treasures lay scattered throughout. My rocks and arrowheads, the toy boat that Pop had carved for me, my slingshot, and the two comic books that I had gotten from the trader on his last trip through. The comics were my favorite. In my eyes, they were pure magic. Pop had told me that before the comet, there were stores that sold nothing but comic books, although I'm pretty sure he was just kidding.

I tiptoed to the kitchen, trying not to disturb my brother and sister. Joey had been so jealous the day before, wishing he would turn sixteen like me, so Pop would take him hunting too.

"You've got to wait until you're older, Joey," Pop told him. "It's not a game out in those woods. It's too dangerous for a boy your age."

Mom had her reservations about it too, which I overheard as I walked into the kitchen.

"What if something happens?"

"Now Shannon," I heard Pop say, stern but patient. "He's not a little boy anymore. He's wanted to go with me since he was six. His heart's set on it."

"But Lloyd, what if one of those things…"

"Honey!" Pop interrupted. "Jason's got a good head on his shoulders, better than I did at that age. Growing up in this world is different than it was for us. He's a man, for Christ sake! I'll be with him, and we're not going out far. Besides, you know our situation. We've got plenty of canned stuff from last years garden, but the meat is running low."

Clearing my throat, I walked into the room. Mom did her best to look happy, but the smile didn't reach her eyes. Pop grinned as I sat down to eat. The bacon tasted fantastic. It was real pig, not the kind we usually had.

With breakfast finished, I shrugged into my heavy wool coat. Pop disappeared into the side room and came back with two rifles.

"Jason, this is yours now," he said proudly, and handed me the smaller gun. Pop's Remington 4-10. I looked at him in disbelief.

"That's the same gun I used to hunt squirrels and turkey with when I was your age. My Daddy gave it to me, and now I'm giving it to you. I've got some punkinball shells for you to use in it. They'll bring down a deer or anything else, as long as you remember to aim for the head."

"Thanks Pop," I whispered, a lump in my throat. The rifle's weight felt good in my hands. I was more excited and eager than the night before. I was also a little nervous. As we walked to the door, Mom made a big fuss over me, giving me a squeeze and making me promise to be careful. She and Pop embraced, and he gave her a quick kiss. She stood in the doorway and waved silently as we stepped out into the blue non-light of the early morning.

Candles burned in the windows of several other homes within the compound. Others departed from them as we walked over to the gate. Joining us was Mr. Norville, our resident doctor. He was a good-natured man, and always had a joke to tell. With him were Mr.

Glatfelter and his son Ron. Ron and I had been best friends since birth. Being the same age, we'd grown up inside the compound together.

This was his first hunting trip as well, and he was just as thrilled. It had been all that we had talked about for the last few weeks. Ron grinned as the adults exchanged pleasantries. He eyed my rifle in obvious appreciation. He couldn't, of course, let on that it better than his own gun.

"Seems kind of small to be hunting anything big with," he said, staring at the rifle barrel.

"That's why I'm using punkinballs. Pop says that as long as I hit them in the head, it'll bring them down. Yours is pretty small too."

Ron had his father's Ruger .22 rifle, which I agreed was almost as nice. While our fathers laughed at one of Doc Norville's jokes, Ron and I bet on who would make the first kill. I couldn't help but notice that Ron seemed as nervous as I felt. Mr. Glatfelter asked us if we were ready, and we nodded in agreement.

"Now you boys remember what I told you about buck fever," Pop reminded us. "Back when we were your age, buck fever could cost us a deer. Nowadays, it could cost us our lives. When we were kids, animals didn't get up and walk around after they were dead."

"People, either." Ron's Dad added.

We walked toward the containment fence, Ron and I both feeling a giddy mix of fear and excitement. Doc Norville looked a little green as well. He'd probably been up late the night before, sampling from his moonshine still.

Pop rolled back the steel security gate and we filed through. The gate closed behind us with a loud clang.

We lined up in the snow. Pop and Ron's dad were in the lead, Ron and I in the middle, and Doc Norville brought up the rear.

"A hunting we will go," he chuckled softly.

With the bitter wind whipping at our faces, we walked into the dark woods. The snow swirled around us, covering our tracks as the first rays of dawn crept over the horizon. Nobody talked. All of us were on the alert for any game. As we walked, I listened to the forest. The silence was broken only by the soft crunch of our booted feet in the snow, and the wind howling through the trees.

As the sun rose, the forest began to come alive around us. The wind died down to a few small gusts. In the treetops, I could hear the morning songs of the birds and the soft flutter of their wings as they took flight.

Both the living and the dead were coming to life around us.

Growing restless, Ron took aim at a robin perched on a branch several yards away. This earned him a stern look of admonishment from his father, and the robin flitted away.

Minutes later, there was scurrying noise in the branches above us. Two gray shapes dashed over our heads. Pop and Mr. Glatfelter raised their rifles and fired. Two simultaneous blasts ripped the air. I jumped, nearly dropping my own rifle. The squirrels plummeted to the ground, landing in the snow, their blood staining it red.

"Nice shooting, Lloyd," Ron's father said to mine.

"That was some nice shooting you did yourself," Pop replied. "Looks like you were too slow, Doc."

"It was a late night," Mr. Norville laughed. "I'll beat you both next time. Look's like these two were still alive when you killed them."

Pop walked over to the squirrels and nudged them with his boot. Tiny wisps of steam rose from the warm bodies.

"Now you see boys," he said. "That's why you have to stay alert out here. If we had been slower, we might have missed those shots. If these squirrels were already dead, or if it had been something else, we might not be standing here right now."

We nodded as Pop pulled out his old Green Beret knife and proceeded to cut the head off the first body.

"It's always important to destroy the brain as soon as possible," Pop instructed us.

"In the old days, we wouldn't have been able to eat meat that had been dead for a while either," Mr. Glatfelter added. "Anything that had been dead for more than a few hours would have spoiled and been unfit or human consumption. The radiation from the comet changed all that. As long as the brain is intact, the meat doesn't rot, no matter how long it's been dead."

Pop pulled the second carcass over and placed the knife to its throat. The squirrel suddenly burst to life, its eyes jerking open with a malevolent glare. Before Pop could pull away, it thrashed in his grip and bit down greedily on his hand.

Pop screamed and drew his hand away. Blood flowed from a ragged hole between his thumb and forefinger. The dead squirrel chewed hungrily on the piece of flesh, holding it in its forepaws like an acorn. Mr. Glatfelter cursed and pulled his trigger. The point blank shot disintegrated the zombie's head.

Pop's face was ashen. I could see the terror beneath his eyes, a terror that he was bravely trying to keep from me.

A terror that was mirrored in my own gaze.

"Pop…" I wheezed. It was all I could manage. I felt like someone had kicked me in the stomach.

"Damn," he said quietly. "I've been bit."

"Let me see it, Lloyd!"

Doc Norville bent to examine the wound, his _expression grave. Ron looked at me with concern as I fought back the tears I felt coming to the surface. I was angry. Why did it have to be my father? Why not Ron's or Mr. Norville? I was ashamed by these thoughts, but also terrified.

"I might be able to stop it," Doc Norville said. "We'll have to get you back to the compound, pronto."

Mr. Glatfelter and the doctor supported him as we made our way back. The squirrels lay tucked away in Ron's game bag. Ron tried to reassure me that everything would be okay. Pop moaned as the poison began to work its way up his arm. The black sludge pumping through his veins was visible beneath his skin.

"Please don't let him die," I silently pleaded.

The rest of the day was a chaotic blur. Mom ranged from hysterical to comatose. Joey and Chrissy cried all day, their little faces dazed with fright. Pop's moans increased, turning into screams of intense agony as Mr. Norville amputated his arm.

Concerned well wishers flocked from the rest of the compound to offer help. Mr. Norville turned them away, assuring them with a smile that everything would be fine. It was a smile that vanished when he shut the door.

He left after dark, telling us that he'd done all he could. Now we would have to wait. He left a poultice for the fever ravaging Pop's body, and gave my mother a consoling hug. He shook my hand and his grip trembled.

"I'm sorry, Jason," he said, his voice tinged with emotion.

Mom stayed by Pop's side and I put the kids to bed, telling them that Pop would be okay in the morning. When I was done, mom called me into the room.

"He wants to talk to you," she said, her eyes brimming with tears. "You better hurry. He might not be conscious much longer."

Slowly, I walked into the room. My heart raced in my chest, my feet felt like lead. Pop turned his head toward me and I gasped. His skin had taken a ghostly pallor, almost chalk white. Dark circles underlined his sunken eyes.

"Jason," he rasped, and held his hand out to me. There was a bloody stump in place of his other arm. In a daze, I floated to his side. A tear ran down my cheek as I took his hand in mine.

"Ssshh. Your mother's cried enough for us all today. It's going to be hard for her to cope with this. You're going to have to help..."

He broke off in a violent fit of coughing. I started to yell for Mom but he waved his hand and brought it under control. I noticed in horror that a rusty colored fluid was leaking from the corner of his mouth.

"You've got a job to do, Jason," he wheezed. "You're the man of the house now. You've got to take care of your mother and the kids. You watch out for them. Take care of me as well."

"Pop, I can't!" I sobbed in protest.

"Yes you can," he said softly. "You're a good son, Jason. I'm proud of you. I know that you can do this. It's not easy, but it's got to be done. Promise that you won't let me come back! Don't let me turn into one of those things."

Unable to speak, I nodded. With fading strength, Pop squeezed my hand. My face was wet with tears.

I noticed that he was crying too.

"Eventually, you'll have to go back into the woods again. I understand if you're scared at first, after what happened today. But remember my example and learn from it." He coughed again, the fluid spraying the sheets in a fine red mist.

"I'm a pretty big man, so you all should have plenty to last you for the next few months. Sooner or later though, you'll have to go hunting again. Remember, there ain't nothing wrong with eating zombies. Once they die the first time, they're not human anymore. Once I'm gone, I won't be you're Pop anymore either, just meat."

I couldn't speak, so I leaned over and hugged him, our tears running together.

"I'm gonna try not to come back. I'm really going to try. Better send you're mother back in," he rasped.

"I love you, Pop."

"I love you too, Jason."

I kissed him softly on the forehead and he closed his eyes. Then I walked slowly to the door and sent Mom back inside. I sat down at the kitchen table and laid the rifle by my side, checking to make sure that it was loaded. Pop had just given it to me that morning. I hadn't even fired it yet.

I wondered if Ron's dad would help me butcher after it was finished. I thought of what life must have been like before the comet.

Before the dead started coming back to life.

I looked out the kitchen window, into the night, and lost myself in a flood of memories.

I waited.

Whitley '04

PARADISE DENIED

John L. French

THE APOCALYPSE WAS A big disappointment: no trumpets, no Second Coming. Maybe somewhere the forces of Good were preparing to do battle with the armies of Satan, but not in Baltimore.

All the signs had been there. Astronomers were suddenly unable to find stars that had always been in the sky. And some quasar that had been 40 million light years distant was now only 39.9 million light years from us. The scientists tried to explain it away by talking of dark matter and refinements in measurements. But the next month that quasar was just a little bit closer and more stars were gone.

And then the Righteous disappeared.

It wasn't like the Fundamentalists predicted. Planes didn't fall from the sky and cars didn't crash into buildings as their operators suddenly vanished. It was more gradual. One by one, a few more each day, people just disappeared. A husband and wife would fall asleep together. One would wake up to find only the pajamas the other had slept in. A family out camping would go for a hike. They'd come to a bend in the trial with the children out of sight for just a second. The parents would be left alone. Or a man would leave his house, go back in for his umbrella and would not be seen again.

Police Missing Persons Units were so that they stopped taking reports. Terrorists were blamed, then aliens. The religious right had an answer, but no one listened to them.

That is, not until all the children disappeared.

By the time everybody figured out just what was going on, by the time the Pope, the Archbishop of Canterbury and the chief rabbi of Jerusalem (all three newly elected) made a joint announcement declaring The End of Days was upon us, the world's population had been reduced by twenty percent, and all children who had not reached puberty were gone.

What surprised most people was not that Judgment had occurred, but that so many had been Taken. Twenty percent? Who would have thought there were that many truly good people in the world? And they were from all walks of life, although there was a sudden and acute shortage of nurses, teachers and religious ministers. Yeah, I know, the last surprised me too. Maybe dedicating your life to God and the service of others pays off.

More poor people were Taken than rich. I guess having money gives you more time and opportunity to commit the really big sins. Prisons were emptier, by about ten percent. Says something about the legal system.

Who stayed behind? Well, let's just say there weren't that many special elections on local, state or federal levels. And those groups that had preached about and looked forward to the Rapture were more than a bit disheartened that no more of them got taken up than anybody else.

After the initial shock went away, a feeling of despair swept through the survivors. We had fought the good fight, we had run the race, and we had lost. Our souls had been weighed and found wanting. We were just not good enough.

Church attendance fell. For who could trust a minister whom God had rejected? Crime went up as the police slacked off. Why bother arresting some when all had been judged guilty? And charities collapsed as donations dried up and most of the remaining do-gooders left to do something for themselves.

The party started shortly after that, one big party that lasted for weeks. When you know that Heaven has been denied you, when there is no hope of a reward after death, why not grab all the pleasure you can? Drugs, alcohol, sex – why abstain? Adultery, theft, even murder – if you wanted to, why not? Do What Thou Will became the first and only commandment for far too many people.

Gradually, though, some sanity returned. A general religious council was called. All were invited – Catholic, Protestant, Jew, Muslim, Hindu, whatever – it didn't matter, every denomination, every faith was invited. There was a God, and He didn't play favorites. By mutual consent it was held in Jerusalem. There, Hope was again found at the bottom of the chest.

God has not abandoned us, it was decided. Those that had been Taken were the ones who at that time had found favor with Him. And they had been Taken for a purpose –to warn the rest of us that the end of the world was approaching. It was a test, to see if we could overcome our faults and weakness, to see if we could make ourselves worthy of Heaven.

We had not gotten off to a very good start. But slowly, things got better. Churches filled up again, and charities found even more donors and volunteers. And people went back to work mindful of the fact that each word said in anger, each lie told about a co-worker, each customer cheated, was a step away from Paradise.

That didn't last, either. Humanity being what it is, things soon leveled off. There were good people, better people, worse people. Mostly, there were just average people, content to live out the days they had left. With all the children gone, and no babies being born, the story of man on earth was coming to a close.

Then the dead returned.

We'd been ready for them. With the Taken gone and the universe growing a bit smaller every time you looked up, it didn't take a divinity degree to figure out what was going to happen next. So when the first of the undead crawled out of his grave, there were people there to meet him.

Granted, some of those people had flamethrowers, just in case. No one knew just what we'd be dealing with. Too many late night movies had everyone thinking "flesh eating zombies."

No one got napalmed. The dead who emerged were more like frightened children – unsure of what was going on, unable to remember what just happened and willing to go anywhere and do anything they were told.

Camps had been set up, and those who returned were lead to them. There they were photographed and fingerprinted, their identities checked against the names over the graves out of which they had crawled.

One thing we didn't know was how many would return. Would all the dead rise, or just some? Would there be centurions wandering Europe wondering just what the Hell had happened to their perfect world and the Pax Romana? Would legions of soldiers rise up and resume fighting the wars that killed them?

It turned out that not everyone came back, just those who had died in the past ten years or so. When a final count was finally made, about the same number returned as had been Taken. Some kind of balance had been made.

It was commonly believed that the recent dead who didn't return were those who, if they'd been alive, would have been among the Taken. The ones who returned hadn't earned Heaven in their lifetime, and were sent back to try again.

One thing that no one thought of was the legal issue. What rights did the Returned have? I guess that's why so many lawyers were left behind, to argue that point. In the end, a heavily conservative Supreme Court ruled that precedent held – that most rights of citizen ended at death, and unless Congress acted, it didn't matter if the dead had come back or not.

Congress didn't act. Mindful of the fact that their living constituents, the survivors and (more importantly) heirs of the deceased could vote and those Returned could not (except in Chicago, where the dead had been voting for over a century), the House and Senate did nothing.

The camps closed. Most of the Returned were taken in by family. Some just wandered from place to place. Still others found their way into the cities, where they took shelter in the poorest of dwellings and did the work no one else wanted to do.

All this had been a year ago. Back then I was cop, a good cop. At least, I thought I'd been a good cop. I guess I was, by the standards of the day. Sure, I'd planted evidence, but only when I knew my guy was guilty. And maybe at times a suspect got roughed up, but he wouldn't have talked any other way. And if somebody ran from me and I caught up to him, well, he had to get a beat down, just to teach him some respect. But I did my job—catching the bad guys and protecting the average citizen. And I never took more than I deserved, and then only when it was offered.

It was back when the big party ended. A lot of people started taking a good long look at themselves, trying to figure out why others had left and they stayed behind. I was one of them. I remember sitting home alone. My wife and I had split and my son, well, he would have been eight this year. I remember looking at my badge and for the first time seeing the tarnish on it.

I almost quit. For a long time I wondered if the kind of cop I was could give way to the kind of man I had to become. What could I do —go private? Same job, same environment, less pay and no pension. I could give it all up and do the 9-5 bit, but that would leave me too much free time to find trouble and get in it. So I'd kept the badge, and did what I could to polish it up.

The first thing was to get out of narcotics and vice. Too many temptations. My record was good, so I was able to wangle a transfer to the Northeast Station as a district investigator. It wasn't a high crime area. A few shootings a week in the trouble spots, the occasional B&E in the residential areas and hold-ups along the Belair Road and Harford Road corridors.

The District Investigation Section office was set up in the old courtroom. When they moved the district courts to a central location the judge's box and prisoner benches went with them, leaving a large empty space to fill. Some cheap drywall and spackle, second hand desks and chairs from city surplus and a few computers with obsolete operating systems and it was office space.

Being the new guy, I got the desk closest to the door. That meant I'd be the person anyone coming in and looking for help would see. I got the cranks, the complainers and the kooks. I also got the people who came in with real problems, the ones who had no one else to turn to, the ones I needed to help.

I was reading reports about a B&E suspect called the Spider for his ability to get into otherwise inaccessible second floor windows when I heard laughter out in the hall. It wasn't the hale and hearty kind that comes from a shared joke told well, but rather the hard-edged laughter that comes at someone's expense.

Then I heard, "Dead man walking." More laughter. After it died down, a slow, deliberate voice asked something.

"Through that door, freak," the desk sergeant answered. "Office on your left. And don't touch anything. Hey, somebody hold the door for this corpse."

Funny that, fear of contamination leading to a basic human courtesy.

I turned in my chair and watched as the zombie came in. He had the same deliberate gait they all did, moving a limb at a time as his conscious mind gave the orders that once came automatically. They might be up and about, but fully alive they weren't.

I stood up and waited while he shuffled over. As he did I took mental notes. He dressed well, a suit with a clean, white shirt and knotted tie. That must of taken some time, given the undead's usual lack of hand-eye coordination. He carried a briefcase, and if it wasn't for his shambling walk and grey going to white pallor, he could have been any businessman coming in to file a complaint.

When he finally got close enough, I held out my hand in greeting. His face showed what little surprise it could, then he brought up his hand and we shook, me trying not to flinch at the touch of his cold grip, him pretending not to notice. Civilities over, I invited him to sit down with a wave of my hand.

"How can I help you, Mister..."

"Foreman," he said, his speech slow and deliberate as his mouth formed one syllable at a time. "Terry Foreman."

"I'm Detective John Scott. What can I do for you?"

"I would like you to investigate a murder."

I was ready for anything but that. Sometimes the undead will come in and try to file a theft or assault complaint. I'd have to explain to them that, being dead, they had no legal standing under the law, so technically, whatever anyone did to them was not considered a crime. Then I'd find out what happened and try to find a way to charge their assailants. Desecrating a corpse is a misdemeanor, so is robbing one. One of those charges generally sticks if brought before a liberal enough judge.

Murder was a different story, and I told Foreman that. "Not my division, Mr. Foreman. If you witnessed a murder or know of one that's been committed, I can call a Homicide detective for you."

He sat there unmoving, not saying a thing. Maybe he was forming his words. Maybe he was waiting to be told to leave.

"Give me the details," I finally said, breaking the uncomfortable silence. "I'll look into it and call Homicide myself. Now whose murder are we talking about, Mr. Foreman?"

"Mine."

This was new. I'd talked to many a murder suspect, but never a victim. And it suddenly occurred to me that a lot of cold cases could be cleared up if we could only locate the victims and ask them what I asked Foreman,

"Who killed you?"

He shook his head. "If I knew I wouldn't be here."

I'd forgotten. In the post-resurrection interviews it turned out many of the Returned didn't remember their deaths, especially the sudden violent ones. And none of them remembered what happened between death and resurrection.

"What do you remember?"

"Not much of that last day. I know I had a meeting with my business partner. After that, a young National Guardsman with a nasty looking weapon was saying something about crispy critters."

I wanted to go further, but then I realized that I might be dealing with a closed case. His murder might already have been solved.

"Mr. Foreman, I am going to look into this, but first I'm going to have to pull the report. Give me you number and ..."

While I was talking he reached into his briefcase and pulled out a folder. He handed it to me. It was a BPD case file, complaint number 06-4G97810. Under the number was the heading "Homicide—Foreman, Terrence."

"Where did you get this?"

He smiled, "It's one of the few rights we have left."

Of course. The Victim's Rights Bill of '03. When the City Council passed it zombie rights weren't a consideration. The bill specified that crime victims had the right to review their case folders. And while Foreman might not be a citizen under the law, there was no doubt he was a victim.

I opened the case folder and took a quick glance. On the first page, stamped in red, was the word "Open." That meant it hadn't been solved or otherwise disposed of. I leafed through the rest of it —police and crime scene reports, lab results, witness interviews—it looked like it was all there. I put it on my desk to read later.

"Who wanted to kill you, Mr. Foreman?"

"I can't think of anyone."

The trouble with questioning zombies is that they show little emotion. Their faces generally don't move much unless they want them to. And with a near expressionless voice it's hard to tell if one of them is lying. I fell back on one of the givens in detective work – everybody lies.

"Mr. Foreman, when I look through that folder I'm going to find two or three people with a reason to have wanted you dead. Why not save me the trouble and tell me yourself. Let's start with the obvious —wife, girlfriend?"

"Wife, we were married five years."

"And how did you two get along."

"Fine."

The answer came too quickly. I started tapping the case folder with one finger. If he were telling me the truth he'd see the tapping as a nervous gesture. If not…

"She'd been having an affair." Something showed on his face that time, a sorrow so deep it had to come out. A sadness that death couldn't ease.

"When did you find out?"

"A few days before I…you know."

"Who wanted the divorce, you or her?"

"No, we were trying to work things out."

That could be true or not. Either way, his wife was now suspect number one.

"You mentioned a meeting with your partner. How was business?" I started tapping again.

"Not good, bad actually. I'd gotten the result of an independent audit and..."

"Your partner was cheating you."

Foreman nodded. Suspect number two.

"Your partner and your wife, were they...together?"

"No, it wasn't him. She wouldn't tell me who, but it wasn't him, I'm sure."

Unkown boyfriend, number three.

I stood up with the folder and made copies. When I came back he was standing. He took his originals with his left and offered me his right. I took it, asking as I did, "your wife, ex-wife, is she..." I fumbled for the right term. Words like alive and dead are losing their meaning.

Foreman forced a smile. "She's alive, not a zombie like me."

My face must have shown my surprise, the undead don't usually use "Z" word. Foreman kept his smile. "I am what I am, Detective. Thank you for your help."

I walked him out, hoping my presence would prevent any more harassment from the desk sergeant.

It did, sort of. The uniformed Buddha behind the desk saved his comments for me.

"You were with that cadav a mighty long time, Scott. What are you, some kinda necro or somethin?"

There was a lot I could have said back. Comments about his large size, small IQ or doubtful parentage came to mind. I even thought about the ever popular "He wanted directions to your mother's house. I told him to expect at least an hour's wait." Instead I turned the other cheek, took the laughter that came my way and went back to my desk.

I called Homicide and told them what I had.

"Foreman, Foreman," muttered the harried detective as he searched through a year's worth of computer entries. "Oh yeah, here it is. It's been dropped into the Cold Case bin. No one's really working it right now, but if you want to bring him down I can see him," I heard him paging through a calendar, "Tuesday a week."

"So soon?" I asked, not trying to disguise the sarcasm.

"Listen, Scott, I don't know what it's like up in the great Northeast, but down here in the real world we're swamped. The murder rate's been going up ever since the dead returned. Word on the street is that it ain't murder if they come back after you kill them. And you try getting a homicide conviction after the so-called victim walks into the courtroom. Baltimore juries never were the brightest, and there's always one of the twelve who can't tell the difference between alive and undead."

He rambled for another few minutes. When he paused to breathe, I made my offer. "Look, if it's that busy how about I look into it? If I get any where I'll give you a call, say, Tuesday next."

I got a "Yeah, you do that," and then he hung up.

I slipped a CYA memo into the case folder noting the date and time that I had been given permission by the Homicide Unit to investigate one of their cold cases then sat back and started reading reports.

Two months and three days before the Righteous started leaving us, Terry Foreman was found dead in his car. The car was parked in his driveway, the motor running. Foreman was slumped over in the driver's seat, having died from a close-contact gunshot wound to the head.

Foreman's body was discovered by a curious neighbor, who noticed the car idling for about twenty minutes before going over to investigate. According to his wife, Debbie (nee Lochlear), Foreman had left the house forty minutes prior to the discovery of his body.

No gun, casings or bullets were found on the scene. The Medical Examiner did recover a .38 bullet from inside of Foreman's head. The bullet was suitable for comparison should a suspect weapon be recovered. The Crime Lab did a nice job of photographing and diagramming the scene. The lab techs also dusted Foreman's car, recovering quite a few latent prints, all of which were matched with Foreman, his wife, the neighbor and the first officer on the scene.

The area was canvassed and of course, no one heard or saw anything. Foreman's wife and business partner were both questioned, routinely it seems, with no mention of either infidelity or embezzlement. But then, that's not the sort of thing one brags about to police investigating a murder.

Updates filed one, two, three and six months after the murder reported little progress in the case. The last update listed solvability as poor, and recommended that the case be placed in the "Pending" file to wait further developments.

There were none, not until the dead returned and one of them walked into my office.

I started with the wife, the ex Mrs. Foreman and now Debbie Lochlear. She'd moved out of the Hamilton duplex she'd shared with her husband into a pricier Perry Hall condo. Perry Hall was in Baltimore County and out of city jurisdiction, but I was only going there to chat, this time at least.

I'd called ahead and she was expecting me. So when I rang the bell she buzzed me in right away.

"Ms. Lochlear," I said when she opened the apartment door, "I'm Detective Scott." She let me in and offered coffee. I took a cup and we sat at the kitchen table and talked.

"You said you had some information about my husband's death?"

"Yes, Ma'am. I've been asked to reopen the case."

"By who?"

"Your husband."

"But I'm not married...Terry's back?"

She was genuinely surprised. I looked at her hard, trying to find some guilt or fear but came up empty.

"He's back," I told her. "You didn't know?"

She shook her head. "I knew it was possible, but thought maybe he'd call. When he didn't, I thought that he'd been one of those that...didn't come back."

"How did you and Terry get along?"

It must have been the way I asked the question, because right away she said, "He told you, didn't he—about the affair?" I nodded and let her continue. "It was one of those things. Terry was a good man, the best. He loved me dearly, gave me everything. But he wasn't— exciting. One day I decided that I needed some excitement and went out and found it. Terry was never supposed to find out."

"But he did."

Her "Yeah," came out like a curse, and her following words grew bitter as she came near tears. "Someone who knew us, a 'good friend' of ours, saw me with my lover one day. I guess we were being a bit obvious. Anyway, he thought Terry should know, so he told him. That night he when came home, Terry asked me about it. I never was a good liar."

"How did he take it?"

"Sat there and cried like a baby. Blamed himself for not being what I needed. We talked and I said all the right things, the things he needed to hear. Told him I'd end the affair, that I'd make it right between us again."

I halfway believed her. She might have just been someone who made a mistake. We all make them. But then she might just be telling me "all the right things" hoping I'd believe her like her husband did. "Did you make it right?" I asked.

"I would have tried, but Terry was killed a few days later."

We sipped our coffees for a few minutes, then Debbie asked, "When you talked to Terry, what did he say happened that night?"

"He doesn't remember." Did a look of relief pass across her face? It was time to play bad cop.

"Ms. Lochlear, what was your lover's name?"

"I don't think Frank had anything to do with it?"

"Frank?"

"Chavis." She gave me the address she had for him. "But he didn't do it."

"Why not? You were his. You might have told him you loved him. He didn't want to lose you. With Terry out of the way..." I let that hang and changed direction. "When your husband died, you got the house, the bank account, everything. Right?"

"Yes, but..."

I interrupted. "And Terry was well insured, he was that kind of person, double indemnity for 'accidents' like murder."

She caught on. "I did not kill my husband." No tears now. The eyes that glared at me were clear and hard.

"Someone did. Somebody put a gun to his head and pulled the trigger. Why not you or Chavis? You both got something out of it. He got you and you got," I looked around the room, "a condo in Perry Hall."

She called me a name, one I'd been called before. "I did not kill my husband," she repeated. "You want someone with a reason to kill Terry, talk to his partner. Talk to Ronald Morrison. That bastard stole from Terry, then was going to leave the firm and take most of their clients with him. Terry was going to sue. He wanted to give Morrison one last chance to make it right. He had a meeting with him the night he died. He never got there. Go see Morrison, and get out of my house."

I thanked her for her time. On the way out I stopped at the door.

"You never asked, you know."

"Asked what?" she said icily, wanting me gone.

"About Terry—how he was, what he was doing, that sort of thing."

For a moment she softened. "Terry's dead," she said quietly, then she closed the door without saying another word.

It was the weekend before I could do any follow-up work. A rash of B&E's in the Glenham area combined with a string of armed robberies along Harford Rd. kept us all busy. Then I got picked for a special detail.

Friday, City Hall. The first Zombie Rights rally here in Baltimore. Anyone who didn't expect something like it soon or later hasn't been paying attention to the last 100 years of American history.

I got "volunteered" as part of the security taskforce, to make sure the prominent undead brought here from other cities weren't killed —again. It had happened in other places, one speaker shot by a sniper, two more blown up in a car. It didn't stop the cause, only slowed it down while everyone waited for the deceased to come back from wherever the newly dead go these days. The terrorism backfired. Nothing feeds a cause like martyrs, and having living (sort of) martyrs makes the cause stronger still.

There was the usual rhetoric—Zombies should give up their old identities and adopt "post-existence" names. There was a call for a Zombie Nation, where the undead could dwell in peace. Even the name "Zombie" was attacked as insulting, a slur based on beliefs fostered by horror fiction and the movies. "Revenant" and "Non-breathing American" were the best replacements offered.

Scattered among the above were some ideas about basic human rights – freedom from harassment, fair housing and employment, the right to vote and own property. Petitions were passed around asking the State of Maryland to grant citizenship to the undead. I signed one. As one living speaker pointed out, zombie rights were in everyone's interest. You may not benefit now, but when you die and come back you will.

The rally broke up about eight. We were released at nine, after the last of the stragglers left City Hall Plaza and any threats of violence were reduced to the normal dangers a Baltimore night has to offer.

Since I was already downtown, I decided to do some work on the Foreman case. Debbie had given me an address for Frank Chavis. A phone call when I go back to my desk the day I talked to her told me that Chavis had moved on. A few calls later I had traced him to his last official place of residence – 111 Penn St, the City Morgue. He had died almost six months to the day after Foreman passed on. Drinking had killed him. That and the tree he hit doing sixty with a 0.24 blood alcohol content.

Chavis didn't have a fixed address. According to government records, he was among the last to leave the containment camps set up to welcome the dead back to this world. When no one came for him, they asked him his city of origin, and when he said "Baltimore," they gave him twenty dollars and put him on a bus headed for the Trailways Travel Plaza. In life Chavis had a history of alcohol-related arrests and problems. Figuring that old habits die hard, and that some come back with you, I decided to check out the zombie bars.

It says something about Baltimore that it's only a short walk from City Hall to the notorious Block. Back in the Fifties and before, the Block was Baltimore's only tourist attraction, the only reason for a businessman to stop in the city on his way north or south. Back then, the Block was really three or four blocks long, and its strip joints and burlesque houses were famous nationwide. Blaze Starr's Two O'Clock Club was on the Block, and at the Gayety one could watch the legendary Ann Corio and Irma the Body take most of it off.

It changed in the sixties, with "free" love and increasing nudity in the movies. Fashion changed too, and by the Eighties one could see more female flesh on the beach at Ocean City than Miss Starr ever showed on stage. Videotapes and DVD's brought adult movies into the home, and camcorders let people make their own. By the Nineties the Block matched its name, having being reduced to that size, the once proud theaters now cut up into liquor stores, small video shops and strip clubs where under-aged girls dance listlessly on stage and middle-aged hookers hustled drinks to a tired disco beat.

Nothing happens in this world that someone doesn't try to make money from it. The Block had revived since the return of the dead. It was still the same size, but the entertainment had changed.

The strip clubs were still there, but now the banners out front proclaimed "Dead Girls Live!" and "The Naked and the Dead!" The bars were a mixed lot – some were for still breathing patrons, who paid for the novelty of having shuffling deadmen bring them their drinks. (And where every night some drunk loudly proclaimed, "Hey, I didn't order a Zombie," then laughs like he was the first to tell the joke.) Other bars catered to the undead crowd, where the Returned could be among their own kind. When one of the breathing mistakenly enters these places, they're stared at by pairs of cold, unblinking eyes until they feel uncomfortable and leave. It was in one of these that I found Frank Chavis.

It was called The Horseshoe Lounge. If there was a reason for the name it was lost three owners ago. The bar wasn't on The Block proper, but rather halfway down on Gay St. It was the third place I tried that night and I was tired. If Chavis wasn't there I'd give it up and start again Monday. I stood in the doorway to let my eyes adjust to the dim lighting then walked over to the bar.

Unlike his customers, the bartender was still breathing. No surprise there. These days almost any skilled profession requires a license, one of the requirements for which is that you have to be alive.

"Beer, please," I ordered once he decided to pay me some attention.

"No beer," he replied mechanically, 'Just the hard stuff."

"Ginger ale then." I knew how hard they served it in these places. He put a small glass in front of me. "Five bucks."

"For soda?"

"A drink's a drink, and drinks here are five bucks." I put a bill on the bar. "No tip?" he asked.

"Maybe," I showed him a photo of Chavis. "Know this guy?"

He knew him. I could that by the look on his face as soon as he saw the picture. Would he tell me, that was the question.

"Maybe. Why should I tell you?"

I flashed my badge. "Because I said please." I was hoping the power of the badge would be enough. It was too late and I was too tired to think of any believable threats.

I didn't have to. He nodded toward a corner. "First booth. What about my tip?"

"You charge too much for drinks." I went over to where Chavis was sitting and stood by the booth until he looked up at me.

"Detective John Scott." I showed the badge. "Frank Chavis?"

"I used to be." He waved me to the opposite seat. "Chavis was my warm name. I'm Frank Thanos now. How can I help you, Officer?"

"I'm investigating the murder of Terry Foreman. I believe you knew his wife."

He filled a glass from a bottle of the hard stuff, then offered to cut my ginger ale. I declined. He took a drink, filling his mouth then pausing to swallow.

"Debbie," he said, putting his glass down. Whatever he thought of her was lost in the flatness of his voice. "They say you always remember your first. Debbie was my last. Not everything rises from the dead. I'm a stiff in everyway but the one that matters." He looked down at the bottle. "The only vice I have left, and it has to be at least 180 proof before I feel any kick." He looked back up at me. "You think I killed Foreman?"

"Did you?" I asked. I had a feeling he'd tell me if he did. It wasn't like I could do anything about it. The courts had ruled that crimes committed before a person's death were not punishable if he returned.

Thanos gave me a slow shake of his head. "No, Debbie was a nice piece, but not worth killing over. When she told me it was over, it was over. Plenty more out there. Of course, after Foreman died I did comfort her for a while. That ended about a week before I did."

"Debbie ever talk about it, say who might have wanted him dead?"

"Just that scum of a partner of his. Other than that, old Terry wasn't the type to have enemies. From what Debbie said afterwards, he was an all around nice guy, a church going Christian sort. He'd have to be some kind of saint to take back a woman who did him wrong like she did."

"For the record, where were you when Foreman was killed?"

Thanos made the effort to shrug. "Nowhere near Debbie's place. Other than that, you find out, then we'll both know. There's parts of my warm life that just haven't come back yet. Anything else?"

I pointed to the bottle. "Just one, who's paying for that? You got a job?"

"Government handout, it's not much but all us cold ones get something to keep us out of trouble. Plus I got a few friends left."

"One of those friends named Debbie?"

He didn't answer, just stared straight ahead. When I got up he was still staring. I left him to his liquor and memories of warmer days.

Despite his denials, Thanos still could be the killer. He did wind up with Debbie. And she wound up with a nice insurance settlement, some of which she could be sharing to keep him quiet. Or she could have killed Foreman herself, with Thanos knowing and not saying. I'd see about getting a court order to look into her financial records. Right after I got back from seeing Morrison on Tuesday.

"Everything I did was legal," Ronald Morrison told me once I finally got into see him. He'd been tied up in a meeting, he said, explaining the hour he kept me waiting. That hour gave me time to review what I'd learned about Morrison & Associates.

The business grew from the remains of Foreman & Morrison. The two partners had run an advertising firm, not the biggest, but it had its share of regional and local accounts. Morrison was the idea man, the outgoing glad-hander who met and woed the clients. Foreman worked behind the scenes, running the business end of things. It came apart when Morrison emptied the corporate account and filed to dissolve the partnership. He planned to start his own firm, taking most of F&M's clients with him, leaving Foreman broke and looking for a job.

"I wasn't my fault Terry made the mistake of trusting me. We each had equal access to the money. He could have cleaned me out first if he had thought of it."

"From what I heard, Foreman wasn't that kind of man."

Morrison let out a hearty laugh, the kind that comes from enjoying a good joke. "No, he wasn't. He was a good and decent fellow, the poor fool. Honest to a fault, considerate to the employees, fair with the clients. Definitely not meant for the business world."

"You used him," I said, my tone accusing him of a crime akin to murder, "to build the business, to get everything running smooth, then you screwed him over. The night he was killed he was coming to see you, to give you a chance to do the right thing."

"And I was waiting for him," Morrison said calmly. "Was surprised when he didn't show. Terry never, ever missed an appointment. Didn't hear about his death until the next day."

"Unless you arranged it."

Morrison took the accusation of murder lightly. "Detective Scott," he smiled, "I'll admit that over the last year of our partnership I slowly drained the corporate account. Terry kept the books and he wasn't a hard man to fool. However, according to my attorney I had a legal right to do so. Terry's attorneys would no doubt see things differently and he was free to sue me. He might even have won, if he had any money left to hire attorneys. So you see, I had no motive to want him dead. In fact, he had a better reason to kill me."

Morrison was so gleefully venal and proud of the way that he'd cheated Foreman that I doubted he'd killed the man. He'd want his victim alive. He would have gloated over the remains of Foreman's shattered career then thrown the man a bone, offering him a job with the new firm. If he had no other prospects, Foreman may have swallowed his pride taken it. I got the feeling that when the Lord called the next batch of us up, Morrison wasn't going to make the cut.

A week went by. In between doing the work the Department paid me to do I managed to get Debbie Lochlear's bank statements. She showed a regular pattern of deposits from her job and withdrawals from both savings and checking. She could have been giving money to Thanos, but there was no way to be sure except to follow her. I also checked on the bullet that had been dug out of Foreman's head. It had yet to be matched to a gun, nor had the Firearms Unit's computer paired it to bullets recovered from other crime scenes.

There comes a time with some investigations when you look at what you've got and realize that you're not going to get anymore. That's when you know it's time to close the case folder for good. I was at that point with the Foreman murder. I suspected that Debbie, Thanos or both knew more than they were telling, but suspicions aren't proof. Maybe it was time to admit defeat and call the real homicide detectives. I'd give them what I had and maybe they could close things out. For me, there were just too many questions I couldn't answer.

I was going over these questions yet again, looking for answers, not really wanting someone else to break this case when I thought of the big question, the one nobody had asked. I signed out a car and drove to Perry Hall.

After the last time I didn't think Debbie would let me in, so I sat in my car and waited for someone else to enter and went behind them.

I knocked on her apartment door. When Debbie answered and

saw who it was she tried to slam it shut. I was a bit faster and had my foot and shoulder past the door before she could close it. "Get out," she told me, "I don't have to talk to you."

"Just one question," I said quietly, not wanting to rouse any helpful neighbors who might call the county police. "What did you do with the gun?"

"I didn't ..." she started to deny it, then looked at my face. "You know, don't you?" I nodded and she let me in.

She gave it all up—what she did, what happened to the gun, all of it. "What happens now?" she asked when she was through.

"I honestly don't know," I told her before leaving.

Foreman lived with his sister in a housing development on 33rd St, near where Memorial Stadium used to be before Baltimore's sports teams moved downtown. On the way there from the station I stopped at Lake Montibello. How, I thought, looking at the placid waters of the lake, did she get the gun past the police? They would have searched her, the cars, the house. Where did she hide it? No matter, every house has a dozen hiding places known only to its occupants. It didn't matter either that the gun was now resting somewhere at the bottom of the lake. Let it lay there. No one needed it.

Foreman was waiting for me. "You have news?" he asked, as excited as his kind can get.

"I know who killed you," I told him. We sat down. I took out a sealed envelope. "Before I give you this, what are you going to do after you open it?"

He thought a moment. "I, I don't know."

"No *Revenge of the Zombie* plans?"

"No. I think that I just want to know."

"Good, because there's nothing the Department can do."

"Statute of Limitations?" he asked.

"Something like that. Listen, Mr. Foreman, before you open that envelope, ask yourself how badly you need to know the name, and how willing you are to forgive the person who killed you." I stood up, offered my hand. "Good luck to you," I said, meaning every word.

The big question in this case hadn't been who killed Terry Foreman. It wasn't whether or not Debbie was paying for Thanos to keep his dead mouth shut. And it wasn't why she hadn't told the police about Morrison cheating her husband. No, it was more basic than that. This is a world where the sky is falling, where the truly good have been taken away and the dead walk among us. So why in this world did Terry Foreman, a man everyone agrees was a good man, return after death? Was it because he had some secret sin, some vice no one knew about? Or was it because in a moment of weakness and despair, having lost his wife, job and future, he got a gun, put it to his head and pulled the trigger?

Debbie told me she had heard the shot and ran out to find Foreman slumped over in the front seat, gun near his hand. Even in her shock and grief, she realized that suicide cancelled Foreman's insurance. So she took the gun, hid it well and waited for the police to ring her doorbell. Later she dropped it in the lake. When the police decided it was probably a robbery gone bad, she let them think that, rather than tell the truth or trying to place the blame on Morrison.

I closed the case out as a suicide. One day someone might read the file and contact the insurance company. If so, Debbie might be in some trouble, but it's not likely.

I never saw Terry Foreman again so I don't know if he ever opened the envelope. If he did, I hope he found the strength to forgive himself, to take the second chance we've all been given to make for the weakness that had denied us Paradise.

Whitley '04

FLESH WOUNDS

Adam P. Knave

THE FIRST TIME I died I was alone, except for my killer of course. The sidewalk was slick with recent rain that made pools of reflected light along the gutters. Reflections of houses shone up at me, and I watched them as I trundled back home. It was late, two or so in the morning, and I knew I wasn't allowed out that late, no one was anymore since the problems began. I was seventeen, a stupid kid coming home late from a party. Half drunk, I left Tom's house to the protests of the other friends gathered there to help send him off to the Army. His last night of freedom, my last night of life. Interesting how that worked out.

It wasn't interesting how it worked out. There was no deeper meaning to it, but sometimes it can be comforting to try and assign one. Regardless, my feet landed one in front of the other with almost no side to side deviation and I could feel the buzz of the night's drinking wearing off slowly. Three, maybe four, blocks away my family slept soundly, sure I was safe at Tom's place for the night.

Scraping and rustling snuck up behind me and I spun around, hoping it was a Captain Jingles, one of the neighborhood cats that refused to actually live in anyone's home. I spun around and saw that I was face to face with one of them. The undead, a shambler, a zombie just looking at me the way a dog looks at a tasty crunchy bone. It wasn't a look I had ever had turned on me before, a look that simply told me I was lunch. I ran.

I took off as fast as I could manage, shouting all the way. I screamed for the cops, screamed warnings that there was a zombie near by, the whole nine yards. I even tossed in a tenth yard for good measure, but by the time anyone could react, could get themselves out of their homes to see what was going on, I had been taken down.

You have to understand, the things are faster than you might consider. They shamble along slow most of the time, true, but they can sprint when catching prey. It was discussed on the news from time to time, mostly after something like this happened. After they had downed a victim. After they had downed a particularly stupid young punk of a victim who probably deserved it.

Rotting teeth found purchase against my skin, pushing in and trying to scrape my neck clean off. I swung out, my fist hitting its head with a wet thump, this wasn't exactly a fresh specimen, and the flesh eater backed off a bit. He didn't back off enough though, as he latched onto my arm instead. His teeth sank into my forearm as his head tore slaveringly from side to side, worrying off a hunk of my flesh. I screamed at the sight and sensation but managed to stay conscious. I threw up when he ate my thumb, splashing the contents of my stomach across the sidewalk. The thing chewed at the severed bone quickly, sickening crunching and splintering sounds filling the night. My blood swam out of my body, looking for a new home among tar and concrete.

His hands scrambled up my body, dirty fingers digging rents in my skin through my clothing with their ragged nails. He climbed my body like it was a rock face and my consciousness swam in and out of focus. I was helpless, lying there in shock and slipping from the world, as his teeth found my neck again. A blood slick tongue probed at me, finding an artery and his teeth tore at me again. The world went black. I died.

I died. No long tunnel with a white light at the end, no choir of angels, just blackness and nothing. My soul fled my body, escaping the prison of meat and soaring upwards into the endless night. Up and up it flew, streaming towards stars, until it snapped backwards, colliding with my body like a high-speed chase ending in a twenty car pile-up.

THEN THERE WAS LIGHT.
Heaven?
A final reward after all?
I opened my eyes to intense halogen lamps shining down on me. I felt a sheet over my body, but found I couldn't guess the temperature of the room. With a realization like a slap in the face, I realized I had

come back. Revived the worst way possible; not some last second save by the police, rushed to a hospital where my wounds were cleaned and treated, restoring me to health slowly while my family chewed their nails to the nub nearby waiting for word that I had pulled through. I had come back as one of them.

I looked around and realized where I was, in the zombie wing of Memorial General, police and doctors spaced around me, waiting for me to come back exactly like this. I knew the procedure, having heard about it on the news before. Once I woke up and proved that I would indeed come back as the undead, I would be put down. It was, they claimed, the only way to be sure. I was nothing more than the latest in a string of zombie infections across the country and, as such, was afforded no special treatment.

The world slid down to a calm level after the first zombie infections of a decade past. At first no one knew what to make of it. The dead rising again? Biblical signs of the end times? There was chaos and mass panic. I remembered it dimly happening all around me, but I was only a kid, ya know? There had been three wars within the first two years of discovery as governments blamed each other for the invention and spread of what turned out to be a very strange disease.

The wars had died down after time, and the world learned to adjust, as it always does. Zombies were hunted, international curfews were in place, and everyone had an agenda of extermination. It made sense, no one wanted the world taken over by zombies. I certainly supported the notion of total extermination, until I became one of them that is. Once I found myself in the communal boat I realized that it was really in need of a good outdoor motor. I needed to live...well...unlive, that is.

The cops waved the doctors back a safe distance.

"Listen kid, we need you to just lie still, ok?" one of them told me. As. Fucking. If.

"Hey, you don't need to kill me, alright?" I told the cop closest to me, "I won't eat anyone, I promise!"

The cop shook his head almost sadly and drew his service revolver. The light glinted off the metal along the barrel of the weapon as it sliced through the air until it pointed directly at my head. I caught another flash of light on metal and saw a second cop had also leveled a gun at me. I did the only thing I could think of, I made a break for it.

I took a bullet in the shoulder as I hopped off the table, the wound stung a bit and messed up my arm some, but otherwise it didn't slow me down. I slammed into a doctor, muttering "Excuse me" as I bolted past him into the hallway.

People in the halls screamed and a few brave folks even tried to tackle me, as the police came screaming up behind me. I hoped they wouldn't try to fire their weapons in a crowded hallway, but even half sure that they wouldn't I could feel an itching in the back of my head, the imagined final bullet. I tried to run faster. I hit the front doors of the hospital hard enough to go through them, glass showering down along me and the street. Shards of plate glass bounced off the sidewalk, but I wasn't so lucky - ribbons of flesh coming off me as I kept running from long slices of glass firmly embedded in my body. I knew what this meant.

Back when zombies had first started to become understood it was realized that while they were technically the un-dead and did feast on the flesh and blood of the living, they couldn't really help themselves. The disease that brought people back from the very brink of death also made them dependant on certain protein chains inside human DNA. Some other animals would do, mostly mammals, but human DNA and bone marrow and the like was the best thing for them. The stuff let zombies regrow some lost tissue and kept their brains going in ways that weren't yet fully understood. The more they ... we ... I ... got hurt the more flesh and bone and blood I would need to keep going. The longer I went without it, the more I would decay, the faster my brain would rot in my skull turning me into a drooling idiot who shambled around with his arms out muttering "*braaaaiiiinnnnnssss.*"

I was feeling hungry.

WELL KNOWN FACT: A lot of zombies still escaped before being "put down," and when they did escape the cops they ran for woods or alleys, somewhere people couldn't find them easily and they tried to pass for the homeless or infirm as much as possible. So I went home. I snuck up on the house, the same way the zombie had snuck up on me. I cased the two-story structure: no cops nearby, neighbors inside, all probably fearful that another zombie was in the neighborhood, as if another of the undead would be lurking—

Oh, right. I was *lurking*.

I fished in my pocket for my keys, having trouble getting them free while missing a thumb. The front door was in front of me, all wood and glass like it always had been growing up. For the first time the situation sank in and I grew afraid. They would reject me, turn me away right then and there. Worse yet, my father would call the cops and have me "dealt with." If blood still fully pumped in my veins it would have run cold. I stopped my hand from shaking and put the key in the lock as quietly as possible. It turned in the lock with a sudden click that I had never noticed as being quite that loud before. Door handle turned, I edged the door open slowly and slid inside into the front hallway.

As I closed the door behind me again, the darkened living room right off the hallway suddenly grew full of light. Mom, dad, my sister Caroline, and even her Chihuahua Sparky all stood there staring at me. Caroline started to move forward but dad grabbed her by the shoulder and held her back.

"Shawn? Is that you?" my mother asked, her voice shaking with fear.

"Yeah mom, of course it's me."

"That isn't Shawn," my father insisted, face growing red with anger, "it's some undead freak!"

"Dad! I *am* Shawn!" I held my hands out in front of me, palm forward to show peace and then quickly pulled them back to my sides as Caroline screamed at the sight of my missing thumb, "I just had an accident."

"An accident?" my father's face was something close to beet colored, "You got attacked by a zombie and you're an undead flesh eater now!"

"But I'm also still your son. We can work with this."

"Carl," my mother interjected, putting a hand on my dad's shoulder to try and calm him, "Shawn is our son, we can't just turn him away at the door like a...like a..."

"Undead flesh eating monster, mom?" Caroline offered oh so helpfully. My mother shot her a look designed to wither humans.

"...Like a stranger," she finished, serving Caroline up with another helping of wither-glare.

"Yeah, see Dad, it's still me. I'm your son, ok? I just need to..." I tried to find a good way of phrasing it but found none, "hide out from the law so I don't get killed...again...you know?" My father scowled and stalked out of the room. My mother turned to follow him, casting a long look at me as she did.

"No, Mom, it's okay. I know where my room is." She sighed and left, Caroline in tow. Only Sparky remained behind to guard me, growling loudly now that we were alone. That dog had always hated me. Sparky took a hesitant step forward. I was so hungry.

I WOKE UP TO loud banging noises coming from the front of my room. I stretched out in my bed, home and safe felt really good, and rolled over trying to ignore it.

"Shawn! Open this door now!" Caroline yelled out. Sighing I got out of bed and pulled the door open. Caroline stood there holding Sparky's leash in her hand. *Uh-oh.*

"Hey, Car, what's up?"

"What's up?" she asked, shaking the leash, "You ate my dog!"

"Well, I didn't really have a choice."

"You did eat Sparky! Oh my God!"

"No, listen to me Car: yes, I ate your dog, but I needed to or I would've died, ok? It was him or me."

"You ate my dog, you undead freak!"

"Hey! Watch the slander. I hear the acceptable term is 'corporeally challenged' now. No need to be rude."

"*Rude? You! Ate! My! Dog!*"

"But I had to, you see…"

"Undead freak!"

"Stop that."

"Brain eater!"

"Bigot!" I yelled at her and slammed the door. I had to think fast, alright, eating the dog was a mistake but I really didn't have a good alternative: Caroline would've fought back harder. Once she told Mom and Dad I knew someone would call the cops. I had to get out fast. I opened the window next to my bed and went back to shove a bunch of clothes in the duffel bag I used to use for gym class. Heading back to the window, I also grabbed a few books and shoved them in next to the clothes. Then I lowered myself out of the window and down the drainpipe to the ground.

I snuck off into the trees by the house and tried to lose myself. I had to get out of town: that much was obvious. The problem was how. I couldn't exactly take a bus or train in my condition, and not many people stopped to pick up undead hitchhikers. We were in upstate New York, I could try and get down to New York City maybe, it was only a three-hour drive. I stopped, leaning against a tree and did some math. A three-hour drive at sixty miles per hour worked out to roughly a hundred and eighty miles. Not too far, unless I had to walk the whole way and it was looking like I would have to.

I walked through the woods towards the highway, unsure of how I was going to manage to get to the City, or even if it was a good idea. The woods were full of chirping birds and the rustling of squirrels and mice. Leaves coated the ground and I inhaled a big draught of fresh air, letting it fill my nostrils. I wandered through the woods, trying to forget my problems and let my subconscious mind work out a solution by itself.

Luckily, a solution presented itself in the form of a car. I could see the small lake that sat near the edge of the woods, a car parked nearby and some people from my school splashing around in the water. The car was an old Dodge, a big iron machine coated with mint green paint, sitting there unloved. I would love it.

I opened the door to the car as quietly as I could, hoping that the folks down in the lake wouldn't notice me. As I sat in the car, undisturbed, I had second thoughts. Was I really about to steal a car? Not even a week as an undead monster and already I was committing Grand Theft Auto? I felt slightly sick to my stomach at the thought, until I remembered that just last night I had eaten my sister's dog. Things clicked into perspective; at least the car was insured and could be found later, and I turned the keys that had been mindlessly left in the ignition. At the sound of the engine starting up, the kids in the lake looked over and started yelling. I threw the car into reverse and peeled out, tires squealing in my wake. I drove through the woods dangerously, not quite following the normal path out, and hit a road with a hard bump of the shocks. The highway was only a few turns in front of me. I got on an entrance ramp and sped off towards the City.

THE DRIVE WAS UNEVENTFUL for the most part. Stopping at tollbooths was interesting though, handing money to booth clerks and trying to make the transaction happen as fast as possible before they got more than a passing look at me. I was nervous the entire way downstate.

I reached the city and headed downtown, to Greenwich Village where I had come once before with an old girlfriend. I left the car on some small side street and just walked off keeping my head low. Sights and sounds assailed my senses, throngs of people on the streets, all passing me by without so much as a glance. I had become invisible in a sea of humanity. Humanity that I was no longer really a part of. When night fell across the city, the number of people seemed to just increase by magic. I had been on my feet all day and was feeling a mite peckish as well as exhausted. Sliding into an alley, I sat down to wait and consider my new options. A few slow-moving pigeons became dinner and as I sat and crunched my way past bone, spitting out feathers unhappily, I saw another body wander down my alley hideout. She was walking almost drunkenly, head hung low and looking depressed. I was determined to not eat her, no matter how much my mouth watered at the sight of someone unprotected and virtually alone.

The stranger walked right up to me and said hello. I sat where I was and fought back instinct. She knelt down until our eyes were level, which is when I noticed she had no nose.

"New in town, huh?" she asked me, her voice full of friendly welcome.

"Uhm, I, that is..." The words were in my head: Yes I have just recently gotten to town and if you don't leave, lack of nose or not, I might have to eat your head but they wouldn't come out of my mouth.

"Don't worry, sniff deep, I'm undead too." She smiled, and I could see that dried blood crusted some of her teeth. I breathed a sigh of relief. "See, you don't want to eat another of your kind, we aren't very nutritious." I nodded at her and held out my hand.

"Shawn Jacobs. Pleased to meet you...Miss..." She took my offered hand and shook it, not caring about the missing thumb any more than I found I really cared about her lack of nose.

"Irene Cummings. No Miss though, ok?"

"Alright. So uhm, aren't we..."

"Hunted? Feared? Abominations in the face of God and man?"

"Well, yeah."

"Sure, but look around, who notices here?" She had a point, no one had given me a second look all day. "Look, want to come hang out with the others?"

"There are others?"

"New York has the largest undead population of any city outside of L.A."

"Really?"

"Sure, it isn't easy to hide in small towns." I groaned at that, memories of how my sister had looked at me before I had run, of how my father had seen me when I had first come home flooding my mind.

"You got that right. Sure." I stood up with her and she led me off to Washington Square Park.

"We have an old underground system beneath the park," she said as I followed her into the public men's bathroom in the park, "the city doesn't even realize it's there." Inside the bathroom she pulled out a key and opened an old dirt-encrusted janitor's door.

A single dim bulb hung from the ceiling giving us almost no light to see by. Irene didn't seem to need it as she walked purposefully across the room, stopped only to glance back at me as I tripped over a mop bucket, and unlocked a second door. A stairway loomed on the other side, dim lighting set at even intervals downwards. I hesitated as she slid into the dimness.

"What are you afraid of? I'll kill you? It happens to be a little late for that, I should think." She was right and I hurried down the stairs after her, following her billowing black curls that reflected the dank light.

THERE WAS A HUGE room at the bottom of the stairs, filled with zombies just sitting around on old chairs or crates, talking and reading and listening to the radio. The light was brighter down here, and the place looked like a little dinner parlor. Irene turned and smiled at me, the skin around the hole where her nose had been creasing around the old wound almost cutely.

"Home sweet home," she told me, her arms waving with a flourish. Some of the zombies looked up and waved or nodded at us before going back to what they were doing.

"How long have you guys been here?" I asked, incredulous.

"I've only been here two years, but old Bingo, he's the guy in the purple chair over there in the corner," she pointed and sure enough there was an old guy in the corner doing what looked like a crossword puzzle, "has been here since the beginning, about four years ago."

"Wait, five years? And no one has noticed?" I shook my head, it wasn't possible.

"Of course not. We stay away and keep to ourselves and the City forgets we're here mostly. Those that still worry, and yeah there are a lot of those, have no real clue where we are. We're careful."

"What about..."

"Food? Pigeons, stray animals, the occasional almost dead homeless people...we're scavengers." There was no shame in her expression as she said it, which made me embarrassed that I had been ashamed of what I was now myself.

"What do you do for living? Just hide out here?" I didn't look forward to the prospect of spending the rest of my unnatural life in an underground room.

"During the day we can shamble around in the city, if we're careful. Some of us even have jobs," she said proudly, "but that doesn't happen too often." I was shocked, to say the least.

"Jobs doing what?"

"Oh you know, odds and ends. Jerome over there"—she pointed off towards a black zombie reading a magazine—"gets some occasional work as a stunt man. The producers don't care, they can ignore a lot of safety rules using undead stuntmen."

"But doesn't he, you know, lose a lot of flesh that way?"

"So long as he can get it back and eat quick enough he can reattach it mostly. It pays and his money helps fund this place, buying magazines and more furniture and new light bulbs." I nodded, mystified. Irene walked me over to meet some of the other zombies and after a while we sat down and traded life stories. A lot of them were like mine, folks that had been taken by surprise or done something stupid to end up undead and then decided that they didn't want to be put down like animals after all.

"Most of us who try, don't make it," said Tom, a young Asian zombie with only one arm, "but we gotta try—you know?"

I did know.

Hours later, after a fine snack of squirrel, Irene led me to a rectangle of blankets on the floor. She told me how many steps away and in what direction the stairs to get out where, just in case something happened in the middle of the night, and left me to bunk down. The lights were switched off in most of the room, leaving us in darkness. Next to me a slim woman called Katarin muttered in her sleep the rest of the night keeping me half awake.

THE NEXT MORNING I decided I needed to get out for a while and Irene came with me. We wandered upstairs and carefully checked out the public bathroom before coming out of the janitor closet. Finding it empty, as it usually was she told me, we exited and wandered around the park. Over near some old fountain that no longer spat water fitfully a woman was performing some kind of show, people gathered in a large circle around her.

"Come see Miss Mysteriosity perform her daring feats of blinding brilliance!" she proclaimed to the crowd that was already gathered to see her. Hopping off the milk crate she stood on, Miss Mysteriosity lit a bowling pin on fire and lit some paper with it. Once she had proven it was real fire coming off the club she proceeded to pass it under her arm, wincing a little as she did. Club passed by her flesh, she raised both arms to the sky and let out a loud "Taa-Daa!" The crowd responded with a smattering of clapping and a few people wandered away. Next she did some card tricks and a rope trick. The card tricks went ok and garnered her more applause but the rope trick fell apart and more people left. She ran through some more tricks, working at about a sixty percent success rate and then passed a hat around what was left of the crowd. A few people put coins in the hat and then everyone slowly wandered away back to their lives. Miss. Mysteriosity sat on her milk crate, sifting through the change, her head hung in defeat.

I pulled away from Irene and went up to Miss Mysteriosity myself, her head snapping up as I drew close.

"Nice act," I told her lamely.

"No, I fucked up a lot, as always."

"No, no…it wasn't that bad," I insisted, staring at her dull blue eyes. "Really."

"You're sweet to say that." Her eyes caught my hand, stupidly left out of a pocket and she gasped, "You—you're—"

"Undead," finished Irene as she came up behind me. Miss Mysteriosity blanched, gathering her things quickly.

"Just stay away from me, okay?!" she yelped, "I know my show sucked but that isn't cause to just eat someone!"

"Hey, now," I told her, taking a step back, "no one is eating anyone, alright?"

"Well, probably," Irene said and I thumped her on the shoulder to shut her up.

"No really, don't listen to her," I said, extending my hand, "I'm Shawn."

"Miss Mysteriosity, but you knew that," she told me, ignoring my offered hand and still packing up her things with due haste.

"Look, you just need some more work and your show," I said with a smile that was only partly false, "could be a hit."

"Maybe," she grudgingly admitted, packing away her clubs and cards.

"What you need," I told her, an idea springing to my mind, "is a willing assistant."

"Someone who can work for nickels and get burned a lot," she said shaking her head at me, "yeah, that'll happen."

"I'll be your assistant," I told her happily, "I don't care if you burn me or cut me a bit, you know?" Her eyes found mine and the look of fear they held was slowly replaced by one of curiosity.

"You're serious?"

"Why not? I don't have anything else to do, and it could be fun."

"Shawn, it's a little too" Irene butted in, jabbing me in the back with her fist, "public. Don't you think?"

"People will be so busy watching the act, they'll assume I'm made up to look like a zombie to fool them even more. It would be great!" Miss Mysteriosity had caught on to the idea too, smiling now and reaching out for my hand. I shook it and to her credit she only turned a bit paler when the lump of my ruined thumb joint brushed her palm.

We spent the next few weeks meeting at her apartment in Queens late at night and practicing tricks. She set my arm on fire, which stung like hell, and then had me douse it in a bucket of water that steamed dramatically when I put myself out. Later we tried cutting me in half, and I was patient until she learned to do it without actually cutting me in half. The first few times she tried it we had to go grab a bird from the cage I made her keep so I could piece myself back together again.

Irene wasn't too happy with the situation, grousing whenever I came back to the park and spending days not talking to me, but she started to come around to the idea too, after a while. Miss. Mysteriosity (whose real name was Sasha I found but she hated it so I just started calling her Myst in private) picked up her tricks a lot faster once she didn't have to worry about hurting anyone. I felt like I had found a way to cope with my new un-life after all and all too soon came the day of our big first show.

IT WAS A CLEAR sunny day and the crowds were pretty good. Myst went into her opening spiel and lit her club. I held my arm out, I was known as the Great Deadgimi to the crowd, and she lit me on fire. There were gasps and cries of shock as I stood there lighting things with my arm, pieces of wood and paper mostly. I dunked it in the prepared bucket and let out a sigh of relief as the stream hissed upwards. The cheers were loud and prolonged.

The box of swords trick went off mostly without a hitch too, and I kept quiet when one went through my side cleanly, so that the crowd had no idea anything had slipped up. I wore gloves, the thumb of my right glove stuffed with cotton so it looked like I still owned that digit; if anyone noticed it never moved, they didn't comment on it.

While Myst did her card tricks, a bit of a pacing problem that we had to change having them come after the bigger numbers, I circled the crowd with the hat collecting money. I shambled around stiffly and whispered "*Bbbbrrrrraaaaaaaiiiinnnnnsss*" to the crowd as I passed, getting little cries of laughter and surprise, along with bills shoved into the hat. We made a hundred bucks that first show, a pure hit.

By the second week we performed, the crowds were bigger, word had spread. Our tricks had gotten more extravagant too with a new finale tacked on before I passed the hat where Myst would run me through with a sword right before the crowd's eyes. We warned them the effect was not for the faint and intoned great deep magic was involved. The sword passed clean through my liver and hurt every time, but doing it almost guaranteed us another fifty bucks of take for the show, so I put up with it.

I'm still there, doing the show Mondays, Wednesdays, Thursdays and Saturdays, like clockwork. I moved out of the park and me and Irene got a small place in Brooklyn where no one knew us or bothered us, paid for by my work and Irene's new job in construction.

We eat out on the town every night, but really what other option do we have?

...FOR IF THE DEAD RISE NOT

Stefan Jackson

[1]

EMILY DODDS STOOD IN the middle of Sack Avenue on a cool afternoon. A patchy gray-blue sky hung over the quiet and still avenue. Nothing moved in the town except the wind-blown traffic light hanging above avenue and the farmer zombie lurching toward her.

The deader had been buried in bib overalls and a John Deere cap; disgust filled her as she looked at the deader. Emily did not want to waste a bullet on the dead human so she pulled her short sword free of its scabbard. Emily's father trained her in Kendo sword style; she made a quick pass attack on the deader. Two swings of her blade had cleanly sliced off the deader's right arm and right leg. Emily whirled and with blinding speed made a third cut, slicing off the deader's left leg as it was falling. Then she chopped off the zombie's left arm. Emily watched the animated torso pull itself along the black asphalt with its chin. She looked at its horrible blue-face. Emily knew that a blue face meant it was a newly turned zombie. This face was pitted with dirt crusted holes, and bits of skeleton poked through thin the paper-thin flesh. Its eyes were unfocused and slimed over with a yellow mucus film. Its mouth fixed agape, ragged teeth jutted from black gums. The deader head had no tongue. It was disgusted her but she could not look away. Its chin dug into the asphalt, its neck strained and flexed, and the bloated torso inched toward Emily.

The wind shifted and forced Emily to breathe in the putrid stink of the ridiculously repulsive thing proceeding toward her. She hacked and semi-choked and tears formed in the corners of her eyes. She turned away, regained her composure and fast walked down the empty avenue. Emily hadn't confronted a deader in a long time. She had forgotten just how horrible they smelled. After thirty-five years, Emily's father was sure the plague would have run its course by now, Apparently that is not the case.

The store window read: BIG TOM'S LIQUOR & SPIRITS. Emily entered the store with sword in hand. Her father—and experience had taught her that deaders do lay in wait for the living. Like lions staking out a watering hole, deaders know where people go: grocery stores, liquor stores, stores in general. One must always be alert to an ambush when inside a store. Her father has instructed her to never enter a mall.

Emily searched the store for her father's favorite brand. Most of the booze was gone; the shelves were pretty barren. She caught a glimpse of herself in the row of mirrors on the wall. Her red hair was streaked with soft blonde tresses, a hold over from the summer's blazing sun. Her skin was caramel colored and firm. The black tee shirt she wore accented her taut and slender frame; her young breasts threatened to burst free of the cotton shirt. Today, for the first time, Emily saw the fine young woman that her father always said she would become. And it's because of her father's love that she's going through all this hell at this moment.

Emily approached the door marked *Employees Only*. She pulled out the Colt .45. She cocked back the hammer. Sword in one hand and gun in the other, she pushed open the employee's door with her foot. It was dark. No electricity to power the lights in Big Tom's storeroom. No electricity in the whole of Dwayne County, West Virginia for that matter. Emily put the sword away and took out a slender candle from the pocket of her army fatigue pants, lighted the wick.

The illumination offered by the candle was better than nothing. Emily checked the front entrance to make sure it was clear. She could see the rear door in the far left corner of the storeroom. It seemed secure. Emily entered the darkened storeroom with only a thin flame of light to champion her will. Emily listened for movement, thankful in her heart that deaders were not too fleet of foot. She also took a deep sniff and found the storeroom musty and moldy but not a whiff of the acrid reek of death. The storeroom was about six by ten feet. So if anything happened, it would be immediate.

Emily located the prize: Black Label Vodka. She grabbed the case of six bottles—then she heard the tinkle of the bell attached to the front door! Emily bolted out of the blackened storeroom and into the main room. Emily saw three deaders amble through front door. She had the case of vodka under her left arm, the candle and Colt .45 in her right hand. She blew out the candle, spit on the wick and quickly stuffed it in the side pocket of her pants. Then, smoothly, Emily raised the gun and neatly placed a single round in the skulls of each deader. The zombies dropped without ceremony. She opened the case of vodka, and removed four bottles. She put the bottles in her large leather pouch. Emily quickly hopped over the dead and scrambled out of the liquor store—only to find the avenue littered with deaders. Emily's old friend, the deader she had only moments ago chopped up and left in the middle of the avenue, had wormed his way to within a few yards of the liquor store. She took two steps and planted her boot squarely in the relentless torso's face, kicking it a few feet down the sidewalk.

Emily easily dodged the turtle like deaders. She made a hasty retreat back to compound she shared with her father. Today was his birthday so she planned something very special for him. The alcohol was the last thing she needed to make the night complete.

5:15. The autumn sun cast shallow shadows through the forest of blackened trees. An unchecked forest fire had swept through this mountain a decade past. The fire was started due to conventional ordinance employed by the United States military to combat the deader infestation along the mid-Atlantic region. Emily's father said that submarines must have delivery the bombs because he doesn't recall planes flying over that day. And her father remembered that day well. It was the day Emily lost her mother and big sister. Emily had been seven years old. She remembered that day as well.

It was eerie walking amongst the blackened trees. Emily remembered the train whistle that would sound as the locomotive come through the tunnel at Grundy Peak. She hasn't heard that whistle in many years. Emily missed the trains.

Emily stopped to rest. She took this moment to inspect the other item she picked up in town. She pulled the tightly sealed package from her hip pocket. Emily held the package like gold. She had scored about three pounds of gunpowder from the gun store back in town. That should make about 100 bullets, split between .45 caliber and .22 long caliber rounds.

She secured the gunpowder and hefted the booze-laden pouch over her shoulder. She set off for home.

———

"AFTERNOON, YOUNG LADY. HAVE you seen this man?" Duncan Maines slapped the photo down on the old wooden table, between the rows of cabbage and squash. "He's wanted by the law."

The willowy blonde looked up at the mountain of a man that stood before her. Maines truly blocked out her sun. He stood at least seven feet tall and was almost as wide as he was high. He wore a long leather duster, jeans and a blue button-down shirt and carried three side arms, a rifle and a machete. He wore a floppy, wide-brimmed hat and a charcoal blue star pinned upon his button down shirt.

"Well?" Maines demanded impatiently.

The young woman scanned the picture of the handsome blonde man. The man in the picture had a week's worth of stubble on his chiseled cheeks and chin. The outlaw's piercing blue eyes aroused the young woman's curiosity. This was the best-looking man she had seen in quite some time. Not like the dour and plain-faced men of her community.

"Haven't got all day, miss."

"No," she snapped. The lawman put a fright into her—yet he wasn't altogether unattractive. Maines was older, maybe in his fifties, but he had a full head of sandy gray hair. He was well-groomed with an easy sloped moustache and soft brown eyes. He was better looking than any of the men in these parts. She starting to warm up to the lawman.

She gave Maines her best smile.

"What's he done, exactly? Oh, my name is Diana. Diana Millcrave. And yours is?"

"Call him Mister Deadhead," answered a man in his late sixties. Thin and wiry, he had the step of a man half his age. He came right up to Maines, took the picture from Diana.

"And who might you be?" asked Maines.

"My father," said Diana. "Everyone just calls him Papa."

"So you lookin' for live folk this time. Last time I saw, oh, about ten years past, you were collectin' deaders. You wouldn't allow us to kill them; said the government wanted to study deaders for a way to beat the infestation. I guess the experiments didn't work. We still got fresh zombies poppin' up."

"I imagine the study is ongoing," Maines replied, a bit annoyed.

"What? Ongoin'. Shit, they don't tell you shit, do they? You just go out and fetch like a good little doggie. Ongoin' my ass."

"It's my job. Civilization is not dead. We still have a chance to beat this disease."

"You can't beat God's wrath! What kinda fool are you? This ain't no Russian drug or Chinese flu. Deaders are God's will. This is Judgement Day!"

"Thirty-five years is one hell of a long day," Maines sneered.

"Thirty-five years ain't shit to the Lord!" Papa snapped back.

Maines pulled a thin cigar from the side pocket of his leather overcoat. He lighted it then spoke.

"A very wise man once said, 'Every new child born is proof that God is not yet done with man.' I see quite a few children here in Fort Norris."

"Yeah, well, that wise man was a fool," Papa spat back.

Diana attempted to break the tension. "So what's he done that's so bad?" Diana pointed to the picture that her father held. "And does the handsome stranger have a name?"

"Girl, keep your panties on. Damn embarrassing, you know!"

Diana looked hurt. "I'm just asking is all. Ain't no harm in asking his name. I mean what if he does come by here, we got food and all. And we sell this food. You don't want me selling food to an outlaw, right? Even an outlaw has to eat. Aint' that right, Mister...mister—?"

"Psssh" Papa handed Maines the picture and the lawman returned it to his pouch. Papa stomped away.

"Name's Duncan Maines," he said to Papa's back.

"Don't mind him, Mister Duncan. Papa's got a lot on his mind. He's responsible for this town. He's always in a foul mood."

Maines sighed deeply. He removed his hat for a movement. He put it back on before he spoke.

"The handsome stranger is Miller Hannon. He staged a mutiny aboard a military vessel, killed his captain during the take over. In his ignorance, he released a deader infestation on a highly sensitive military outpost."

"Wow."

"How much for an apple?"

"Two dollars. American money only."

That surprised Maines. "You get much foreign currency here?"

"Sure do. 'Bout a week ago, we had two guys tryin' to pass off Canadian money. And a few months ago, there was a nigger with English pounds! He was handsome and all. Papa didn't care much for him. He worked the fields for room and board just like everyone else. He didn't complain none. But he's gone now."

"Gone? What do you mean, gone?"

"He left after his debt was paid off. Most people here are just passing through. Everyone believes there's a better place'n this. A place with no deaders. That's what everyone is lookin' for when they leave here."

"But Papa doesn't believe there's a better place, does he?" Maines asked.

"That's right. He says the whole earth is like this. You've been around right Mister Duncan... is the whole earth like this?"

Maines placed two singles in Diana's small palm. He took the shiniest apple in the pile, firm with a deep red glow.

"I can't confirm the whole earth, but from my own eyes, I know North and South America suffer this plague," Maines told her. Then he walked away.

Diana was crushed. Maines had just doomed her to a life sentence in Fort Norris, West Virginia.

Maines slowly walked through the lively bazaar. Canvas tents supported by metal and wooden poles kept the late afternoon sun off the bountiful produce of fresh fruits, vegetables, and bread, as well as dried fruits and meats. Food was not all there was for sale. Clothes, shoes, blankets, oil paintings of Jesus and banal landscapes, wood carvings of deer, bear and birds in flight. Simple jewelry made of finely polished and brightly colored stones. Tools and books on wilderness survival and Bibles could also be bought for reasonable price. Maines was impressed by the way the community of Fort Norris, West Virginia had secured itself from the undead infestation. A fifteen feet high, three feet wide, stone and rock wall surrounded the community. The only gate was made of flat iron and stood eight feet high and five inches thick. There was a small iron door at the south wall, which abutted the Stanos River. The river was the community's source of fresh water.

Maines heard soft strumming from a guitar. He followed the tune and found an old woman playing to a small crowd. Her hair was snowflake white, long and thin. She wore it loose, pulled back from her ebony weathered face. Her slender fingers moved easily over the frets as she plucked out a sorrowful tale. She sang in a voice of cold fire:

"Lest you forgot, not that past nor long ago
A'for death walked open
A'for the passed on returned
A'for the Great Dream became the Great Nightmare.
We built cities of concrete, glass and steel
We danced in fields of golden grain and we swam in seas of blue.
But we were not thankful for the Creator's gift
We abused, raped and killed all we touched."

All of the gathered, young and old, child and adult sang out the chorus:

"So now, Judgement is upon us
So now, our ancestors awake
From the good sleep to feast unholy on us—
The black sheep."

The old lady was a graceful guitar player; yet, purposely, she hit a dour soul chord that cramped Maines's spine. He could not walk away fast enough from the haunting melody she played with masculine verve.

Maines showed Miller Hannon's picture to many residents of Fort Norris. No one had seen Miller - yet all the older people, they all remembered Maines as the man who had once collected deaders for government research. That was true of Maines's past, and it seemed so long ago. A newly-created branch of the FBI called Homeland Security had recruited him. His mission had been to collect politicians, and scientists that had been vital in current affairs and that had turned zombie. The scientists of Homeland Security wanted to see if useful information could be extracted from deader brains. They believed it was possible to capture and download memories and information from the human brain. Of course, the doctors would also study deaders in hopes of defeating the infestation. Yet, there was truth to Diana's father's blunt statement, "You don't know what the hell is going on." Maines was never given information on the status of these experiments. He did what he was told and did not ask questions. As far as he knew, the experiments were ongoing. Yet, he was no longer asked to collect deaders.

Maines approached the small iron door at the south wall. It was the entrance and exit for solo travelers. Once the all clear signal was flashed from the man at the top of the wall, the gate was unbolted and opened, allowing Maines to take leave of Fort Norris.

He consulted his map as he stood on the rocky riverbank, the strong flowing water just a few feet away. He decided to continue south along the river Stanos. There are more communities along the river.

[3]
EMILY'S HOME WAS CARVED into the side of a large and rocky hill. The last fifty yards up the Dodds' hillside stronghold was laced with anti-personnel mines, which were triggered from within their home.

Emily's father, Carson Dodds, had been a corporal during the onset of the deader infestation. His troop had been assigned to protect the nation's capitol from deaders. It was the first time that US troops were employed on American soil. Carson went AWOL immediately because it was more important to him to protect his family than the whole of America. He took a great deal of explosive ordinance as well as bullets, rifles and pistols from his base camp in Salmyra, Virginia. He found a small cave in a hillside back in his home of Dwayne County, West Virginia. Carson used some of the explosives to blow out the cave and enlarge the cavity; fashioning a defensive home for his wife and her parents, and his own mother. Emily and her sister had not been born at that time.

Late day shadows claimed the countryside. Emily knew the position of each explosive device, yet was in no trouble of tripping the anti-personal mines. The mines were not pressure sensitive.

Emily walked straight up the hillside to the front keep. The keep was a metal cage affixed to the front of the stronghold. It was six feet deep, seven feet tall and twelve feet in length. Thick plastic sheets attempted to shield the keep from the elements, but the plastic was old, shredded and torn, and completely ripped away in some places. The metal door of the keep was the size of a normal door. Emily put her key into the slot and quickly turned it. She swiftly entered the keep. The front door of her home was an iron sheet, four feet high, two feet wide and two inches thick. It was also set firmly into the stone. Before Emily went into her home, she had to use the toilet. The outhouse was within the keep, to the right of the front door. She put down her backpack and the case of vodka, secured her weapons. Then she entered the outhouse.

Emily put her key in the keyhole of the front door and turned it right, then quickly to the left. She immediately withdrew the key. The door hissed as it was pushed open by a pneumatic arm. Emily quickly rushed into the cave as the door urgently shut behind her.

Emily walked through the sparse living room. There was a wooden table in the middle of the room. There was a long couch, which doubled as her father's bed, and two short sofas. One sofa is Emily's bed; the other one had been her sister's bed. Emily laid her booty from town upon her bed. Emily went deeper into the cave and found her father in the kitchen.

"Emily! Where were you?" Carson stopped slicing the large flank of raw meat and turned to his daughter.

"I'm okay, daddy. I went into town for some…stuff. Happy Birthday!" Emily presented her father with a birthday card.

Her father sighed and said, "Thank you, Poppy. But you know how I feel about you going into town alone!"

"I know, but you trained me real good. I can fight and take care of myself. I'm a big girl now!"

Carson looked at his daughter. A soft smile traced his lips. "Yes...Yes you are." He opened the card and read it slowly. He smiled big, then quietly placed the card atop the wooden counter.

"What kind of meat is that, daddy?

"Well, seems the Lord also gave us a present on my birthday. This is Red Deer. Shot a six-point buck back on the east forty. Had to work quick because you know the smell of blood carries far and fast. We got a good twenty-five pounds of meat from that buck."

Carson returned to his task of salting the meat. He cut the meat into small salting blocks, and patted the course salt in. Carson laid the meat piece by piece in the small kegs, careful that the meat slabs did not touch each other. He laid them like bricks, and pounded salt in the spaces.

Emily was happy to see it. They have been eating dehydrated and canned goods for so long that she had forgotten the taste of fresh meat. In fact, she was ready to chow down on a tiny chuck of the juicy raw meat spread out over the kitchen table.

"You gonna make jerky, too?" she asked her father.

"You bet I am, Poppy."

"Wow. I can't wait! I'll be in the big room. I got some more stuff for tonight. I didn't just to into town for a birthday card."

Carson turned to look at his daughter. "I didn't think so. Can't wait to see what you got." He turned back to salting the meat.

Emily left the kitchen, walked back into the living room. She had to prepare for this special night.

[4]

A PACK OF WILD dogs charged Miller; silent save for untrimmed claws clicking maniacally upon the dark asphalt.

Miller was used to this. He casually grabbed his revolver, aimed and fired two shots at the advancing canines. The lead dogs fell dead. The rest of the pack halted their charge, peeled back and regrouped. The dogs studied Miller, and they studied their fallen comrades. The dogs hunched closer together, their runny black eyes on Miller.

Miller sighed as he realized the dogs were going to charge him anew. He raised his revolver—the dogs stiffened and snarled as one furry beast. Miller fired two more rounds, killing two more dogs. This time the pack ran from Miller without looking back.

Miller reloaded the single-action revolver; then secured it in the black leather holster than hung at his waist.

Miller Hannon continued to walk down the lonesome main road of Slurry, New York. At one time, this had been a hard working industrial town. Now, like all of America, it was a ghost town.

The setting sun cast tricky shadows across the avenue. The approaching dusk put a touch of dread in Miller. He was looked around for that familiar sloppy jerk walk that was the deader gait. He did not see any and that was always a relief. Day or night, it didn't matter to deaders, they lumbered about twenty-four/seven. It was just that the dark seemed to work in their advantage, even though they moved slowly.

Miller spotted the car as he walked by the auto lot. It was a '68 Shelby Mustang. Kelly green with thick chrome rims. He knew a working car was a pure fantasy, but he had to have a look at it.

The keys were hanging in the ignition. "Unbelievable." He said softly. Miller got in the car. He turned the ignition key and, of course, the car did not respond.

"Let's take a look under the hood?" Miller said. He had about an hour of daylight left, so whatever had to be done, would have to been done fast.

He popped the hood and cursed to himself. No battery.

Miller looked around the auto yard and saw a wooden storage shed in the back of the lot. He walked toward a shed. When he got to the shed, he found it was locked. At least there would be no deaders inside, he thought. He shot the lock off the shed door. He slid the doors opened and looked inside the shed, thankful for the sparse rays of sunlight that broke over the mountain top. He spotted a wooden locker on the floor of the shed. Next to the wooden locker was a battery charger. Upon examination, he found it was a gas powered battery charger. Miller saw two large red plastic containers in the far corner of the shed. He checked out the containers and sure enough, it was gasoline. He set the containers outside the shed. He then opened the wooden locker. He was surprised to find the inside of the floor locker was lined with a lead sheet. He was truly surprised and a bit happy when he saw three new batteries resting comfortably in the lead lined locker. He picked up one battery. He hauled the battery and battery charger out of the shed.

Back by the car, Miller twisted off the gas tank cap from the battery charger and found the tank full. Smiling, Miller tugged on the ignition cord for a minute until the charger sputtered then chugged to life. He placed the charger clamps on the car battery terminal posts.

He poured the gas from the red containers (about ten gallons) into the Mustang's tank.

Then he waited.

Miller placed the battery in the carriage next to the engine. He attached the positive and negative cables to the battery posts.

Miller got behind the wheel of the car and tried the ignition.

The car body lurched and the engine seemingly twisted - then a loud bang! The engine spurted and coughed. Black smoke jetted from the exhaust but the engine did not die. Miller gunned the engine and it roared with authority.

"Hot damn!" Miller yelled. He had a car.

———

Now it was dark.

Miller set the candle down on the countertop. He grabbed a packet of beef jerky from the spring rack. He ripped it open and quickly bit off a chunk of dried beef. He chewed the meat as he approached the cash register.

"You never know," He said aloud.

Miller set his sawed-off shotgun on the countertop. He glanced toward the front door, fifteen feet due east, the city street was black. Nothing moved outside. He did not hear the sick siding walk of the dead; those awkward slurs of dragging flesh. He picked up the candle and viewed the cash register. He pushed a few buttons on the antique machine. It sprung open and voila! Money! Sixty-three dollars total. He stuffed the cash into his pants pocket.

"Damn! This is a fucking good day."

Miller grabbed his shotgun and left the convenience store for the dark street. He was surprised by the lack of deader action in the town of Slurry, New York.

He set the candle against glass of the Mustang, making sure a deader had not climbed into the car to lay in wait. Finding the interior clean, he opened the door and got in. He blew out the candle. He wet his fingertips, then held the wick, pitched the candle into the front seat. Miller switched on the ignition, then put the car in drive and began to slowly roll down the avenue. He did not turn on the headlights.

"This is so much better than walking," He said.

Miller grabbed the bottle of whiskey, uncapped it, and took a mighty swig.

Just for kicks, he turned on the radio, and spun the dial. He was surprised when he found a voice around 810 on the AM dial.

"—Again, this is Joe Fisher in Masters, Pennsylvania. Me and a few others have a working community here in Masters. For the wandering that can pick this up, it is a safe haven. We're about seventy strong, with women and children. We're God-fearing Christians. We accept and understand that this is Judgement Day. The rapture…"

Miller spun the dial.

"Hey, to anyone that can hear me. This is Carl."

"And Danny!"

"Yeah, this is Carl and Danny. We're in Felton, Delaware. Our group is eight strong. We're set up pretty in the Woolworth's shopping center. We got fresh water and plenty of canned foods."

"We need women!"

"Yeah, Danny's right - we need women so we can turn the population back to the land of the living! Fuckin' zombies everywhere! But we got the weapons to deal with that shit. We took control of Felton's largest gun store!

"We have live landlines. Telephones for you none technical speaking people. So if you can hear this call three-oh-two, two, nine, four, eight, three, oh, oh."

"Danny with the phone number. This is Carl and Danny—and Joey, our engineer, has just informed us that we're low on power. Gas generator folks, so we don't have a lot of time. We're gonna sign off with a little music. It's from a band called, The Doors. This one is for all the ladies. "Hello, I Love you!"

"Call if you can hear us—especially women!"

A heavy repetitious organ accompanied by thumping drums pulsed through the Mustang's speakers.

"Damn, haven't heard this in a long time." Miller said to no one. He took a pull from the whiskey bottle.

He found it interesting that telephone lines were working. He had heard that rumor about six months ago, but had not confirmed it. Every public and private telephone he has tried was dead.

Miller moved down Edson Avenue at 5 M.P.H. Small town community with a bank, post office and police station right in a row. Dress shop, Dairy Queen, McGhee's Restaurant. He did not spot a single deader on the cool, darkened streets.

He saw another pack of roving dogs. This was a large group of twelve or more.

It was good to have a car.

He took another pull from the whiskey bottle.

The Mustang hummed smoothly as he cruised down the street. He turned right. To his right were more small business, like a dentist office and a jeweler. There was an open field to his left; flat meadow that at one time held horse or maybe cattle. Now it was wild and thick with bramble. The rising moon cast a shade illumination over the landscape. Miller saw one perhaps two deaders wade through the dense underbrush.

The music stopped. Miller spun the dial. Nothing but static.

"It was good while it lasted."

Miller stopped the car. He reached over to the back seat and selected a bolt action rifle from his weapons cache. He had also raided the local gun shop since he now had a vehicle. He has a combined total of seven pistols and revolvers, also five shotguns and three rifles. He has bullets for all of these weapons. Miller figured the town of Slurry went down without a fight. The rifle was loaded (as were all his weapons); he aimed and immediately fired a round. The deader jerked and stepped back but stayed on its feet.

He adjusted the sights and fired again.

Clean head shot; the deader dropped to the ground. He fired another round and the second deader dropped into the underbrush.

Miller put the car in drive in continued down the road.

He sipped his whiskey.

He thought about where he was going to sleep tonight. He reasoned he should get on the interstate and drive. He had a map of known communities. He was a few hundred miles north of Fort Norris, West Virginia. He had passed through there once, maybe five years ago. If memory served him right, it was one of the best communities he had encountered. He reasoned he could make it there in four, five hours tops.

He drove the car down the street in perfect silence, and near perfect dark. No street lights. No lights in shops or homes. No buzz or power through the thick cables that hung above the avenue.

Miller fancied with the idea of driving west; then quickly discounted the notion. West meant San Diego to Miller. And San Diego was not where Miller wanted to be.

Perhaps Alaska.

Miller saw a sign pointing to the interstate. He moved that way.

He saw a single deader ambling across the front lawn of a blackened house.

Miller stopped the car. He grabbed the same rifle he used a moment ago. Aimed and fired. The deader immediately dropped to the ground.

He put the car in drive in continued down the road.

He took another pull from the whiskey bottle.

———

[5]

EMILY POURED HER FATHER another shot of vodka.

Carson was drunk and damn proud of it. "I haven't been this tight in a duck's ass!" he said and laughed.

Emily felt warm and a bit giddy. She poured herself another shot of vodka. It was her second. She spent the better part of an hour with her first shot.

Carson was mesmerized by Emily's full lips. Her lips were painted soft red. (The same lipstick her mother had worn.) And Emily had combed her red hair and pulled it back into a perfect ponytail. He always liked her hair in this style.

Carson watched his daughter take a demure sip of vodka. It made him smile.

Carson watched her every move. He noted how firm and upright Emily's breasts were, the way her thick nipples proudly punched through her thin white blouse.

Carson knocked back a vodka shot, set the glass back on the table.

Emily reached to fill it, found the bottle empty.

"Good thing I got a whole case," she said with a simple smile.

Carson watched his daughter open a new bottle, fill his shot glass.

Emily handed her father the shot glass. She saw a look in Carson's eyes that both frightened and excited her. Emily noticed that her father had an erection.

Carson slowly sipped the vodka. "What's going on here, Poppy?"

Emily spoke slowly, she had been taking about this night for a long time. "Lot laid down with his daughters after his wife was turned to salt," she said as she reached for her drink. "It's just comfort, daddy. Lord knows you deserve it." She sipped her vodka. She left a hint of lipstick on the rim of the tiny glass.

"You are beautiful."

"Thank you, daddy."

Carson laid the empty shot glass on the table. Emily refilled it.

Carson relaxed and let the vodka wash over him.

The soft scent young overwhelmed Carson. Then he was seized by a fevered sensation; something he had not known for what felt like a hundred years.

[6]

THE FAT MOON WAS yellow-orange and hung low in the black sky; the rapidly flowing Stanos River dismembered its reflection

Miller flashed the Mustang's headlights as he approached the gates of Fort Norris. Miller saw two lights flash from the tower gates.

He repeated the signal. The reply was an unblinking white light. Miller slowly approached the gates.

The mustang's headlight caught about a dozen deaders standing before the gate. Miller came to a stop. He looked around and saw the tall grass shimmer with the walking dead. The zombies seemed to sprout from the trees, from the dirt and even from the riverbank. Within moments deaders besieged Miller's car. The deaders weakly banged on the windshield, rear and side windows, and the flat darkness did not hide the rotting, fetid faces of the living damned pressed against the glass of his vehicle.

Suddenly columns of fire erupted from pits in the ground before the gates of Fort Norris. The abrupt blazes torched about a dozen deaders. Suddenly the front gates were flooded with bright lights. Then shots rang out from atop the tower gates and more deaders fell.

Miller continued to slowly roll forward. He felt he had run over three or four deaders, but three times more clunk to his vehicle: on the hood, the roof and the trunk. Miller stopped the car, sharply put it in reverse and raced backwards. He quickly stopped and the remaining deaders were ejected from the car. He punched the gas pedal and sped off down the now illuminated dirt road, roaring toward the quickly opening gates. He slammed a few deaders as they stumbled into the path of his racing metal dart. The Mustang rushed through the opened gates. Miller hit the brakes and came to a screeching halt within the town square. Miller quickly got out of the car with a revolver in each hand. He scouted the car for deaders. There were none to be found. About a dozen or so towns people approached Miller and his car.

"What the hell is this?" asked Papa; he held a bright candle close to Miller's face.

"Thanks for opening the gates, old man. I couldn't think of any place else to go." Miller said.

"Roaring in here like a bat outta hell," Papa stated. "And where did you get this car?" He held the candle out to inspect the car.

"From Slurry, New York. Beautiful, right?"

"It's got deader shit all over it. I'll get a better look at it in the morning. You got money, or are you prepared to work for your room and board?" Papa asked looking Miller over in the candlelight.

"Well I got some cash but I'm not opposed to working."

"Very good. Montgomery will put you up. You can work out the arrangements with him."

A man stepped forward. "I'm Angus Montgomery. Come with me."

"What about the car?" Miller asked.

"Angus'll take care of ya," Papa said.

"He's got a lot of guns, Papa," Diana stated, her candle illuminated the well-stocked back seat of the mustang.

"Good. We need guns," said Papa.

And the matter was settled. Miller, driving the Mustang, followed Angus Montgomery to a large wooden structure.

"My name is George. You can park the car right against the west wall of the shed."

"Yeah, thanks. How the hell do you guys have lights?" Miller asked. He turned to look back at the front gates. The flood lights were out. The front gate and town square were dark, save for candlelight.

"We harness the river for energy," George said as if he were talking to an idiot.

Miller picked up on it, grudgingly realized it was deserved.

"Forgot about the river," Miller said defensively.

Miller watched the candles go their separate ways, entering homes and shops.

[7]

MAINES HEARD DOGS barking in the distance. Howling at the large, yellow moon.

Maines had secured himself a sleeping space high in thick and plenty branches of an elm tree. Deaders have been known to climb, but that fact did not concern Maines. He was sure he would hear and feel any deader approach up this tree. From his vantage point on high, and aided by the bright moonlight, he could spot dozens of the living dead ambling across the countryside. Aimlessly walking nowhere; like gazing sheep or cattle. Yet, this herd was trying to catch a scent of fresh meat. Some zombies stood motionless, seemingly waiting for some phantom switch to spur them forth.

If he wanted to, Maines could easily eliminate twenty or more deaders within a two to three hundred yard range. He turned away and closed his eyes.

Maines thought about his mission. He realized that it was truly a futile effort, but what choice did he have? He could just pack it in and come to rest in a community like Fort Norris. Yet, somehow, he believed that man would overcome this dire situation and reclaim the land for the living. He did not believe that this was Judgement Day. He did not believe that the Lord Almighty would set this evil upon the land. No, somehow, mankind was responsible for this dark travesty. Somehow, mankind must right this wrong. He decided to stay the course and continue with his mission.

A shot rang out. And another and another.

Maines looked around. He saw the muzzle flash of gunfire and watched deaders fall. He spotted one lone gunman riding a dark horse. The horse's gait was nonchalant as the gunman fired at will but made each shot count.

"What kind of man would shot deaders in the West Virginia mountains at three in the morning?" Maines said in soft awe.

Maines thought about climbing down the tree to confront the lunatic, but then ruled it out as he realized the lunatic shooter would fire on him before a word could be spoken. He decided to stay secure, high in the tree. Out of sight of deaders and lunatics.

[8]

CARSON AWOKE WITH A hard groan and a dry mouth and there was a dense pulse echoing through his skull. He sat up in bed—immediately felt her warmth and looked to his left. Carson stared at his sleeping daughter. Her red hair fell easily across her porcelain complexion. Her face pressed softly into the pillow, Emily's full lips framed a perfect kiss. Carson's member swelled and he gently eased out of her sleeper-sofa bed.

Carson put his pants on (he was still hard; he never took his eyes off Emily). Then he put his boots on. Emily moved in bed, now the thin sheet silhouetted the hard curves of her body.

Carson left the room.

Muted light streamed in from above as he approached the front door. He had installed a skylight above the door. The skylight was secured by cement, rocks and a steel mesh grate. He then turned left of the front door, into a tight alcove. Gray light streamed in from above here also. He ascended the short stairs, reached out for the crank in the top of the ceiling. He turned the wooden crank. The skylight rose until it made contact with the steel mesh grate. Carson ascended the stairs and looked out over the landscape. It was an overcast sky with a slight wind from the north. Strong scent of ozone suggested it might rain. The bright side: not a deader in sight. He lowered and skylight and descended the stairs.

Now that his libido had calmed down, Carson was able to perform his morning constitutional. He opened the front door and rushed for the toilet.

Carson chewed on a strip of salted venison as he checked his weapons. Three revolvers, all fully-loaded, eighteen shots. He reckoned that he would not encounter more than eighteen deaders on this trip to the river. The most he has ever seen at once was five, and that was at the old well. They were seemingly laying in wait for him. He has since abandoned the well and has returned to fetching river water. The river is better than five hundred yards due east. Carson grabbed two plastic five-gallon tanks. The whole trip should take him forty minutes.

On the message board hung beside the door he wrote Gone hunting, erased it with the heel of his hand, wrote Gone shopping, erased that. He finally settled on Gone for water.

Carson opened the front door, walked out into the keep. The front door hissed to a close behind him. He opened the keep door and stepped out into the dead world.

He easily descended the hillside, and once on level ground, set a swift pace through the blackened trees, heading for the river.

Carson tried to recall last night but it came to him like a broken dream, repeating vague fragments instead of a complete picture. He remembered drinking. He remembered Emily's pouty lips as she sipped vodka. He remembered the sweet scent of her skin.

A loud thunderclap shook Carson from his reverie. A moment later fat rain drops pelted Carson. Then sheet lightning illuminated the dark gray sky. Carson felt that this was just a passing storm.

————

The rain continued, harder now. Brilliant lightning bolts streaked earthbound.

Carson looked up and down the riverside; he did not see a deader or a wild animal at the river's edge. He quickly approached the river. He began to fill the first of his five-gallon water tanks.

Task complete, Carson hauled the water tanks from the river's edge. The rain was strong and constant, nearly blinding. The thunder shook Carson to the bone, and the lightning seemed to be pitched in his direction. He wondered if this was the Lord's retribution for sin he committed with his daughter last night. He knew it was wrong, but his soul was weak, his desire and lust insurmountable.

And Carson remembered calling out the Lord's name in the fevered clutches of his ecstasy.

Carson saw the forest shine star bright for a split second. The booming thunder masked the cracking of the lightning-struck tree. The flaming cleft tree fell upon Carson. He never knew what hit him.

[9]

The booming thunderclap scared Emily awake. She looked around like a frightened rabbit before she realized that she was in her bed. She took a deep breath and fell back onto the mattress. A moment later, she realized her father was not sleeping beside her. She sat back up and looked around.

Her voice echoed flatly against the stone walls when she called out "Daddy!"

Emily set her feet on the floor. She stood but was hit with a sharp pain between her legs that quickly subsided. She took a few baby steps, and felt all was okay.

She saw the board and felt better knowing that her father had simply gone out for water. (She had feared that he had left her in shame of their affair.) She put on her shoes and a robe, then opened the front door. The rain was falling hard and the keep was not secure against the elements (the plastic sheeting was about fifty-percent effective), so Emily used an umbrella as she stood in the keep. She searched the rain-blurred landscape for her father. Thunder boomed and rolled in the black clouds, as those same storm clouds spat out thin streaks of white heat. After a minute or two, Emily went to the toilet.

Emily had an uneasy feeling when she did not see her father upon her exit. She went back into their home. She dressed for the weather. She noted that her father had taken three revolvers. That still left her with a good cache of arms. She took two semi-automatic pistols (twenty-four bullets total), and this time she took her father's US Army Calvary sword.

She caught a glimpse of herself in the mirror. She thought she looked different...somehow. And it wasn't her hair or her weight.

She felt surer of herself, and in control. She felt...she felt *right*.

Emily donned a dark green army poncho and a western-style, wide-brimmed hat.

In the keep, staring out into the pouring rain, concerned, as she looked for her father. She did not see him so she exited the keep; and carefully walked down the minded hillside.

Emily secured the hat to her head by cinching up the small clasp. Then she broke into a steady run. Despite the violent falling rain and debris on the forest floor, she achieved and maintained a quick pace. She had trained with her father in just such conditions. Carson had put Emily through a hard physical regimen since she could walk. Within moments, Emily was in the zone and cruising toward the river.

She spotted a pair of deaders off to her right. The duo slugged toward the river. A sickening wave of dread flooded Emily. She pulled out her gun and, never breaking stride, fired two shots. The dead pair fell to the wet ground with quiet, soggy thuds.

Emily rushed on toward the river. She saw one, two—no, *five*—

deaders marching toward the river. Ahead, she saw soft smoke rising and smelled burning wood. Emily pulled out the other gun. Now she held a gun in each hand, running at a full gait, she hit each zombie, one bullet to the head.

She approached the smoldering tree and saw seven or eight zombies gathered around. Emily saw her family's water tanks off to the side. She ran up on the deaders shouting like a madwoman, "Get away from my father!" she screamed, without having seen a body. She fired her guns with extreme anger, punching the air with each pull of the trigger, and each shot was a direct hit to the head. She reached down into the pile of rank bodies and pulled the smelling, rotting flesh back away from what see did not want to see. She grabbed a corpse and pitched it aside. Emily grabbed a deader woman by her white hair and the scalp pulled away with the nasty nest of hair—the odor of a ton of steaming baby shit overwhelmed Emily. She vomited while still holding the decomposed scalp, then pitched the thing far into the forest. Emily tugged at the heavy, rain soaked, discolored, and corrupt flesh. Wrists, forearms and whole arms tore away from their host corpses as Emily worked like a garbage man on speed, pitching the trash to the side with phenomenal ease. She now had clear access to her father—and was rewarded with her ugliest nightmare. Her father's face was nearly eaten clean like a chicken bone. Carson's skull, blood and brains were spewed wanton upon the wet ground like confetti.

Emily howled in pain. She cried, forgetting where she was.

Low thunder rumbled in the distance and sheet lightning frosted the dark sky.

A rotted hand touched Emily's back—she spun around and shot the deader three times in the face. The deader, once a young boy, fell to the rain-soaked ground with a sick plop.

Emily stood over her father's body as tears and rain stream down her face.

She put a bullet through her father's ravaged skull.

More deaders stumbled through the dead forest toward her. She gathered her wits and looked at her guns. She recalled the shots from each weapon. She had four bullets left. Then she realized that her father had three revolvers on him. She fired on the three zombies, felling each one.

Suddenly there were three more deaders closing in on her. She fired her last round into a fat green skinned zombie. She put the empty gun in its holster. She withdrew her sword from its metal scabbard. She drew strength from the ringing sound of metal on metal.

Emily took a deep breath while the rain washed over her.

Then she rushed toward the white faced mother type deader and decapitated it with the same effort it took to pull the trigger of a gun. A few feet beyond that, Emily swiftly cut off the ashen-brown head of another deader.

Emily hurried back to her father. She inspected the body and found two revolvers. She checked for the third weapon but reasoned the gun was beneath the heavy tree, like the rest of Carson's corpse.

Emily grabbed one of the water tanks and hastily ran from the scene. She did not look back. She did not cry.

———

Emily opened the gate and quickly entered the keep. She dropped to her knees in exhaustion. Only then did she mourn.

———

She grabbed the handle. She realized this was another skill her father had thought her, bullet swaging, that was now an automatic, effortless task for her, like drinking water. She sighed, but would not the let the sorrows take her again.

Emily pulled the clamp down, capping the last .22 caliber shell. She removed the copper-jacketed bullet from the die. The bullet was smooth, no wrinkles or stress lines. Another perfect bullet. She looked at the scale; not enough grains of gunpowder left for another round. Her initial estimate had been correct; the three pounds of gunpowder that she got from town yesterday yielded ninety-nine bullets: sixty .22 caliber shells, and thirty-nine .45 caliber shells.

Emily grabbed the shot glass. She quickly knocked back the vodka shot. It was her third one and she really did not feel it, not like she felt the alcohol last night. Last night the drink had been intoxicating. Today it was just vodka.

Emily had a total bullet count of one hundred and seven bullets, counting the two loaded revolvers she had retrieved from her dead father.

She put the .45's and .22's in separate pouches. She stood up and walked away from the table.

Emily studied the gun rack like she never had before. These weapons will be a permanent decision.

Emily had decided to leave home.

She picked up the Colt .45 with a blue finish barrel and eagle stocks. It was heavy but felt good in her hands. She set it on the table; as a keeper. She reached for favorite semi-auto, the Walther PPK, a .22 caliber. Almost the exact opposite of the Colt, as the PPK was light and fit tightly in her grip. It had a polished chrome barrel and black, hard plastic stocks. Another keeper.

Emily studied the rifles then quickly decided on the Winchester Model 73. The rifle had a solid walnut stock and a thirty-inch, forged steel barrel. It was also a .22 caliber.

She lined her guns on the kitchen table. She set the Calvary sword next to the Winchester. These weapons would defend her on the road.

Away from home for the first time, and perhaps never to return.

––––––––––

"So, you guys are doin' alright?" Emily said into the microphone.

"Yeah, we're doin' real well," replied the ham radio operator. "Please, come and join our community!"

"What's you location again?" asked Emily. She scribbled down the coordinates that flowed from the speaker: 39° 16' N. 81° 34' W.

––––––––––

Emily cinched up the backpack straps. It stuffed pack was firm against her back and did not restrict movement. She could reach both guns and the sword with relative ease. (The PPK nestled against her right breast. The Colt hung long against her right thigh. The sword rested on her left hip.) It did not take her much more effort to pull the Winchester from its place on the right side of the backpack. She took a deep breath and pulled open the keep gate. She stepped out of the keep, closed and locked the keep gate. Emily began down the hillside, trying not to cry.

The morning sun bathed the hills in soft sunlight; the sun's heat had not yet touched the earth. Emily headed for the river, careful to avoid the usual path, as not the visit her father's "grave". Her father has been dead two days now.

She had decided to head for Fort Norris. Her father had taken her there once, many years ago. She reasoned it would take her better than three days to walk there. She had enough food and water for seven days.

She hoped she had enough bullets.

[10]

EMILY CHEWED ON MEAT jerky; then took a healthy swig of water. She stretched, arching backward and extending her arms. Then she slowly swung forward, arms outstretched, until she touched her toes. This was the second break she has taken since leaving home. The plain face on her Timex watch read 11: 50. She looked skyward and watched fat, high clouds with dark gray bellies race before the noon sun. She listened to the rushing Stanos river at her right, it was wide and dark and topped with whitecaps. It was a very blustery day. Once, when she was very young, her father had taught her how to fly a kite.

It was only a plain red triangular paper kite, but it was so magical dancing high in the sky.

It had a very long tail decorated with clips of colored cardboard. She remembered that the spool was on a thick rolling pin with lots and lots of string...

A sound contrary to the rustling tall grass alarmed Emily. It was not natural, not at all like a wind blown stir. Emily quickly put the meat in her side pocket and pulled out her guns. The Colt heavy in her right hand, the PPK snug in her left.

The wind pushed the tall grass. Something else whispered against the grain. Emily did not smell anything, but one could not rely on the foul scent that deaders produced. Her father had once told her that the older deaders did not kick the funk like the younger and newly risen. The weak green-yellow blades were only three feet at peak. Whatever approached had to be snake-like. Maybe a half-deader. Maybe a damn big snake.

The wind whipped over the landscape and pushed Emily a half step, filling her ears with white noise. The grass was bent near flat. Thankfully, her thick hair was tied back; she quickly scanned her sur-roundings. Looking for something...anything. The guns seemed to be her third and fourth eyes as they roamed independent of her vision, more than ready to eliminate the threat.

The wind eased up.

Nothing.

Emily stood at the ready, listening to the wind and the tall grass.

Listening...

Nothing.

Emily realized that life alone was...*hard*. She hung her head, shut her eyes.

She put the guns away.

In time, she donned her backpack and moved on.

[11]

Emily saw the horse and rider in the distance. The horizon shimmered like still water, but she saw sure about her vision. She grabbed her Colt .45. Now she felt secure.

The horse and rider approached at a hard trot then suddenly broke down to a fast stop.

Emily and the rider looked at each other across the span of twen-ty yards of tall grass. The rider saw Emily's gun in hand. Emily noted that the rider had a single shot revolver in his left hand, which lazily rested on the saddle horn.

"What in God's name are you doin' out here?" asked the rider.

"I'm going to Fort Norris." Emily said. "What the hell are you doing out here?"

The black horse closed the gap between them. The rider holstered his revolver. He sat tall in the saddle. Emily guessed he stood about six feet, six inches. The rider was thin, strong veins poked through the skin on his bony hands and bald head. He was in his fifties, maybe sixties. His skin was tight, and of light brown complexion. He eyes were jet black and clear. He is voice was as deep as he was tall.

"I'm doin' God's work. I'm Pastor Bob."

"My name is Emily Dodds." Emily secured her gun.

"Nice to meet you Miss Emily. You say you headed to Fort Norris. You got about another day's walk."

"That's what I figured. Well, Pastor Bob, you sure gave me a stir there."

"You surprised me also, Miss Dodds. I don't see much livin' folk walkin' in the low valley."

Emily nodded knowingly. She smiled at the thought of the sight of them. Two live people standing in a field of tall grass. How absurd was that! She looked at Pastor Bob's horse and said, "I haven't seen a live horse in years."

"Not many left in these parts. I hear tell that they aplenty in Texas and parts west. I'll see for myself one day. My ministry will carry me west of the Mississippi soon 'nuff."

"What exactly is your ministry?"

"I sen' the walkin' dead back home."

"You kill deaders?"

"Yes, ma'am. That's another way to put it."

"All the living do that."

"True. And blessed be the livin'. For it is written in the first book of Corinthians, chapter fifteen, verse sixteen, 'For if the dead rise not, then is not Christ raised.' So you see, Jesus walks with us this very day. When you kill a deader, you ain't just survivin', you are cleansing a path for Jesus. But I go one step further. I ferret 'em out, no matter in a building, or in a field. I find the walking dead and put'em down. That's the Lord's work!"

Emily saw the fire and Pastor Bob's eyes, she remembered the way deaders had mauled her father. Emily got a bit of religion.

"You need a disciple?"

"Aw, no child. You best be on your way to life. You doin' right by Fort Norris. Ain't a better patch I've seen in all my travels. I stopped there many a time. They all know Pastor Bob. Ask for Tim Billits. He has three daughters. Pretty, like you. He'll set you right. Tim Billits. Remember that name."

The horse pissed and shat without so much as a how do you do.

Emily coughed from the quick stink. She moved away from the horse.

Pastor Bob, realizing what was going on, offered a weak smile to Emily.

"Sorry, Miss Emily. Nature's callin'. I'm sure you understand."

Emily nodded.

The pale sun dipped a bit lower in the sky, now half of it was below the horizon. As if on cue, Emily and Pastor Bob noted a pair of deaders slogging toward them through the tall grass.

"Did they just rise from the ground? We should have seem that pair a long time ago!" Emily said.

"Well, they're barely taller than the grass. But sometimes, yes, they do just rise from the ground. I've seen it with my own eyes. And it must be case with this pair. Stay still child. Be right back." Pastor Bob tugged gently on the reins and the horse broke into an immediate run.

Pastor Bob pulled up short, to get a good look at the pair of deaders. Sure enough, they were dirty and blue-faced. The deaders were dressed in fancy black suits with lace lapels and cuffs. Their shoes had a fat silver buckle in the center. They had gray hair, runny yellow eyes and taut skin. They stood about four feet in height. They had probably been young brothers, perhaps twins.

The zombie pair looked at Pastor Bob as if they were alive.

Pastor Bob put a single lead bullet through each of their pinched skulls.

Pastor Bob urged his horse passed the fallen deaders. Soon horse and rider came upon freshly tossed earth. The small graves were unmarked and fully covered by the tall grass. Pastor back turned around and rode back to Emily.

"They were newly risen." Pastor Bob told Emily. "I found their freshly turned graves just up the way. You gotta be wary of the tall grass, it hides things."

Emily nodded, recalling the moment earlier this afternoon, when her mind played tricks on her. "So the curse is still upon us. My daddy was so sure that it was over. He thought we just had to endure it a little longer."

"Sorry child, but you're daddy was wrong. This ain't over by a long stretch. Where is your father now?"

"Dead. A tree fell on him. I found him...by the river." After a long pause, she said, "I made sure he wouldn't rise again."

Pastor Bob nodded. "I've also shot a loved one. It's the damn hardest thing to do. Blessed by your father, for he is now truly in the Lord's care."

"Thank you." Emily sighed, then said. "I guess I should be getting on. I'll head for those trees and bed down for the night."

"That's a good idea. Don't know why, but they do seem more active at night than in the day. Night's when I do my best huntin'. You be careful now and remember Tim Billits when you get to Fort Norris. God speed, Miss Emily."

"Bless you Pastor Bob."

Pastor Bob smiled then slowly rode away.

Emily walked toward the trees as long shadows scarred the land.

———

Emily tied the canvas to the thick branch. Confident that it was secure, she gingerly stepped on the canvas and was relieved to find it tight and strong. She checked the knot on the rope about her waist; this rope was secured the tree trunk. She stretched out upon the canvas and let out a huge sigh. The sun was just a bright, orange-yellow line on the horizon. She looked straight up into the blackening night sky. Stars were breaking through the dark velvet space. She knew planets were solid and did not twinkle, but she was not an avid stargazer, she did not know the positions of planets or constellations. (Other than the Big and Little Dippers, Orion's Belt, the Seven Sisters, and of course, the Milky Way.) Emily reached into her backpack and pulled out a thin plastic tarp. She tied two ends to the branches above the canvas tarp. She let the plastic tarp fall free. The sky was clear, so Emily doubted she needed rain cover, but just in case, she quickly tied down the plastic tarp.

Emily looked out over the dark landscape. She could hear the rushing river in the distance. The scent of wildflowers, rhododendron and oak was heady, almost intoxicating. She felt her self relax, her muscles loosening as tension eased away.

She thought about Pastor Bob and considered him a very intense man, but she liked him nonetheless. She wondered what the horse's name was. She wondered why she had not asked Pastor Bob more about his horse. Emily laughed in spite of herself as she recalled the horse shitting right in front of her. Then she remembered the horse's enormous dick. That was amazing.

Then Emily saw it, just to the left, a single deader lurching north through the tall grass. She thought about this land of her birth; she recalled what little history her dad had thought her. The Shenandoah Mountains were northeast of her current position; marking the fact that some of the bloodiest campaigns from the American Civil War (Harper's Ferry, Summit Point, Shepardstown and bit further, the Bull Runs and Antietam) took place, figuratively, in her backyard. Her father had said that hundreds of thousands of men had died in the Shenandoah Valley and vicinity. She reasoned those battles were the cause for most of the walking dead in West Virginia. (Emily knew that regardless of the battles, time itself would have taken the lives of those men, but like her father, she believed that the truly righteous did not rise from the dead. Warriors, despite the cause, were not righteous for they broke God's order that man not kill man.)

Emily pulled the Winchester rifle from her backpack. She took aim from the prone position on the canvas. She sighted up the deader, made an adjustment for height and wind. She exhaled and smoothly fired. The single shot blistered the air and slammed directly through the deader's skull. The zombie clumsily collapsed, disappearing into the dark, tall grass.

"Doing God's work," she said.

[12]

THE MIDWAY WAS FINALLY quiet. Fort Norris was asleep for the night.

Miller walked along the top of the stone wall, eastside. It was his first tour of security, from midnight to six in the morning, his charge for room and board.

Miller's Mustang had been the hot talk today. The adults had not seen a working car in decades. For the children, touching the Mustang was akin to petting a unicorn. (Some had dubbed it God's Chariot. The Mustang simply should not be running. Yet it did run, as well as if just off the assembly line.) The car also awarded Miller his pick of the eligible women of Fort Norris. Miller had a breakfast date after his security tour. The young lass was named Moonana Billits. She was a thin blond with breasts much too large for her tiny frame. She had a wonderful smile. She promised Miller the best hotcakes he had ever tasted. After breakfast, he had a lunch date with Pamela Longquist, a full-figured redhead. Pamela's features were not as refined as Moonana's. Yet, Pamela gave Miller a comfortable feeling. Miller felt she would be fun. He had also promised a bit of his busy afternoon to one Denise Macky, a petite brunette who told him straight out that sex was the only thing she had planned. (Miller wanted Denise for breakfast, but she would not have it.) Then it was dinner with Clara DeBouis. Another blond, but less aggressive than the other women. In fact, Miller felt she was a bit on the prissy side, but she was beautiful so he had to take a shot.

"Got a full schedule tomorrow, Miller?" asked Garson , a tall, bulky man in his late forties with a face full of beard.

"Yeah, I was just thinking about that." Miller sighed and smiled. "I haven't had this type of action before!" He gave Garson a sideways glance. "I hear Denise Macky is a bit of a whore."

"Hell, she's not the only one. Just the prettiest one." Garson thought carefully before he spoke. "She is the best lay your gonna get."

Miller nodded slowly. "So, are there any virgins in Fort Norris?" he asked with a smile.

"Not that I know of."

"Damn! Not even Clara DeBouis? She seemed a bit to, fancy, to give it away."

"None of them give it away." Garson got close to Miller. "We take it man. What are they gonna do? Where are they gonna go? You can lay claim to anyone you want to, and the rest of us will respect that. But if a woman is free, then she can expect any man to call on her. Many a night I've shared a woman with more than one man."

Miller swayed in disbelief. He stepped back from Garson and digested what the big man just dropped on him. He would have never imagined...the town seemed so...normal and righteous.

"What about the girls, I mean, the young ones..."

"Fathers first."

Miller leaned against a stunted stone partition. His heart was in his throat; he felt it pounding in his ears. The surging, thumping rhythm made his dizzy.

"Shit man, whadd'ya think? We fuck all of 'em. Fat, skinny, ugly, pretty, smart and dumb. All of 'em get fucked. Why the hell do you think there are so many kids runnin' 'round here?" Garson shook his head in disbelief of Miller's naivete. "Look, we give 'em respect. We don't knock 'em around; we ain't mean to our women. We just fuck 'em. That's all there is to it. See man, it was ordained in the bible. Genesis nineteen, chapter fourteen, verse thirty-two; Lot's daughters are with him in a cave after the destruction of Sodom and Gomorrah, "Come and let us make our father drink wine, and we will lie with him, that we may preserve the seed of our father." Women know it's the right thing to do. So, if you want some pussy, go get it. No big deal. Just be polite, you know, say please and thank you. They're more responsive to that shit."

Miller was stunned silent. At first, he thought of himself as a celebrity. Someone important, he had an old fashioned gasoline fueled car in mint working condition! He was a big shot. (He figured the prestige of the car was the reason he was not slopping the hogs or working the fields.) Now Miller felt more like the mythical knight in shining armor riding a white stallion. For the women of Fort Norris, Miller and his Mustang were the very real and tangible fantasy flight; the one way ticket out of the prison that is their home.

"I still can't believe that car of yours. It shouldn't be running, not at all! Gas don't last forever. It goes bad after a few years. And batteries, hell man, lead lined box or not, those batteries should not be good. But George said the other two you brought along are also good. They took a charge! Well, you sure started something. George and some of the others are gonna run into town and try to bring back a car or two."

"What's the big deal. You guys got vehicles. Sure, they run on ethanol and other bio-fuels and can't go very fast but they run."

"Yeah, but you got a Mustang! A fuckin' cherry rod. Every man in here wants one now. We had forgotten all about cars. Just didn't matter—where you gonna go? Now you got people thinking that maybe gas doesn't break down like they figured. Maybe all that gas in the gas station across the nation is good. That means you can go anywhere."

"That's my plan."

"Damn good one. I tell you man, if you want a good piece of ass, and someone that would be a good traveling partner. I'd take Molly James. She's a plain Jane but she's got a good sense of humor and she's a crack shot with both rifle and pistol."

Miller was not sure how to accept this suggestion, yet to be polite he said, "Thanks." He rubbed his temples in exasperation. He had had sex with Molly right before the start of this security tour. In fact, they both made a joke about the fact that he was relieving her of duty. And Garson was right—Molly was a good fuck. Now Miller could not wait for his date with Denise Macky.

[13]

EMILY AWOKE TO SNARLING, barking dogs. She grabbed the Colt as she sat up. It was early dawn. A sticky mist rested heavily over the land. She looked over the canvas, down at the ground. A pack of wild dogs were feasting on deaders. Emily counted ten, maybe a dozen deaders circling her tree. She counted seven dogs. The dogs were content with the blue flesh deaders, lustfully ripping and shredding the corrupt carcasses. The bone white deaders were untouched. Those deaders looked up at Emily. The undead seemed to emit a guttural humming, but she could not clearly hear it over the mauling canines. The white-faced deaders reached and clawed at the tree, yet they could not climb the tree for they were unable to reach the lowest branches. (Emily took care of that the night before. by cutting off a few branches of the wild oak tree.) Emily counted six white-faced zombies looking up at her. Six deaders and seven dogs. She knew everything below her had to die.

Thirteen bullets.

She stood on the canvas and prepared to leave.

Once her backpack was secured, she dismantled the canvas tarp.

The dogs broke away from the dead feast and started barking and snarling at Emily.

She left the backpack strapped to the trunk, climbed down the tree to stand on the lowest branch. Then she crouched down and simply looked upon the easy targets. The dogs jumped and crawled at tree never missing a beat to growl and snap at Emily. The deaders were knocked over the leaping dogs. She laughed, then started firing on the dogs and deaders with both handguns.

Three dogs sprinted away from the carnage. Emily took aim and fired the remaining two shots, one from each gun. Two of the fleeing dogs dropped. The last breast continued to run hard, disappearing into the tall grass and deep morning mist.

Emily secured her guns, climbed the tree to get her backpack.

She lowered the backpack to the ground with the rope.

She stepped on the knobs from the branches she had cut off the night before. She then leaped easily to the ground.

Emily walked the flat ground between the tree line and the tall grass. It was a wide path worn by many travelers. She tired of constantly looking back and around for threats. Wild beasts and deaders. She wanted to be in a secure place where she did not have the constant stress of each moment. She reasoned she had about another six hours travel to Fort Norris. Emily wondered what Pastor Bob was doing. She reasoned it was easier travelling by horse, but that it would be better to go by car. Her father had told her all about them. She knew what they were, she has sat in dozens of them, cars littered the streets of all the towns and cities, as well as dirt roads, expressways and thoroughfares. Yet, she has never ridden in a working vehicle.

She pulled the pouch from her side pocket. Emily pulled the venison jerky from the pouch, then quickly bit off a chunk of meat.

Six hours of walking to go. She should reach Fort Norris around sunset.

[14]

MAINES SHOT THE DEADER point blank in its skin-flapping, blotchy blue face. The animated corpse pitched violently backward and slammed to the ground. Maines turned the stainless steel barrel of his Smith &

Wesson .44 Magnum, pulled the trigger and erased the head of a dead-er dressed in a dirty white dress. Flesh and bone wet the black street. Maines shot another deader in the face. Splash back splattered Maines's leather overcoat and dripped from the wide brim of his hat. Finally, he dropped his arm; the hot gun came to rest at his thigh. Five deaders laid to eternal rest on Elmhurst Avenue. Maines spit on the still corpses.

"Damn these things stink! Never get used to it!" He walked away from the gut-wrenching odor. He discharged the spent shells, reached into his leather pouch and withdrew six bullets, reloaded his gun.

The sun was ten minutes from setting. He had to get somewhere for the night, but first he wanted to clean the deader crap from his coat and hat. He looked around, saw what he needed. He walked over the overgrown, weed thick lawn of a once enviable suburban home. He walked by the opened front door and looked into the home, ready for a deader to spring from the darkened entrance. He walked over to the wall spigot. A hose was attached to the spigot. Maines picked up the hose. The rubber was stiff and all color had faded from it. He pulled the hose to him and he soon had the open end. He turned on the spigot, brown water jetted from the hose, then the water turned yellow, and that was as good as it got. Maines ran the dirty water over his jacket. He took off his hat and washed it.

He turned off the spigot. He looked into the home. His years of this type of life style had thought him that structures are not good places to seek refuge. Yet, rooftops were usually safe. He had tired of sleeping in trees. The canvas spread was havoc on his back. Maines wanted something firm to rest on tonight. He considered looking for a flat rooftop.

Maines wondered where was Miller was at that moment. Was he in the next town, or in Mexico, Colorado, Kentucky? The trail that brought him to Northeast America had grown cold about a month ago. Maines had no clue how to find Miller. He knew he had to stay on the course. He had to show the only picture he had of Miller, to what-ever pocket of people he found, and ask if they had seen this face.

Maines saw the trio of deaders shuffling down the sidewalk, grabbed his Smith & Wesson and walked to them.

As Maines neared the dead trio, he could see that they, were newly dead and newly risen. They wore contemporary clothes and had puke-blue faces. Maines fired the Magnum. The zombies viciously jerked and spun from the mean force of the large bullets.

Maines stepped through the deader slop as he continued down the sidewalk.

[15]

"A TALL MAN WAS lookin' for ya the other day." Diana Millcrave said.

"What! What are you talking about?" Miller had a fistful of Diana's titty, and was greatly annoyed by any conversation that didn't begin and end with, 'fuck me'.

"Some guy named Duncan somethin'." Diana pulled rapidly on Miller's manhood.

"What is he...bounty hunter?" Miller sucked and tugged on Diana's salty flesh.

"Government agent. Said you let deaders loose on some military base."

"Bullshit! An unfortunate set of circumstances. I'm a scapegoat."

"Okay. Jus tellin' you is all."

"Yeah..."

"Yeah... Fuck me."

"Now you're talkin' to me."

———

Miller walked the top of the wall. He had been fifteen minutes late for his security tour but no one was on his ass about it. Everyone knew his schedule. He was dead tired but his cock still twitched with the thought of any of this day's sexual encounters. Food and sex. Home grown wine, grain alcohol, marijuana and sex. No sleep. Just sex.

"This place is fucking insane." He said to the wall. "I love it here!"

He thought about what Diana had told him, about the government agent looking for him. He shook his head in dismay. He was not guilty of setting deaders free on a military outpost. The guard had not secured the corpse before locking the dead body in the freezer. The body reanimated and infected others. It doesn't take long after that.

"Hey, you okay, Miller?" Turner asked. He was standing right next to Miller, but Miller had not noticed the short, compact face and body of Turner Sonnhan. Miller had talked to Turner earlier in the day about the Mustang's, cobra V8 engine.

"Huh. Yeah, I'm just beat, man," Miller said with a sleepy stare.

"No doubt! Hear you've been everywhere today! Way to go man. I haven't done that in a long time. Makes you feel good to be alive."

"Sure. Sure does."

Turner pulled out a silver flask. He took a quick pull from the flask, then he passed it to Miller.

"Thanks." He took a long swig. "Damn!" He said then coughed hard and harder. "Shit, man...*Whew!* That's some mean fired up whiskey."

"Courtesy of Uncle Sal. He's the man for whiskey." Turner received the flask back from Miller. Turner took another pull.

Miller leaned out over the wall. Even-though the sun had set, he could still see whitecaps on the rushing river. Miller felt the flask against his shoulder. He took the flask from Turner, but before he took a swig, he paused and studied the path next to the river. Something moved out there. And it didn't move like a deader.

"Turner, you see something out on the path?" Miller pointed in the general direction he referred.

"Yeah. Yeah, I think so. Moves like a human. Damn! I'll send up the alarm." Turner ran off to the nearest tower. Miller stowed the flask in his side pocket. He made his way toward the south gate.

Shots rang out. Miller looked over the wall and saw gunfire flash from the river path.

———————

Emily fired her PPK as she ran along the path toward Fort Norris. Then the PPK was empty, and the Colt was low. She couldn't stop to reload. She had the sword but the backpack messed up her center of balance. Her legs were tired and felt like thick steel cords. Her shoulders were sore, heavy with fatigue. She thought about losing the backpack, but there was no time for that, either. The rifle was loaded but it was useless strapped to her back where she couldn't reach without stopping. She had to keep running. She felt drunk and stupid and oxygen seemed in short supply. Deaders lurched and clawed at her. Empty guns clutched tightly in her hands, Emily punched the deaders in their patchy, maggot-ridden faces, punched them in their dusty chests. She ran and punched. Punched and kept moving.

Sweat stung her eyes—then blinding light flooded the path. Emily reflexively raised her hands to block the intense white light. The deaders all paused and pitched away from the bright light. Emily took advantage of the distraction and pushed herself to run harder, her feet pounding hot and angry on the hard soil, running wild for the light. She heard faint gunshots, saw deaders fall all around her—dead slop with half a skull fell before her and Emily deftly skipped over the corpse. She kept running.

The steel door swung open and Emily raced through like a mad wind.

Miller slammed the gate shut and Turner dropped the metal bar into the catch. The gate was secure.

Emily crashed to the ground and just laid there.

Candlelight illuminated the scene. Many women immediately came to Emily's aide. The women quickly removed her backpack. Emily had a death grip on her weapons. It took three women to gingerly ease the guns from Emily's fists.

"Hey child—what's your name? Can you hear me? What's your name, honey?"

Emily was too tired to respond. She silently looked at the ladies that cared for her. Human faces. She was so happy to see live human faces! She gladly took the cup of offered water, but coughed it up as she tried to swallow too much.

"Easy girl. We got ya. You'll be fine."

They put her on a stretcher and carried her away.

"Damn! That's one hell of an entrance." Miller said.

"Yeah, tough call between you and her. Love your Mustang, but she's damn pretty!" Turner said with a hard smile.

A smile that turned Miller's stomach.

[16]

EMILY AWOKE WITH A start. She sat up in bed with a throbbing headache. Then her body quickly checked in with heavy, tired muscles. She had soreness in places she had not known she had. She sighed. She was on a bed—a *real* bed. She looked around the room and thought she was in a fairy book story. Candles hung from the stone walls, bathing the room in soft yellow light. The walls had paintings of green fields, vistas of sunflowers and wheat, but there was one picture that made Emily's heart leap with joy. It was a picture of a beach. Emily had always wanted to go to a beach. She laid her head down and stared at the bare ceiling. She wanted to cry but she was too tired. She felt relaxed and thanked God for delivering her here.

She closed her eyes.

———

He pawed her breasts like he was kneading stiff dough. "Hey now, girlie!"

Emily snapped away from the man. She reflexively kicked him away from her. The man slammed to the floor and banged his head against the stone wall.

"What the fuck!" The man groaned rubbing his skull. "This is my home, bitch. You owe me something. And I don't want no money!"

"What—what!" Emily scrambled off the bed. She stared harshly at the man. He was in his fifties. He was thin but well defined, and he was nude. Emily scanned the room and saw her backpack on the floor; noted her guns on the floor next to the backpack. She figured the guns were empty. She thought about the rifle but reasoned against it. She didn't see her sword.

"I want some of that thing of yours! That's a fair trade for room and board."

"No."

"What?" The man stepped toward her. "That ain't your option! I say yes." He grabbed his rigid manhood. "My dick says yes! Damn hard tits. You got some pretty red hair. Let me see that bush, girl."

"You come any closer and I'll put you down." Emily said flatly.

"You welcome to try. This is kinda fun. Ain't had to fight for it in quite awhile."

He rushed her. Emily moved to the left a step, she used the edge of her hand and planted it into the nude man's throat. The man crashed to the stone floor, hacking, wheezing, and holding his throat. Emily grabbed the man by his dirty, long blond hair and pitched him face first into the stone wall, right under the picture of the beach. The man's face left a red smear on the wall. The man lay on the floor, wheezing, moaning. twitching and clutching his throat.

Emily sat on the bed, her head in her hands. "What the hell!" She said to no one.

Suddenly the door opened and a young man stuck his head into the room. "How is she, Pa?" The young man said. Then he saw his father in agony on the floor. "PA!" He rushed into the room and to his father's side. He turned bitterly to Emily.

"What the fuck happened to him? What did you do?" The kid yelled at her.

"He attacked me! He tried to rape me!"

"What!"

"He tried to force me to have relations!" Emily looked at him like he was an idiot.

The young man looked at her as if she were the devil. "You supposed to love a man—especially a man that let you into his house! You ungrateful whore!" He returned his attention to his father. The man wasn't dying, in fact his breathing was less labored. He face was severely beaten. He nose was broken, both eyes were blackened, and he was missing a front tooth.

"You people are sick." Emily stated. She went to her backpack and quickly found the bullet pouch. She grabbed the .22 cartridges.

The young man jumped on her back. Emily spun the skinny kid off her back and tossed him against the wall. He was a few inches shorter than Emily and maybe a few pounds lighter. The kid picked him self up, and never saw Emily's right fist coming at him. She broke his nose and he crumbled, unconscious, onto her backpack. She picked the kid up like and hurled him onto his recovering father. The son's dead weight slammed the father's chin against the stone floor, knocking him out cold.

Emily loaded both her guns. She put on her gear. She figured the father stole her sword. She carried her backpack out of the room. Leaving the broken men on the floor.

She found her sword on the big wooden table by the front door. She put it on. The she left the house.

She walked down the mildly lighted path. Candles hung from the eaves of homes, or set in glass cages fixed atop metal poles. Yet, the true light was from the breaking dawn. She kept looking back, to see if she was being followed.

Emily entered the quiet bazaar. The tents were folded down. The tables were covered or bare. She looked under one of the covered table and found an apple. She grabbed it and immediately bit into it. She savored the sweet, juicy fruit. This was the only thing she has eaten other than salted meat and jerky. She took a few more apples and stowed them in her backpack. She could not believe what had happened with those men. They made is seem as if she was wrong. It that was the case, if all men here in Fort Norris believe they had a right to her body, well she was not going to stay here. She would rather sleep in trees and fight wild dogs than be used like that.

"Hey, what are doing up? What you doing? Where you going?" Miller said to Emily's back.

Emily spun around, PPK in her hand. "I don't want no trouble." She stated.

"Whoa, hey, I don't want no trouble either. I just saw you come in last night! I'm the one that opened the gate. I'm getting off my security duty and saw you here. You okay?"

Emily sighed. "Look, I don't know...I don't want trouble. Just let me go."

"What happened?

"Some guys...I don't know—he expected me to have sex with him. I said no. He came at me so I beat him up. Then his son came in and I had to put him down too."

"Wow. Okay...I think I understand. Look, that's the way it is around here&"

"Yeah, well, that's why I'm leaving!"

"I understand. I just got here a few days ago myself."

"Must be heaven for you then."

Miller looked away. He was not going to lie to her. "I'm thinking of getting out of here too. I got a car and it runs of gas, not bio-fuels, so we can fuel up at any old gas station. We can go anywhere we want."

"Yeah."

"Yeah."

Emily slowly, cautiously put the gun in her holster.

Miller relaxed. "My car is in the garage over there." He pointed as he spoke. "Let's hurry up. Before the town wakes up."

Emily quickly looked under the tarps of the covered tables. She found dried and jerked meats. She took a half dozen pouches of the sealed meats.

"Good idea." Miller grabbed dried fruit and pouches of nuts.

Miller and Emily rushed through the bazaar.

In the garage, Miller opened the trunk. Emily's put her backpack, along with their ill-gotten supplies, in the Mustang's trunk. Emily held onto her sword.

"I've never been in a working car." Emily said. She looked around the garage. She counted five other vehicles in the garage.

"Do all of these run?"

"Yeah, but on ethanol. They can't go fast or very far because bio-fuels are not easy to come by. C'mon, let's go." Miller said with urgency.

"Wow." Emily said casually. She then got into the front seat of the car.

"Jump into the backseat and lay down." Miller told her. I don't want these guys to know you left with me." Miller looked around the garage. He grabbed a fairly clean cloth tarp. Emily climbed into the backseat; Miller covered her with the tarp.

Miller put the car in neutral. He pushed the car out of the garage. There was a slight slope to the garage's exit ramp. He rolled the car down the ramp and let it silently cruise down the path. Miller turned the key and the engine purred to life. He drove for the south gate

The guard asked, "You taking off already, Miller?"

"Yeah man. I can't take the excitement," he replied.

The guard smiled. "You ain't taking a woman, are yah?"

"Hey, I'm a loner. It was fun, but figure this is for the best. "

The guard nodded. He waved to the tower.

Slowly at first, then the gate was wide open.

Miller punched the gas. The green Mustang roared out of Fort Norris.

[17]

"Name's Miller—Miller Hannon."

"Emily Dodds."

The sun was breaking over the eastern mountains as they drove down the desolate highway.

"Did you kill the men who tried to rape you?"

"No. Broke some bones, though." Emily took a healthy pull of vodka straight from the bottle. It was a bottle she had brought from home. She passed the alcohol to Miller.

"You came in hard and loaded down. Where'd you come from?" Miller asked, then hit the vodka bottle.

"Upstate. I walked for about three days. Killed a lot of deaders along the way."

"Yeah...*damn!*"

They drove on in silence. The gas gauge was riding empty. Miller saw a gas station about a mile up the road.

Miller pulled into the Texaco gas station. He parked by the pump, then shut the car off. Miller and Emily got out of the car.

"I need a bath." Emily stated.

"I could use one too." Miller grabbed the gas nozzle and put in the Mustang. He turned the pump on and was surprised to see it work. He pumped gas into the car. He hoped this would work.

Miller jumped when the shot rang out. He turned to see Emily holding her Colt. A little whiff of white smoke emitted from the barrel of the .45.

Emily looked over to Miller. "Deader," she said.

Miller nodded. Fuel spilled from the gas tank. Miller let go of the clutch. He set the nozzle back in the niche on the gas pump.

Miller started the car. He waited for the engine to choke and sputter to a grinding halt.

He shut the engine off after a few minutes. The gas was good. He wanted to shout out in righteous jubilation. He settled for searching the gas station for one or five gallon gas tanks.

"What are you looking for?" Emily asked Miller.

"Small gas tanks. I want to carry a few gallons of gas just in case."

"Good idea." Emily looked around the garage. "So where do we go from here?"

"Anywhere. Perhaps north is better. I got a feeling the dead don't like snow."

"Not true. I've seen 'em slug through the snow. Snow, rain, heat— the elements don't matter to deaders."

"So Alaska is out."

"Hey, I'm up for the trip. Just don't expect the snow to keep the dead at bay."

Miller found two, empty, five gallon gas tanks by a row of tires.

Emily looked at the tires. "You got spare parts for that chariot?" She asked.

Miller looked at her with a blank stare. "No. Nothing."

"Well, let's see what we can get here." Emily said.

Miller grabbed the gas tanks. He realized that Emily was a good catch. He had not even considered spare parts for the car.

In a gun shop. Emily grabbed .22 and .45 caliber shells. Miller looked over the guns. Miller held up a .38.

"I like it." He said.

Emily gave it a soft sneer. "If you like it, get it."

"You don't like it?"

"I'm sure it's a good gun. Take it."

Miller put the gun down. "What do you suggest?"

Emily pointed to the silver barreled forty-five. "The Smith and Wesson. That's a death dealer."

Miller grabbed the gun. He was heavy but he liked the feel of it. The gun had a nice wood grip. "Yeah, okay, I'll take it."

The Mustang raced down the interstate. Emily turned on the radio. She scanned the dial. She did not find a signal. "Every now and again, I used to pick up stations back at home, but we were high on a hillside."

"I got a few signals the other night." Miller took a pull from the whiskey bottle. He passed it to Emily. Emily took the bottle. She took a quick swig of the brown liquor.

Emily coughed. "Damn!"

"Yeah. Makes you feel warm all over." Miller took the bottle from Emily.

"So where was your home?" Miller asked.

"Back in Holocomb. My daddy built the shelter into the side of a hill. He was in the Army Corps of Engineers. He left the army after the Nightmare began in '68."

"Amazing. Where is your father?"

"Dead. That's why I was going to Fort Norris. I was all alone. I guess I thought it was a good idea to be around people."

"It is a good idea. But Fort Norris is...well, I didn't know nothing about it. I gotta admit— it works for the men."

"I can imagine." Emily scanned the woody landscape as they sped down the cement road. She saw deaders wandering among the trees.

A deader stood in the middle of the road. Miller eased the Mustang to the left to go around it.

"Run it over." Emily suggested.

"No way! I'm not getting deader shit on the car!"

Emily nodded. "Fine. Stay close to it." Emily reached in the back seat and grabbed her sword. She pulled it out of the sheath. She leaned out of the car, braced herself against the cool wind, sword ready to strike.

The Mustang ran a tight line.

Emily made a simple, clean cut.

The headless deader stood for a few moments before collapsing lazily onto the tarmac.

"That was fun!" Emily shouted.

Miller nodded. He took a long swig of whiskey, passed the bottle to Emily. She took a healthy pull.

"I see you're very proficient with weapons." Miller said.

"I'm my daddy's girl. He thought me everything I know." Emily snatched the whiskey bottle from Miller. She took a big gulp of alcohol.

"Where we heading?" she asked.

"Currently, west." Miller replied.

"West is good," Emily said. "Never been west."

The Mustang chased the sun down the quiet highway.

Whitley '09

RESURRECTION HOUSE

James Chambers

Of 19,453 prospective buyers Red Moriarty chose Peter Carroll to purchase the notorious property at 1379 Hopewood Boulevard, better known as "Resurrection House."

No one was more surprised than Peter.

Carroll only met Red at the closing when the great man swept into the office, trailing a team of assistants and lawyers in his draft. For a man said to be in his eighties Red got around like an athletic fifty year old, his body commanded by a mind still sharp and facile. He moved with the effortless superiority and inbred poise of royalty, the unspoken assurance that all in his path belonged to him or could be made to belong to him should he only desire it. Moriarty's presence transformed the powerful, wealthy men he employed, powerbrokers hated and feared by those with whom they did business, into fawning children, who shrank from his gaze.

But not so Peter Carroll.

From the moment he met him Peter felt something akin to warmth and paternal affinity from Red, even as the man used his ethereal blue eyes to pick him apart from across the table.

Satisfied, Moriarty sported Peter a wink. "Wondering what you've gotten yourself into, Mr. Carroll?" he asked.

"Well," Peter stammered. "It is a...a big day, isn't it?"

"Did you know that your offer was the third lowest one I received?"

"Oh," Peter said. He hadn't thought it had been that bad. "It's really all I could muster. It's my life savings."

"Hmmm," Moriarty purred, reducing the sum of Peter's efforts to less than words.

The lawyers shuffled papers past Peter like tag-team blackjack dealers. He signed each one, some more than once, his wrist growing numb and his fingertips tingling. The incessant explanatory chatter rattled on too fast for Peter to assemble the details. He would sort it all out later. He was determined now to forge ahead, the course of his life plotted and fixed after so many years of aimlessness.

The paperwork took nearly an hour to be done, and then the room fell quiet except for Moriarty's soft voice speaking German into his cell phone. Peter gazed out the window while they waited. Swaying green leaves caressed the vacant blue sky, and he thought of his new home and its garden, which would soon be in full bloom. He wondered if he wasn't getting himself in over his head.

Red pocketed his cell phone and resumed speaking to Peter as though the interruption had never occurred. "Not everything is about money, of course," he said. "How funny is it that I had to make billions before I learned that lesson?"

Peter started to answer, but Red cut him off. "A laugh riot, right?"

"Money isn't everything," said Peter.

"Maybe power is the thing, eh? That's what you've really bought here today. That's what the others bid on—the power to decide the fate of 1379 Hopewood Boulevard. Roughly a quarter of them wanted to raze the place, salt the ground, scorch the earth, and remove the blemish of Resurrection House from existence. An almost equal number proposed plans to enshrine it, turn it into the destination of pilgrims worldwide, complete with space for spontaneous prostration and prayer, speaking in tongues, and the burning of biers. Most of the other offers came from folks who wanted to make it into an amusement park or a museum, a meditation garden, a low-cost day care center, for Christ's sake, a concert venue, a night club..."

Red's voice trailed off as he faded deep into thought. A haze of distance spread over his eyes as though an ancient memory had kidnapped him into the past. And then it was gone.

"The owner of this house must be someone very special, indeed, Mr. Carroll. There is no place for the banal at 1379. Do you know how many other people tendered offers with proposals like yours?"

"No, sir, I don't. How many?"

Red held up his thumb and index finger to form a zero and clucked his tongue against the roof of his mouth.

"Three simple words you wrote told me that you were the one, no matter what you could pay." Red slid his chair back and rose to his full height of nearly six and a half feet.

"The all-important question," he bellowed and spread wide his arms. "What do you plan to do with 1379 Hopewood Boulevard and its residents?"

Then he swooped forward like a diving kingfisher, stretching over the table toward Peter, his figure propped on his lanky arms. "Your answer? 'I don't know.'

"You were the man I was looking for—a man with an open mind. Honest. Unafraid of the unknown. We had you checked out thoroughly, of course. Watched you for several months. Background investigation and credit check. Dug up your history. Reviewed the orphanage records. All to be solid and secure that you are who we think you are."

"You had me followed?" Peter said, half standing. He flashed a look of concern at his ineffective but affordable lawyer, Finnerty. The attorney shrugged.

"Tut-tut! A formality." Red wagged his index finger. "Don't get indignant when you're on the verge of getting what you want, son. You've been searching a long time for something. Why risk losing it when you've finally found it?"

"I don't understand," said Peter.

"Come, come, my boy. Two years in a seminary, a year volunteering at a hospital in India, two-and-a-half years spent drifting across the good old U.S. of A—sounds like you were looking for something all that time, something extraordinary." Red settled back into his chair. "What goes on at 1379 Hopewood is damn hard to understand, and especially so for anyone maimed by preconceptions of reality, convictions of faith, or plain old stubbornness. You're as close to being free of these traits as anyone I've ever met. You're a rootless loner with more intelligence than your station in life indicates, and you've never even committed to an opinion on whether the phenomenon is genuine or not. That's exactly what's called for. The house will explain itself if you let it. Events will unfold. Secrets will be revealed. And you must be prepared to follow where they lead. Are you...prepared, Peter?"

Peter hesitated, caught off-guard by Red's insight into his life, and then he said, "I'll take good care of the place, Mr. Moriarty. You have my word."

"I hope so, my boy. I'd hate selling to you to turn out to be... a mistake." Red looked to one of his associates. "Is the paperwork done, Tomas?"

The lawyer stepped forward. "All in order, sir. We have Mr. Carroll's check. The house is now his."

"Magnificent," said Red. He exhaled the word like fine cigar smoke, his eyes closing to narrow slivers, his lips curling in a wry smile. "You're aware of your civic and legal obligations as owner and manager of the maintenance fund, Peter?"

"My client is fully informed on all such matters," Finnerty interjected with an air of accomplishment.

"Yes, well, I'm going to assign one of my team to you for three months, free of charge, to advise you and help you get on your feet," said Moriarty. "He'll report to the house tomorrow morning. Consider it a housewarming gift."

With that Red Moriarty stood and walked to the door. His cadre of suits swiveled and followed. Peter and Finnerty rose on polite instinct.

Red paused to shake Peter's hand with his dry palm and bony fingers and said, "I almost envy you the journey you're beginning, Peter. There's a lot I could tell you, but it's better to learn it for yourself. I will share a word of warning with you, however."

Red leaned in, wrapping his free arm around Peter's shoulder and pulling him close. Peter's eyes fell to the odd metal bracelet encircling Red's wrist, its luster something like that of polished gold but diffuse and fluid. It shimmered like a heat mirage. Palpable warmth radiated from the thick metal band as though it conducted heat from Red's body. Or, Peter thought, to Red's body.

"The dead walk their own paths," Red whispered.

Then he and his entourage left. Finnerty and Peter stood alone in a room that felt like it had been flushed. And that's how Peter Carroll came to own the house where the dead live.

EXCERPT FROM CHAPTER 1 OF THE FORTHCOMING BOOK
A History of Resurrection House: The Odd Events at
1379 Hopewood Boulevard and What They Mean to You
by Padraic Irwin O'Flynn

Thirty years ago 1379 Hopewood Boulevard was just another well kept home on a sleepy residential, middle-class, suburban street. The three-story, World War I era house stands off-center in its lot, a bit too far back from the road, shaded by oaks and pines that have grown there since the time of its construction. A low picket fence borders the property and a tangle of rose bushes spreads to either side of the front gate. Its garden is old-fashioned, a seemingly random combination of plants, flowers, and shrubs that becomes charming in the bloom of spring. A wide front window, draped with lace curtains sewn by Carla Montgomery, looks out over the narrow brick path to the front door.

The house's first residents were the Köehlers, a family of German immigrants who lived there for ten years before vanishing into the shroud of history. No trace of them exists following their departure, purportedly to New Jersey where Mr. Köehler had obtained employment as an engineer. The Montgomery family took up residence in the home in the twenties and occupied the house for several decades, staying, in fact, until the strange events in the summer of 1972.

At that time Carla Montgomery was the house's sole occupant, her husband some years dead from an industrial accident, her children all grown and off in pursuit of their lives. The Montgomery family is best described as average—the father, an electrician and small business owner; the three children, a recording engineer, an advertising copywriter, and a high school gym teacher; the mother, a homemaker. None of the Montgomery children agreed to be interviewed for this book, and in past statements, they have uniformly maintained their disbelief in any of the unusual events recorded at their homestead, particularly those directly involving their mother. It is, they declare, a cruel hoax, and they were apparently eager to accept Red Moriarty's generous financial offer for the house and property in late 1972. They wanted nothing more than to put all the stories behind them and get on with their lives.

Their mother was well liked by her neighbors, who looked after her and gave what help they could. And yet, in August of 1972, three days passed before anyone knew Carla Montgomery had died. Finally, bored waiting to be found, she went outside and announced it.

"I'm dead, you know. Feels kind of funny," she stated. A group of local kids who were playing nearby at the time recalled the event in recent interviews with the author.

They didn't believe her. No one did.

Not until Carla started to rot.

By then others like Carla had come to visit and, finding the homey environment to their liking, decided to stay. Where those early few came from remains part of the mystery of 1379 Hopewood Boulevard. No one saw them arrive. No one has ever identified them and the bodies are long gone. Perhaps they came in the dark when the shadows concealed their hideous, decomposing features. Possibly they tunneled underground from the confines of their graves in the cemetery half a mile away. Or maybe, still living, they slipped inside looking for a warm, hospitable place to die. Whatever the explanation, events were well underway at the house before anyone realized what was taking place.

The first identifiable body, after Carla's, was that of Douglas Hollander, an accountant from two houses down. One night soon after Mrs. Montgomery's demise, Hollander joined a group of neighbors confronting Carla about her ranting in the front yard, which had begun to scare their children. They thought she had gone senile, and they wanted to help. Carla did her best to play genial host despite her shriveled larynx. She found it hard to make introductions among her neighbors and the half a dozen or so animated corpses—all in various states of decomposition—that had settled in with her since her passing. While Mrs. Montgomery huffed and puffed, four of the dead seized Hollander, beat him to death with a candlestick, and began plucking away bits of his flesh and stuffing them in their ragged pockets.

The rest of the stunned neighbors fled and called the police.

Officers arrived to find Carla Montgomery at her front gate, wheezing and spitting apologies. Though quite flustered, she somehow conveyed that she'd given her guests a harsh talking to and that no such attack would be repeated. Her word proved good when the officers entered the house to investigate. Carla's guests stayed on their best behavior while the police interviewed Hollander who pointlessly tried to convince them that he was, in fact, dead. Their report quotes him as saying, "Apparently it was a misunderstanding, but that doesn't bring me back to life does it? I'm fucking dead, now." Given his talkative state, the police were understandably skeptical. What they made of the house's decaying residents was never recorded.

Hollander, however, finally made his point when the police removed him—despite Carla's warnings—to the waiting ambulance. The very moment Hollander passed through the front gate, he collapsed. All signs of life immediately departed.

People then began to shed their illusions about Carla and her sickly, old friends.

———

Morning sun limned the yard with delicate fire. A butterfly danced in the hazy air around the buttery flowers of a low, rotund azalea by the front stoop. A girl of sixteen—when she died—knelt by the shrub, her glassine eyes intent on the insect. One of her ears dangled from her skull where an old scar had rotted apart like a split seam, and a shred of muscle dangled out like loose padding. She was oblivious to the coughing motor of the overworked Saturn that rolled into the driveway and chugged into stillness.

Peter Carroll emerged from the run-down vehicle, swallowed a great big breath of warm air, and looked upon his new home.

A trio of withered men shuffled from the backyard with curiosity.

A middle-aged woman, her wounds still fresh and flowing, stood from where she had been reclining by the garbage pails.

A young man missing his left leg dragged himself across the front lawn.

Others came from the side yards. Some spilled out the front door in a slow, lumbering line. They rose from the places where they had fallen in repose behind the hedges or in the basement window wells. Soon they had Peter encircled. A few were rotted into unrecognizable armatures of bone, coated in slick decay and toughening muscle. A handful of the older ones were dry and mummified. Several could have passed for living but for the pallor of their flesh and the dullness of their eyes. And then there were the children, too many children. How many dumped by grief-stricken parents who then never returned to face the unthinkable?

Peter cataloged the visible wounds and injuries, the crushed skulls and severed limbs, the bullet holes and torn throats, the disease-riddled flesh, telltale needle marks, and long fatal gashes. A fair number he guessed had died of less-telling causes, heart attacks or poisons. The stench of the dead consumed his senses. He pressed a handkerchief to his face and wondered if he would ever get used to the smell. Uncertainty lanced him. Moments passed in which he convinced himself that he had made a horrible error. The urge to flee fluttered in his heart.

But then his will asserted itself.

This was home, now. He was its master, and he had duties to attend to.

"Good morning," Peter announced. "My name is Peter Carroll. I'm the new owner."

No response came but the unyielding indifference of the dead.

"I'm moving in today," he continued. "My things will be coming this afternoon. I don't have very much. I've been instructed to inform you that all the established rules remain in effect. Any living person to enter this property is to be considered my guest unless I specify otherwise. None of you will be turned out so long as the rules are obeyed. Is that understood?"

Peter sputtered a bit on the last part. Handing out orders was a new experience for him.

He awaited acknowledgment, but none came. The mob simply dispersed. The dead folk returned to their places, folding back into the property like elements of the landscape come briefly to life but now exhausted of energy. In their absence the kneeling girl remained, her gaze steady in the direction of the flowers though the butterfly was nowhere to be seen.

Peter weaved gingerly around her and climbed the front steps. The door was open. He peered down the hallway into the bright kitchen where George Gail, head of the house's security team, sat sipping a cup of steaming coffee while he read the morning paper.

EXCERPT FROM CHAPTER 3 OF THE FORTHCOMING BOOK
*A History of Resurrection House: The Odd Events at
1379 Hopewood Boulevard and What They Mean to You*
by Padraic Irwin O'Flynn

Who is Red Moriarty?
This is undoubtedly one of the most important questions regarding Resurrection House, perhaps second only to the question of the true nature of events that have transpired there and what they bode for the future of humanity.

Old "Monster" Moriarty enters the stage toward the end of 1972 at the peak of the ravenous success that earned him his nickname. By then the inhabitants of 1379 Hopewood had grown significantly in number. Carla Montgomery had decomposed to a state of bare bones and was no longer up to the running of the household. Yet, things seemed to carry on fine without her, since there wasn't much to be done. The walking dead proved to be surprisingly tidy and promptly tended to the remains of their comrades who reached such advanced states of decay as to no longer be considered among the "living dead." (See Chapter Seven for their means of disposal.) But this behavioral tidbit gave lie to one of the most oft-repeated myths of Resurrection House, that those who dwell there are granted eternal life. In truth they receive something more in the nature of a life extension—putting aside for the moment all theological debates of the nature of "life" after "death"—good only until their withering bodies ultimately dissolve into useless dust.

This, of course, leaves unanswered the question of whether or not their consciousness or soul then ceases to exist as well or goes on to survive in yet another form.

Hopes for the answer drew Red Moriarty to the Resurrection House. The dilemma coincided rather strikingly with research endeavors into the nature of thought sponsored by several of his scientific and pharmaceutical companies. Whatever connections these firms and their studies might have had to clandestine government experiments in mind control and human psychic ability stands as firmly in the realm of dubious conspiracy theory today as it did thirty years ago. Such discus-

sions are beyond the province of this book. Suffice to say that whatever potential Red saw in Resurrection House was enough to sustain his
long-term interest.

In only a few months' time events had conspired toward the
destruction of the house. The Montgomery children refused to take
responsibility for the property or the residents, who they considered
squatters. Thus members of the neighboring community formed a
committee and lobbied to clear the grounds and seal them perma-
nently. The ranks of the curious and devoted swelled as people from
around the globe arrived, overwhelming the small town and causing
horrendous traffic jams, ludicrously long lines at the supermarkets, and
many sleepless nights for those who could not block out the sounds of
the visitors's comings and goings. Worshippers arrived faster than
police could shoo them off. Strange religious ceremonies often began
at midnight and carried on until dawn. Chanting was a mainstay.

The most crucial factor, however, was the abject refusal of any official body to recognize the events at the house as unusual, supernatural,
or miraculous. Every level of the United States government regarded
Resurrection House as the work of publicity seekers and hoaxers. In a
bizarre episode of electoral politics, 1974 gubernatorial candidates in a
neighboring state attacked each other for weeks in an effort to pin the
hoax on each other's party. As a result, a third party candidate won in
that state for the first time in forty-five years. Meanwhile, the Vatican
condemned the place as a dangerous fraud, whose misleading theological implications would surely imperil the souls of any too eager to be
persuaded to belief. Other established churches and religious leaders
issued much the same opinion. Scientific organizations downplayed the
events, stating quizzically that the phenomenon would merit further
study only if it could be proven not to be a hoax, something no one could
confirm without further study. In essence, everyone looked the other way
for fear of ridicule or going on record and looking the fool a year later
when the truth surfaced. Further, persistent rumors point toward the
possibility of bribery and pressure brought to bear—whether by
"Monster" Moriarty's organization or other powerful factions on the
world scene—in keeping bold officials from approaching Resurrection
House with any credibility. Though unproven, these allegations may
point to an explanation for why the place has gone unmolested by
bureaucratic interference for more than thirty years.

There were exceptions, people who protested the summary dis-
missal and mockery of the phenomenon, but their voices were often
squelched, their opinions dismissed with the same casual humor that
greets reports of flying saucers, Bigfoot, crop circles, and the Loch Ness

monster. A regional news anchor lost his job after refusing to report the case as a fraud. The town mayor was one of the few local voices in favor of preserving the house, and the town residents, for their first-hand experience, seemed far less convinced that it was all a put-on. Most others protesting the scam theory came from fringe groups involved with alien visitations, transgressional theologies, UFOs, and other extreme and minority perspectives.

Thus the door hung wide for one of the richest men in the world to step in and take on the full expense of properly securing the house and property, seeing to its upkeep and security, compensating the neighbors for their inconvenience, and launching a full investigation into the matter.

What a collective sigh of relief was breathed.

However, thirty years later and three months after Moriarty's announcement of his intention to conclude his study and put Resurrection House on the market, the public yet awaits the results of his research. It is inconceivable that, with three decades to investigate and the enigmatic Moriarty's resources to draw upon, no progress was made. What is that the old man hiding?

———

George Gail lit a cigarette then deftly managed to wield it with the same hand with which he held his coffee mug and morning paper as he clapped his free arm around Peter Carroll's back and ushered him out the door. The backyard was larger than average for houses in this neighborhood. Peter was unprepared for the number of corpses milling about, perhaps fifty or sixty, all of whom turned and looked at him. Some of them only had empty eye sockets, but he could feel their stares. They looked frail and hungry in the glare of the late-morning sun. Sparrows flitted among them, plucking worms and grubs from the crevasses of their polluted flesh.

"So's not much to it, really," growled George. "Twelve-foot, chain-link fence running on three sides of the property, more to keep 'em out than in, you understand. And Mr. Moriarty, he sunk vertical concrete slabs seven feet down below all the property lines. Still, we get a new face now and then, though I can't say for sure exactly where they come from. Got my theories, you bet, but that ain't what you pay me for, is it?"

George twisted Peter sideways and pointed across the yard. "Up there we got the platform and one of two monitor stations for the cameras. Fifteen feet high. Always a man on watch in there. The other monitors are in the cellar safe room. I'll show you that later. The guard on the platform is always armed, though we've only had call to draw our weapons maybe a dozen times since I've been on the job. Most of those were to scare away vandals."

Gail dragged Peter off the porch and walked him toward the driveway. Every few steps he paused to point out a nook or corner of the house where a small black camera peered down at them.

"We got cameras on every angle of the building and grounds, and twice as many covering the grounds off-property. Those are the ones that matter. Law says we're responsible basically for two things. One, no one live gets hurt by anyone 'dead,' which isn't much trouble as long as we keep the live ones off the property and you make sure to enforce the rules. And, two, we ain't allowed to accept dead bodies on the property. That boils down to doing everything we can to discourage corpse dumping. If they get by us, though, well, ain't much we can do about that. They come back to life, they're welcome to stay. Law says they ain't dead if they're moving. But we're not permitted to store 'em otherwise, even if they've been properly embalmed. But, now, I ain't telling you anything you don't already know, am I, Mr. Carroll?"

George and Peter rounded the front of the house and closed full circle toward the backyard. Peter eyed the sturdy framework of the security platform. It could've passed for an overgrown patio deck, but for the concrete, steel, and glass. Gail dug his fingers into Peter's shoulder, spewed smoke, and gazed up at the structure against the glare of the sun reflected in its windows.

"I'll tell ya, Mr. Carroll, eight years I got on this job, and I still can't understand why they want in here. I mean, Hell, I'm getting paid to be here or you wouldn't see me within five miles of this place. Not that I'm complaining, mind you. Not at all. Oh, some I get it—the ones who want to sneak in with the bodies of their loved ones and bring 'em back. But it's the live ones that baffle me, the ones that sit vigils all night outside the front gate. Like they just enjoy being around death, you know? Like they got some sick urge to fulfill or some unhealthy questions they're looking for the answer to. This whole neighborhood is full of them, you know, folks who moved here just to be near this house."

Peter blushed and looked away.

"Oh, not that I mean you, sir. No, you're the owner, and this place is one of a kind. And that I get, too. Owning a place like this? It's kind of special. And who knows? Maybe you'll figure out how to turn a buck or two off it. Now, let me show where all the alarm boxes are. Officially the dead don't come back to life, but I guess somebody high up is smart enough to hedge their bets. So, we got direct lines to the fire department, the police department, the hospital, and, my personal favorite, the Centers for Disease Control. Soon as they put one in for Lazio's Pizzeria, we'll be all set."

Gail unleashed a raspy chuckle, slapped Peter on the back, and steered him toward the house.

They passed an outside entrance to the cellar, covered over by a pair of cyclone doors painted dark blue and set in a sloped concrete frame.

Have to look around down there, Peter thought.

OBITUARY

Rudolf Mann, Physicist and Founder of
The Society of the Second Death, Dies at 80

Rudolf Mann, whose scientific contributions include *Kinetic Delinquency: A Treatise on the Transfer of Energy*, but who is better known for founding the cultic Society of the Second Death in 1953, died Friday in Hamburg. The cause was a cerebral hemorrhage. He is survived by his granddaughter Dotti Gruenlotter.

Mann, whose philosophical beliefs took their roots in fin de siecle Millenialism and bastardized principles from established world religions, was a proponent of the concept that human beings might move materially into the next world. His unorthodox mix of science and rogue theology placed him firmly outside the academic and scientific mainstream. Yet, in 1953, Mann founded a society whose membership numbers more then 75,000 worldwide today.

Mann spent the better part of his youth journeying through Asia, before returning to his native Dresden at the end of World War II when he gathered a following of men and women devoted to his ideas. Though no formal records of military service exist for Mann, controversy has long surrounded his activities during the war. Historians have purported that Mann's travels were connected to covert efforts of the Third Reich or that Mann was engaged by Great Britain as a double agent. His official biographer, Ute Meineke, claims Mann was neither and that his journey was one of spiritual and self-discovery.

Following the death of his wife in the 1960s Mann became a recluse. In his writings he often pointed to the influence of family legends concerning his great-grandfather, Avery Mann. The Mann patriarch committed suicide with half a dozen others in a cottage outside Dresden on New Year's Eve 1900. Mann alternately characterized his progenitor as a brilliant spiritualist who foresaw the end of the world and just another victim of the odd apocalyptic mania that seizes upon the soft-minded at century's end.

Mann leaves behind a body of work consisting of numerous scientific treatises and monographs, two novels that were banned for several years in numerous countries, and many volumes of privately published religious writings, including a disturbing creation myth that has inspired generations of subculture artists and musicians. At the time of his death, he was reportedly at work collating forty years of his journals for what he intended to be his final statement to the world.

————

Moriarty's lawyer had dubbed the hulking, one-armed corpse that sat in the cellar like a king perched upon his throne the "Scowl." Still and silent as a statue, only the dead man's perpetual glower and the radiating intensity of his eyes indicated that he belonged among the living dead. His tattered clothes suggested nothing of his former life. No one among the security detail could recall his arrival at the house, though George Gail placed it at more than six months ago. But the Scowl seemed too fresh and too little decayed to be so old.

The men who worked the basement security station tried to avoid him. His unblinking stare made them uncomfortable. Peter Carroll found it fascinating.

He came to think of the Scowl as the gravity of the 1379 Hopewood Boulevard, the mass around which the other corpses orbited, and perhaps the vessel that contained the key to the secrets of the house. During the second week of his residency, he began daily observations of the dead man, at first sitting beside the guard, observing the solitary figure, while also keeping an eye on the monitors. In this way he adjusted to the routines and cycles of the household. The dead moved in fixed orbits. Days or weeks long their circuits took them through the rooms and corridors of the house and its grounds like cells coursing through the veins and arteries of a circulatory system. Their inexorable motion made the stillness of the Scowl seem all the greater.

Then there were the "shades" to wonder about, dark figures that danced briefly across the monitor screens or hovered in patches of darkness on the fringes of perception. Glimpsed from the corner of his eye, they seemed to Peter like the figures of men, but viewed head on, they shifted into amorphous shadows like smears of soot on the screen. One moment they were present and the next gone. They only appeared on camera. The guards ignored them, but Peter suspected a connection existed between the shades and the mysterious comings and goings of the dead who vanished without a trace as often as fresh corpses appeared out of nowhere.

The "scraps" were harder to overlook. Scattered willy-nilly within and without the walls of the house were the lost limbs and loose bits

of animated flesh or organs that decomposing residents sometimes
trailed behind them. Or when a body became too damaged to go on,
the others would tear it to shreds and spread the quivering remains
around the property. The pieces never lasted long before withering
into dry nubs of old skin and sinking away into the cracks of the house
or holes in the earth that the dead dug by hand in the yard. Peter sur-
mised that this disposal process marked the central preoccupation of
the dead. He steeled himself to investigate when he could.

For now, though, it was the Scowl that obsessed him.

Carroll had done his research before placing his bid for the
house, and he knew things were changing. The rate of decay among
the dead had been slowing in steady increments over the past
decade. The corpses were walking longer. Their numbers were growing. If Gail's timeline for the Scowl was accurate, then he was the
best-preserved corpse yet to inhabit the house. Peter could not
escape the sensation that something more than the rudimentary
thought processes apparent in the other corpses was taking place
inside the Scowl's mind.

Before long Peter moved out of the guard station to sit eye-to-eye
with the thing. Those first few sessions lasted minutes, but he found
himself staying a little longer each day. The Scowl was unlike the other
corpses. It possessed warmth to their cold, and weight, as though its
physical presence, rather than decreasing in death, had become denser
and more substantial. Its skin shone like veneer. Peter's imagination
filled to bursting with ideas about who the Scowl might be, where he
had originated, and why he seemed so powerful.

When a month had passed, an hour-long staring duel with the
Scowl had become well entrenched in Peter's daily routine. He took
to recording in a notebook the ruminations and ideas that often
flashed through his mind during that time. Visiting the thing had
become a form of meditation, and Peter wondered if some days he
wasn't subjecting himself to a subtle self-hypnosis facilitated by the
unnatural steadiness of the corpse's nacreous eyes. He found that
the immutability of its cold stare bordered on reassuring as though
it understood who Peter was and intended soon to deliver some telltale gesture or revelation.

But after weeks of observation Peter's hope began to fade that any
sign of the creature's thoughts might reach its surface. Maybe,
thought Peter, this one is different in other ways.

One Thursday as Peter sighed, closed his notebook, and rose to
leave, the Scowl grabbed him by the arm.

Peter barked in surprise. Its touch was hideous. Biting cold penetrated Peter's flesh, and an icy sweat broke out on his back. He dropped his notebook and pen to the floor.

The security guard rushed from his post. Peter waved him back.

The Scowl made no other move. He simply held Peter and stared at him.

And then his stiffened mouth opened, shedding flakes of brittle skin as he said, "God...has not abandoned...you...why have you...abandoned him..." His voice floated like a whisper down an endless tunnel. Then the dead thing growled and a flat, rolling uproar billowed from deep within the Scowl's torso. Peter recognized it as laughter. The dead man let go of Carroll's arm and lapsed once more into quietude.

Rattled, Peter retrieved his notes and fled upstairs.

EXCERPT FROM
Seven-Fold World (1955) by Rudolf Mann

And Ailo wept for the loss of Anlo his mate with whom he had created all the aspects of the Seven-Fold World and given seed to the multitude of beasts and spirits that populated it. For Anlo had forgotten the warning of the Great Thing that lived below the sea, the one thing to which Ailo and Anlo had not imparted existence, and she had traveled too near the Fiery Heart of the Earth. And thus Anlo was burned and did vanish while Ailo slept.

Upon awakening Ailo called out for his mate. But only silence like that of the great empty gulfs amidst the galaxies responded.

And Ailo searched for her, receiving word from the beasts of the mountain that Anlo had touched the Fiery Heart of the Earth and had thus been seared from the land.

Upon hearing this Ailo vowed to reclaim his mate from the depths of the underworld and restore her to life for their work stood unfinished. The world remained imperfect.

And though many months did pass and the seasons change, Ailo's conviction burned without wavering. One day after weeks of wandering the utter darkness of the underworld and passing through the many tricks and traps of the slithering shades that inhabit the unlighted realms, he came upon a chamber whose blackness reeled back from the glow of red-hot metal. Its source was the pendant that once he had gazed upon so often where it hung from Anlo's neck. This was where her body lay. The metal of the charm still bore the atomic heat of the Fiery Heart of the Earth. It glowed like a young sun perceived from a planet's distance.

Upon seeing Anlo there, Ailo wept tears of joy. But as his eyes grew accustomed to the baneful light and took in the fullness of his mate's decay, the sight of her shattered his elation. All sign of her former beauty had been vanquished by decay. Those parts of her meant to nurture and spawn life were spotted with rot and ruin. The wreck of Anlo's flesh repulsed Ailo. He cried out in anguish.

And Anlo awakened and asked, "Why have you come seeking me, my love? Do you not know I am not yet finished dying? My life above is ended. Now I must face my second death before this world we have fabricated together might free me in body and soul. Return! Your place is no longer at my side for you have many sins yet to repent."

Upon hearing Anlo's voice changed so by the ravages of death, Ailo seized the fiery charm from his lover's neck and fled back to the surface where he expressed to all the beasts and creatures of the earth his cosmic sorrow that not one death but two must claim them all before they might know peace. And so from the creatures who had drawn around him, he chose seven and declared them divine heralds. Into their hands he assigned governance over all those things of the underworld and delivered to them the freedom of passage through the unlighted channels of the night. Then he cast the burning charm among them and doomed all things to suffer its horrible power.

"So, how do you pay for all this, Mr. Carroll? You're not a wealthy man."

Padraic Irwin O'Flynn pushed his teacup aside and prepared to jot notes on a yellow legal pad. A mini-cassette recorder whirred faintly on the table.

"Ah, well, first question and it's already about money, Mr. O'Flynn? I consented to this interview to help your research, not your royalties. Please don't forget that," Peter retorted.

"It's relevant to my research to know who's backing your ownership and maintenance of Resurrection House. But a poor choice for my first question. Let's start with something easier. How long have you lived at 1379 Hopewood Boulevard?"

"Six months," answered Peter. "And the house is supported by a fund established by Red Moriarty. I contribute every cent of my own earnings, minus expenses, but as you noted, I'm not a wealthy man. Red assured the support of the house independent of the resources of its owner."

"Thank you, Mr. Carroll," said O'Flynn.

He had begun work on his book three years ago, determined to dispel the cloud of half-truths and rumor that obscured what was really happening at Resurrection House. O'Flynn had no doubt that dead bodies did indeed return to life on the property, and he feared that it marked the advent of something monumental. The denial of the place's significance by the world at large only bolstered his conviction. He intended to set down the most factual account of the house's history that he could assemble, at best to expose the truth behind the phenomenon, at worst to awaken the interest of the self-obsessed public. Moriarty's organization had routinely stonewalled his investigative efforts and requests for interviews. It had taken him four solid months of persuasion to arrange his meeting with the new owner. He could feel it was going to be worthwhile.

"Do you like it here? Does it feel like home?" he asked.

"I'm quite comfortable. It's a charming house. Of course, I'm still adjusting to the others but we get along fine," Carroll said.

"So, you, what...?" asked O'Flynn. "Get up in the morning, brush your teeth, come down to breakfast? All while the dead carry on around you?"

"Pretty much. The others keep to themselves. They're like ghosts, in a way, but ghosts with substance. Anyway, I'm well occupied. There's plenty of work to tend to as the house's caretaker. Administrative affairs, fielding requests for visitation, and other duties."

"I'd imagine keeping contact with lawyers takes up a good deal of your time. Last I checked there were 734 pending legal actions connected to the house."

"You've done your homework. But we're up to an even 750 as of this morning. Not everyone wants to see the house continue to exist. Not everyone is happy that I own it. Most of them are crackpot cases that will never see the inside of a courtroom."

Padraic took a leather-bound scrapbook from his briefcase and flipped through stiff pages of newspaper clippings. "It raised quite a stir when Moriarty chose to sell to you. Here's one," he said, stopping at a page. "The headline reads: 'Moriarty Sells To Incompetent.'" And another, 'The Headless Household: Visionless Amateur To Buy 1379.' Do you feel there might be something to the criticism?"

"I understand it," said Peter. "But I've never cared about what people say. I'm not here for publicity or to play public servant. This is my home, and if the public doesn't like the way I choose to run it, they can take a flying leap. It's none of their business. I keep everything in complete compliance with the law and I take good care of the grounds. These people all have their own agendas. They don't understand what the house needs."

"But you do?"

"I'm learning," said Peter. "Something miraculous is taking place here. It should be perceived for what it is, not for what we hope it to be."

"What is it?" O'Flynn asked.

Peter pondered the question for a moment, then said, "It's difficult to describe. The dead do return to life. They're not mindless shells, but they're not the people they were before they died, either. They have purpose."

"Which is?"

"I haven't figured that out, yet. They've told me some things but it's a jumble."

Padraic decided to shift gears. He wanted to gather as much information as he could before he dropped the bombshell he had been sitting on for the past nine weeks. "How do you get along with your neighbors?"

"Very well. They've all been rather unexpectedly supportive."

"Most of them only moved here to be closer to the house. Two of them were bidding against you, weren't they?"

"Yes, but they've been good about the way things went. They're genuinely involved. I won't tolerate anyone whose sole interest in the house is to make money."

"And what interested you, Peter? What drew you to bid on the house in the first place?"

Peter laughed. "If you had asked me that six months ago, I would've told you the same thing that won it for me, 'I don't know.' But I have an idea, now. Something special is happening here, and I think I've always known that. One of the world's grand mysteries is playing itself out before our eyes. I've learned quite a lot about myself since moving here. I'm meant to play a part in whatever is coming."

The candor and conviction of Peter's answer surprised Padraic. He faltered a moment before his reporter's instincts took over. "Then the business of Resurrection House is a matter of faith for you?"

"Faith is belief in that which cannot be proven," said Peter.

A woman whose chest had been shorn open in a car crash staggered up to the kitchen doorway. She peered in at the two men. Padraic paused and waited for her to withdraw. Instead she stayed, observing them without the slightest trace of self-consciousness.

"Do you know where Red Moriarty got his wealth, Peter?" continued O'Flynn.

"Not really. From his businesses, I assume."

"Do you know where he was born? Or who his parents were?"

"No," replied Peter. "Is it important?"

"No one knows. That's the thing. For all practical purposes, Moriarty came into existence fully formed in 1947 as the head of a small Zurich-based financial company. There's no trace of his life before that date, and no one who works for him will discuss it. I've known a number of journalists who've tried to investigate him, but all of them dropped the story sooner or later and never went back to it. I've only found one shred of evidence of Moriarty before 1947, and quite frankly, I'm not sure what to make of it."

O'Flynn again opened his briefcase. He withdrew a transparent envelope containing a yellowed, black-and-white photograph, which he slid out and passed across the table to Peter. The sleeve of Peter's shirt drew back as he reached for the paper, and O'Flynn noticed the unusual band of bright metal worn around his wrist. It struck him as unlike any substance he had ever before seen.

"Interesting bracelet," he commented.

"A gift from the dead, believe it or not. Moriarty wore one like it, too," Peter said. "Now, what am I looking at here?"

"It's a copy," said O'Flynn. "I purchased the negative from a man in Dresden whose grandfather was a news photographer. I had it restored. It was taken in 1900."

———

Peter examined the photograph. At the center of the image Red Moriarty lay dead among a group of bodies scattered awkwardly around a room in a ramshackle cottage. From the clothes and décor, Peter could easily believe the photo was a hundred years old.

"I don't understand," Peter said.

"The dead man at the center of the room? The one who looks like Red Moriarty? That's Avery Mann, great-grandfather of Rudolf Mann."

"Rudolf Mann?"

"The physicist and cult founder. Lived in Germany. He died last year." O'Flynn reached into his briefcase once more and produced another photograph.

"Are you suggesting that Moriarty is related to Mann?" Peter asked, as he accepted the second photo, leaving it face down on the table.

"Not quite," explained O'Flynn. "I'm suggesting that Moriarty is Avery Mann. I think "Monster" Moriarty has been dead for a century and no one has caught on."

"That's ridiculous," Peter sneered. "The phenomenon began in 1972 and it's contained to this property. Besides, even if Mann had come back to life, he would've decomposed entirely decades ago."

"Well, it's an imperfect theory, I admit. I was hoping you might help me clear away the murk of history," O'Flynn said. "There's one thing I am certain of, though. See that man by the fireplace?"

Peter looked at the image of a well-dressed man, lifeless and slumped by the hearth.

"I see him," he said.

"He's your great uncle, Wilhelm Köehler."

Padraic tapped his pen against the table and his right leg started to twitch. The kitchen grew cold, and another broken figure appeared in the doorway. Outside a trio of pale bodies passed by the windows, dimming the sunlight with carousel shadows.

"That's not possible," Peter said.

"Actually it is. Wilhelm's brother, Ernst, came to America in the 1910s. His family lived in this house for a time. Ernst was your grandfather. Your ancestral name is not Carroll, but Köehler. Have you ever read Rudolf Mann's Seven-Fold World? Do you know about the seven heralds?" O'Flynn continued.

"No," retorted Peter. "Why should I?"

"Because I'm sure there's a connection to Resurrection House. I just haven't worked out what it is," said O'Flynn. "That second photo, by the way, is Rudolf, taken a year before he died. They say he went mad after his wife burned to death in the sixties."

Peter flipped the picture over. He attempted but failed to stifle a gasp.

"What is it?" O'Flynn demanded.

Peter composed himself. "I'm sorry, but we're done. It's time for you to leave."

The walking dead filled both exits from the kitchen. Their heavy stares bore down on O'Flynn. He retrieved the photographs, slipped them away, and left a manila folder filled with papers in their place. "All right, I'll go. But look through this folder, Mr. Carroll. The documentation of your ancestry is irrefutable. I know Moriarty had you investigated before selling, and if I could dig it up, you can be sure his people did, too. So you have to ask yourself, why didn't he tell you?"

O'Flynn stood and approached the corridor with caution. The dead parted to let him pass. A small group of them trailed him all the way to the front gate, and he was sure that had they been free to act, they would've torn him limb from limb.

In the kitchen Peter collapsed at the table with his head in his hands.

He could not be mistaken.

The person O'Flynn had identified as Rudolf Mann was the Scowl.

EXCERPT FROM
Seven-Fold World (1955) by Rudolf Mann

Consider that the worship of death is the essential, underlying foundation of every significant religion in the world, and the question of existence becomes crystal clear. We live to die. Life is a chrysalis. Death is the end state.

In many Asian cultures people treat their deceased ancestors as though they are still among them. They bring them food and presents and implore them for their assistance and blessings.

Dozens of societies in the past, such as the Egyptians and the Celts, have buried their dead with worldly goods, fully expecting those who had passed on to have need of such things.

Christians worship the one who conquered death, who held in his hands the power of a second life, the one who returned to the Earth after his own demise and promised one day to impart the same gift to all his followers.

And what of reincarnation? I purport that it is the repetition of the act of dying not the act of living that achieves spiritual advancement.

Throughout history, throughout the world, peoples have constructed their beliefs around human sacrifice, whether abstract or concrete. Unknown quantities of blood have been spilled over the concept that life springs from death, renewal is born of decay, and that only through the act of killing do the living become fertile and enriched.

So our purpose is clear.

Life and death must become one.

The flesh must not be left to rot and wither and the soul loosed aimlessly into the universe.

The dead are worshipped, and so in order to become gods, we must die.

A frigid draft braced the diner. Outside rain poured from the night. O'Flynn sipped his coffee and stared at the torrent of shadows beyond the water-rippled plate glass window. He sat in the last booth of the diner three blocks from Resurrection House, precisely where Peter Carroll had asked him to be. It was pushing one o'clock in the morning and with the bad weather, the place was deserted.

He started to doubt if Peter would turn up after all. Weeks had passed since the interview, and he had fairly given up hope of hearing from Carroll again despite the information he had delivered. He agreed to the meeting without hesitation when Peter contacted him.

Soft bells jangled as the front door opened. A blast of damp cold spit through the entrance, and Carroll entered, his slender body hidden beneath the glistening folds of a thick raincoat. A waitress started her way around the counter to seat him, but Peter ignored her and trundled toward O'Flynn. He slid into the seat, leaving his hood in place so that his eyes peered out from darkness like the headlights of a distant, oncoming car. His shoulders slumped.

"Thank you for seeing me," Peter said in a faint, withering voice. "It's a miserable night."

"It's fine. I was pleased to hear from you," offered O'Flynn. He raised his hand, beckoning the waitress. "How about some coffee?"

Peter seized O'Flynn by the wrist and slammed his arm to tabletop, pinning it there. "No. That's all right. Nothing, thank you."

"Well. Okay. Guess you don't really need the caffeine," O'Flynn chided. "You can let go of my arm, now."

Peter grunted and released his hold. "Heard your book is done."

"That's right. There's a lot more I'd like to have done with it, but it's a start. I think people are really going to open their eyes when they read it. I'm already planning a follow-up."

"I see," Peter said.

Rain pattered a nervous beat against the window glass.

"There were so many of them after you left," Peter exhaled. "Shoulder to shoulder in the cellar, spilling from every room, the entire house filled with living corpses. You didn't know what it was you were doing, did you, Mr. O'Flynn?"

"What are you talking about? What did I do?"

"The photographs, the papers. The information. I had nightmares for days afterward."

"Dreadfully sorry if I upset you," said O'Flynn. "I didn't mean to."

"Not me. Them. The dead," Peter corrected. "You spoiled their fun. Forced a revelation." He sniffled and wiped his wrist across his lips. The motion drew his sleeve back, uncovering the same milky, bronze bracelet O'Flynn had first seen during the interview.

"Peter? Are you all right?" O'Flynn asked.

Drops of blood fell to the table. A fresh crimson smear was visible on Peter's sleeve.

"He was there in the house all along, and I never knew," Peter rasped. "Had never even heard his name. But he knew who I was. He knows what I'm meant to do. He was playing with me, amusing himself. They all were for a while. Time doesn't mean the same thing to the dead as it does to the living."

Peter jerked back as the waitress set a coffee mug down in front of him. She filled it then topped off O'Flynn's cup. "It's okay with me if you sit and talk, fellows, but you gotta order something. Coffee's the cheapest. All done with your pie?" she said. She reached for the crumb-dappled plate in front of O'Flynn and strained for a glimpse beneath Peter's hood. He turned away. She took the dish and retreated behind the counter.

"Even you could sense the truth," Peter uttered.

"Are you sick, Peter? You don't sound well. And you're bleeding."

"You must think me quite the fool."

O'Flynn placed his hands palm down on the table. "I don't think you're a fool, Peter. I never did. What are you getting at?"

"You're right about Moriarty. He's been dead for more than a century," Peter breathed. "Rudolf Mann is one of the living dead, too. He lives in my basement. They've been hard at work down there making up for lost time. My father made a mess of it or it would've started years ago. But he got frightened, so he took their secrets and ran. It should have been him in that picture, not my uncle. Father's dead, now, of course, but he hid well when he was alive. They traced him to America after World War I, but from there…nothing. Not until 1972. Not until someone died in Resurrection House. That's where my father buried it, underneath the cellar floor, but not deep enough. Once the first of the dead rose there, it beckoned the others like a radio signal. And they came. Even Moriarty showed up in person to take back his long-lost possession."

"What did your father steal?" O'Flynn said.

"A seventh of Anlo's charm," said Peter.

"The charm is real?"

"Yes," Peter whispered. "They won't tell me where it came from or how long it's existed. Moriarty found it in 1873. Its powers are… unimaginable. They call it the Fiery Heart of the Earth."

"Then, Dear God, all of it could be real," O'Flynn said. "But how has Moriarty lasted so long?"

"A piece of the charm. He bears it on his person. It sustains him."

Peter stuck a spoon in his coffee and twirled it idly in a steady circle. Padraic eyed the ghostly pallor of his skin. "Do you know there are other places like Resurrection House? Consecrated ground where the dead walk? They're remote and not widely known."

"I had my suspicions about that," said O'Flynn.

"Well, they exist. They're much further ahead than Resurrection House. They haven't been missing their heralds for a hundred years. The soil there has been properly blessed with the flesh of the dead and the blood of the living," Peter muttered. "That's what the dead do, you know. Day and night. Their flesh soaks in the power of the charm and when it rots from the bone, it serves to fertilize the land. Now the concentrations are high. The decay is stopping. The bounds of the soil can be cast off."

"What do they want?" said O'Flynn.

"What they planned more than a century ago. The heralds are all present. The sale of the house was a test. Red knew who I was, just as you said, but he wanted to know if I would come on my own. And I did. It's in my blood. This power, energy, radiation, whatever it is—it's part of my being. It always has been. It courses through me."

"Listen to me, Peter," blurted O'Flynn. "Come with me. Now! Don't go back there. We'll get far away and we'll tell the world the truth, whatever it is, about Resurrection House. Please, Peter, before there's no chance for you, leave with me."

Peter said nothing. His hand ceased twirling the spoon and dropped to the table, dragging the coffee cup onto its side. Hot coffee pooled out and dripped over the aluminum trim.

"Peter?" O'Flynn said.

The patter of coffee dripping onto Peter's raincoat joined the rhythm of the rain. O'Flynn reached across the table and swept back Peter's hood. He recoiled. Coagulating blood trickled in sticky streams from Peter's nose. One of his eyes was bruised. The right side of his neck had been torn away. There were bite marks in his flesh. Peter's chest was still. The blood leaking from his throat slowed to a trickle.

The man who owned Resurrection House was dead.

O'Flynn turned away, looking out the window. The dead watched them from outside. They filled the street. Dozens plodded through the puddles and downpour, marching along the darkened sidewalk like a troop of rusted automatons.

Bells jingled. Cold air rushed in.

The waitress screamed. One after another the corpses filed in, silent and voracious.

O'Flynn skittered sideways and fell to the floor. He groped at the table, grabbed a knife and brandished it. "God help me!" he cried.

"God is dead, Padraic."

O'Flynn looked up to see Peter Carroll pulling himself free of the booth.

"And God will help you," he finished.

Splattering blood all around him, Carroll snatched O'Flynn by the shirt collar and lifted him, slamming his skull against the overhead light fixture. Cold flowed from the dead man's fingers, but a nauseating heat radiated from the bracelet at his wrist, toasting Padraic's skin like the noonday sun.

The waitress shrieked twice more and then her voice was not heard again. One of the dead clambered into a seat at the counter and gnawed on the cracked end of her leg. Fresh sounds of fear gurgled from the kitchen staff in the next room.

The dead congregated in the diner, their eggshell stares intent on O'Flynn.

Peter righted him on his feet and straightened his clothes.

"The seventh herald has returned," Peter declared. "We are your gods, now. Worship us. Die for us."

Padraic's heart pounded. Blood crashed through his head, clouding out his thoughts. He averted his gaze and shook his head.

"No..." he whispered.

Padraic lashed out, every muscle in his body quivering with fury. His blind thrusting arm knocked loose a bit of flesh from a corpse standing beside Peter. It barely noticed the blow. Carroll snarled in anger. He seized Padraic's wrist and snapped it. The knife clattered to the floor. Pain exploded in Padraic's arm as Carroll squeezed until bone crushed against bone. With his other hand Padraic reached for the cross around his neck and spoke the words of the Our Father.

The dead blanketed him. Their bodies blocked out the light.

EXCERPT FROM THE AFTERWORD OF THE FORTHCOMING BOOK
A History of Resurrection House: The Odd Events at
1379 Hopewood Boulevard and What They Mean to You
by Padraic Irwin O'Flynn

My interview with Peter Carroll was meant to be the final piece in this puzzle of a book to which I have dedicated my life. In receiving it I had anticipated something akin to a sacrament, the last great enlightenment, the lifting of the shroud that I had always, blindly, associated with access to Resurrection House. For so long I had convinced myself that with entry would come knowledge. Answers I sought, and answers I would have.

How could I have known that all along I had been asking the wrong questions?

Is it too late, now, to turn the tide? I fear it may be, yet, I'm unwilling to forfeit the spark of hope that lingers in my heart. Few will listen and even fewer will act, though, and so I suppose it is inevitable that I will see that light extinguished before long. Mankind carries on like a wild herd of burrowing animals, their senses too clouded by the grime of their own lives to notice the expansive, indisuadable doom plunging down around us all.

The full set of clues to the mystery has eluded me for now, but when the full picture is finally assembled, I have no doubt it will shatter the foundations of all our beliefs about the world.

In the time since my visit to Resurrection House, I have caught the first inklings of other such places in the world. In India and France, perhaps in Japan and Belize. Word carries now of secret places where the dead walk in South Africa and the Ukraine, Argentina, Great Britain, Somalia, New Zealand, and on and on. Are they but more lies and rumors? Or is there in every part of the world, a Resurrection House, where the dead carry on in imitation of those against whom they plot? The idea is incredible to the most credulous and to the skeptical, it smacks of inebriation.

But why not?

Peter Carroll once told me that the dead travel their own paths, the roads and trails unknown to living men where the secrets of their power dwell. Imagine the ranks of the unliving, mustered to action by a single-minded will, organized, granted power and energy from sources beyond the knowledge of science, and set in motion. Resurrection House is our future. Humanity walks the edge of a knife—the blade that parts humility and grace from arrogance and subjugation.

And thus what Resurrection House means to you depends on which you have worshiped.

For as the past, so the future.

CRIME & AUTHORITY

C.J. Henderson

"The strongest bulwark of authority is uniformity; the least divergence from it is the greatest crime." – Emma Goldman

Lightning fragmented the evening sky, illuminating the clouds, terrifying children. On the ground, Miles Strass hid in an alley, as terrified as any child. But not by the lightning. Strass was tall, a good 5'9", but he was also thin as a rail, and that was in the sickly sense. As he cringed, his longish, dark hair whipped his face in the sogging wind. His glasses, coated by the rain, were practically useless.

Actually, Strass was no longer in the alley. He was but remembering the moment, relating it to the man across the desk from him.

"I remember I was hiding," he said, trembling, sniveling. "*Miles, come out, Miles,* they called to me. *Nobody wants to hurt you, Miles.* I had been running from them for so long…"

Strauss spoke on about the ominous figures, striding forth through the rain, searching for him. As he told it, it seemed that no matter how far he ran, he could never get ahead of them.

"No matter how fast I traveled," he whined, "or in what direction, still there were always more."

This sad fact proved to be Strauss's downfall, for eventually he ran into a group of them, or more specifically, into a mailbox near a group of them. He hit it hard, slipping on the rain slick cement, going down in a clumsy tangle that looked particularly painful even to those closing in on him.

The odd thing about the walking dead pursuing Mr. Strass was that they were not dressed in rags and graveyard tatters. Indeed, if they looked like anything, they seemed to most exactly ape the appearance of office workers. Of course they had the same dark-circled-eyes of their cinematic cousins, but other than that they were intact. In other words, no peeling skin or bones showed, their look was not jaundiced. They merely shuffled forward, from every corner, in pursuit of their prey.

"They came from everywhere. I was amazed at their speed, all things considered." Strass took a breath at that point, sucking down the dry, air-conditioning all about him. His head still hanging down, eyes studying the floor, he continued on.

"I swung at them, beat at them, did everything I could to drive them back. To be honest, I was surprised when I actually managed to get away from them."

"Yes," came a voice from across the desk. "And then what happened?"

"That was when I finally caught a break," he continued. "When I got away from them then, I actually managed to turn a fast corner and lose them for a moment."

Finally, Strauss looked up, his gaze fixing on the eyes of the man across the desk from him.

"That's when I realized I'd actually made some kind of crazy circle and come back to the office. That's when I decided to come and tell you everything I'd figured out."

The man across the desk was in his early fifties. What was left of his hair was still dark, and he swept it across his shining pate in a desperate attempt to disguise his growing crop of skin. Like too many wealthy individuals, he suffered keenly from his misfortune. He was not thinking about his hair at that moment, however. No, for once, his attention was firmly off himself, and firmly on Miles Strass.

"And what is it that you've figured out, Miles?" The man leaned forward, spreading his open hands before himself to show his sincerity. "Tell me everything. Start at the beginning."

"Well," the wet and shaking man said, "it all started a few weeks back. I was working late one night, like usual. Like everybody. But that one night… I worked too late. All the places I usually eat, where everyone eats after work, they were already closed. So I had to eat someplace else. That was when I got the food poisoning. You know… when I was out sick for two weeks last month…"

The man behind the desk remembered. Strass was not indispensable, but his absence had been noticed.

"When I left the hospital, they gave me a long list of dos and don'ts. No coffee. No sugar. No heavy starches, no meat, oh God… no anything. I mean, yeah, I almost died, and I understood that it was going to take a while to get my system back to normal, but still, at first it was just hell."

Indeed, deprived of all his favorite foods, especially the life-giving medicine known as "the first cup of the morning," Strass had felt as if life was no longer worth living. But, as he told his story, suddenly things got unexpectedly better. For no reason he could discern, he found himself with more energy. He was smiling more, moving with confidence, new vim and vigor added to his step. For lack of a better word, Strass was simply happy, happier than he had been in a great long time. He found himself doing simple things like taking walks, petting strangers' dogs, simply sitting in the sunlight. All of it pleased his soul in ways he could not remember.

"I couldn't eat much, but what I could eat tasted better than anything had in ages. But, that wasn't all I noticed."

The man across the desk from Strass nodded sincerely. He still had security ready to pounce upon his visitor, but his finger had drifted from the hidden call button under the lip of his desk. He was not certain Strass would offer no trouble, but he was beginning to feel more comfortable. Still, he listened to the nervous little man's story with half his attention on his safety button.

"Suddenly," Strass said in a faraway voice, "television didn't seem to be entertaining any more. For some reason none of my favorites had their old zing, you know? Sports weren't any fun anymore, either. I mean, if I went to the ballgame, which I used to love to do, instead of seeing my heroes, all I saw were a bunch of millionaires playing a kid's game."

He left out some of his tale, like his visit to his favorite strip club, but he remembered it. He could see it in his mind still. All his buddies drooling, screaming, pounding their fists, and himself… not. Not doing any of it. There, but just not very interested.

But, though his mind reserved that one embarrassing story, it did not stop him from telling others. How McDonald's restaurant, and all his usual fast food hangouts simply did not taste the same anymore. How surfing the Net, hanging out with the guys—how absolutely nothing had that same old zing for him. It had been the same when he finally returned to work. His fanfare strewn return to the salt mines was greeted by the usual gathering of office guys and gals, the typical cake, the required gag gifts, and the standard plastic smiles all around.

"No offense," he said as he reached that part of his story, "but I never thought the best thing in my life would be coming back to work."

"None taken, Miles," responded the man behind the desk. "You just speak your mind. Just tell me everything."

He did. Strass talked of returning to work, of the numbing piles of paper he found on his desk, of the day-to-day of his re-immersion into business as usual.

"At first," he said, "it seemed wonderful to be able to tear into my work, to be useful again. But, as the days dragged on, and the piles of paper came and went, I started to feel... I don't know... *dissatisfied*. I don't mean any disrespect to the company or anything, but it was, it was like there simply was no point to what we do. To any of it."

His mind flashed back then, back to the first instant to when his real problems began. Seeing it clearly in his mind once more, Strass viewed the same scene again. Looking out through the eyes of memory, he watched his co-workers dragging themselves about the office, moving in slow motion. It was a heavy, lead-legged shambling he had seen somewhere else. Everywhere he looked, everyone he looked at, it seemed as if nothing had any purpose, as if no one had any drive, as if they were simply staggering through their work perfunctorily, without joy or caring or satisfaction.

His mind flashed back to the strip club, his eyes focusing on his pals. Looking past their carefree G-string stuffing, he noted that their eyes were glassy, their motions mechanical.

"At first I thought maybe it was just because we were at work. Everyone was just sluffing off, sticking it to the man, so to speak." Strass let out a long, wistful sigh at that point, then added, "But it wasn't that. I wish it was that simple."

His mind whirled through the club once more. Although he hoped it would not, memory insisted that the dancers and all the other patrons were equally bored, equally dead-eyed, as his co-workers. As everyone around him. Everywhere.

"Nothing thrilled anyone. Nothing moved anyone I knew. Oh, they responded to the nightly news with the correct gravity, made the right jokes around the water cooler, filled out their Christmas cards on time, but no matter what, nothing—I mean *nothing*—actually seemed to mean anything to anyone."

His mind still revolving around the night at the strip club, the moment when his eyes finally came open, he said;

"And then, then I finally figured out the truth."

"The truth, Miles?"

"Yeah, the truth that everyone I know—everyone period—I don't care who they are, or where they are, whether they're wearing mink coats or biker jackets, have shaved heads or mohawks—*whatever*—they're all *zombies!*"

The man behind the desk gave a small cough, his hand almost triggering his security alarm. As Strass sank back into his chair, however, the balding man relaxed, encouraging him to keep speaking. Gulping down a deep breath, Strauss obliged him.

"Every day, we all go through the same dulling madness. We go to work, go back home, eat, watch TV, sleep, get up, go to work, go back home, eat, watch TV, sleep... get up..."

Tears formed in Strass's eyes. As he talked, a collage of life in America flitted through his head. He saw his high school days, college times, his first fast food job, his second, the eventual upscale step to his "better" corporate job, and all the other myriad steps in between.

"All our lives are planned out for us," he told the man behind the desk. "Schools and work, love and marriage, take the kids to Disneyland, retire and die, replaced by your kids who drudge into the same madness..."

For a moment, Strass was overwhelmed by the pieces of the puzzle he was assembling. Behind his desk, the balding man said nothing, his poised finger relaxing almost completely. In a quieter voice, Strass said;

"I can see in your face that I'm right. That I figured it out. All our food is prepacked, every office provides free coffee... they make sure we get enough of whatever it is that turns us into zombies."

Strass's mind focused on his television, showing it to him as it never had before, vomiting its never-ending parade of commentators and super models, athletes and comedians, and products, products, products in a never-ending flood across a helpless countryside.

"The boob tube tells us everything," he added weakly. "Doesn't it? What to think, how to live, what to wear, who to vote for—and we just do whatever it says like the obedient little robots we are."

Strass sank back into his chair—tired. *Defeated.* Across from him rain splattered against the twenty foot high windows, its patter almost soothing. Realizing it was time to tie a bow of one color or another around the package before him, the balding man finally asked the question he knew he would have to ask since Strass first arrived in his office.

"Interesting, Miles," he offered calmly. "But, if you're right, well, wouldn't all that make me one of these, what would one call them, *oppressors?*"

Strass smiled like a sick dog.

"Of course it would," he agreed. "That's why I came to you in the first place."

The balding man did not quite know what to make of Strass's statement. His eyes gleamed with their normal confidence, but a wash of fear showed around them. His finger still near his button, the CEO asked;

"Why, Miles? Why did you come to *me*?"

"Because," the crying man shouted, "I want my life back! I want to be a zombie again like everybody else!" Dropping down out of his chair, Strass began begging, his hands folded in prayer to the god of his world.

"Please," he sniveled, "I want food to taste good again. I want to root for my team and not feel like an idiot. I want to care about who gets elected like it makes some kind of difference, I want to know that wearing the right clothes makes me one of the smart set..."

Crying, pleading for all he was worth, Strass screeched;

"*I want television to mean something again!*"

Giving up then, Strass folded in on himself, sobbing in his chair. Across the massive desk of polished oak, his boss smiled down upon him with compassion.

"There, there, Miles—we can take care of all of that. In fact, for someone sharp enough to have figured everything out like this, we might even has a promotion available."

Strass perked up appreciably at the unexpected news.

"Really?"

"Certainly," the balding man assured him. "Nothing but the best for a team player like you."

Strass unfolded then, suddenly beaming from ear to ear. His boss, smiling expansively, moved his finger slightly, hitting a different button on the intercom on his desk.

"Kitty," he said, "fetch a cup of coffee for Miles here, would you?"

And the world turned, as it always does, one crushed soul at a time.

WILLING PARTICIPANTS

JAMES CHAMBERS' ("The Dead Bear Witness," "Resurrection House") tale "A Wandering Blackness," published in *Lin Carter's Dr. Anton Zarnak, Supernatural Sleuth* received an Honorable Mention in The Year's Best Fantasy and Horror, 16th Annual Collection. He lives in New York. *www.jameschambersonline.com*

JOHN L. FRENCH ("Paradise Denied") is a crime scene investigator for the Baltimore Police Department. He has been writing short fiction for over ten years. His stories have appeared in *Alfred Hitchcock's Mystery Magazine*, *Hardboiled*, *Futures Mystery Anthology Magazine* and many more. His first book, *The Devil of Harbor City*, was recently published by Wild Cat Books.

C.J. HENDERSON ("The Last Best Friend," "Crime And Authority") has been a professional writer for over a quarter of a century. He has produced everything from novels to comic books, including an encyclopedia. His works have been translated into a half dozen foreign langauges, and yet he will still work for food. His work here is but his latest attempt to coax chicken legs out of the public at large. *www.cjhenderson.com*

ERICA HENDERSON (cover artist) is also the cover artist of *Lin Carter's Dr. Anton Zarnak, Supernatural Sleuth* (Marietta Publishing), illustrator of *Baby's First Mythos* (Z-Man Games), and contributor to *Slamm! The Hard-Boiled Fiction of C.J. Henderson* (Moonstone Books), among many others.

STEFAN JACKSON ("...For If The Dead Rise Not") was born of a cold North Wind, west of Hell. Called Nothing at birth and promised nothing as well. Found a home in stone and now etches pictures on the walls with bone.

BRIAN KEENE ("Hunting Season") is the Bram Stoker Award-winning author of *The Rising, Terminal, Fear Of Gravity, No Rest At All,* and many other books. He is also the fiction editor of *Horrorfind.com* and edits their popular anthology series. Several of his works have recently been optioned for film. His website, *www.briankeene.com,* contains household decorating tips for zombies and favorite recipes.

ADAM P. KNAVE ("Flesh Wounds") is a Writer of Things in NY where he lives with his wife and two cats. He dabbles in interpretive dance, competitive mocking and fibbing in bios. He welcomes hearing from readers via *pulse@hellblazer.net* and openly admits to having more of his writing up at *www.hellblazer.net.*

ROBERT M. PRICE ("The Righteous Rise") leads a double life, obsessed with both weird fiction and theology. By day he is Professor of Scriptural Studies at Johnnie Colemon Theological Seminary; by night he is editor of the revived *Strange Tales* and author of horror stories to appear in the collection *Blasphemies & Revelations* from Mythos Books.

VINCENT J. SNEED ("Just Like In The Movies," editor-in-chief) first saw *Dawn of the Dead* in 1979 at the impressionable age of 16—the book you now hold in your hands is a direct result of that incident. He is the co-creator of the comic series *Forty Winks,* as well as designer and associate editor of *Allen K's Inhuman Magazine.*

NEAL PATTERSON ("Zombie Beach Party") toils anonymously by day as a worker drone for a large investment firm and struggles by night to work out his pop culture psychosis through his writing. He lives in Baltimore with his ever supportive wife, Kathy, and their three cats: Pete, Linc, and Julie (a.k.a *The Mod Squad*).

JASON WHITLEY (illustrator), award-winning illustrator and informational graphics artist, lives with his wife and daughter in Charlotte, NC. Jason's work appears in *The Charlotte Observer* and *The [Myrtle Beach] Sun News* and has graced the pages of *The [Harrisburg, PA.] Patriot-News, The Washington Post, Golf PA. Magazine, Caliber Comics, Champawat Pictures, Hellcar Comics, Undercurrent Comix* and more. He's currently working with writer Scott Eckelaert on *Sea Urchins,* a daily comic strip, and with writer James Chambers on *The Midnight Hour* supernatural adventure series, as well as a new series of oil paintings. More information regarding *Sea Urchins* can be found at *www.seaurchins.net; Before Dawn* at *www.greenflyproductions.com.*

OTHER BOOKS FROM DIE MONSTER DIE!

Mooncat Jack *by James Chambers**

The Dead Bear Witness *by James Chambers**

The Last Best Friend *by C.J. Henderson**

Pretty Female Assassin Pixie, vol. 1
by Vince Sneed and John Peters

Pretty Female Assassin Pixie , vol. 2
by Vince Sneed and John Peters

The Midnight Hour
by James Chambers and Jason Whitley

chapbooks; available through shocklines.com